BUTTER

Butter

ANNE PANNING

SWITCHGRASS BOOKS   NORTHERN ILLINOIS UNIVERSITY PRESS   DeKalb

© 2012 by Switchgrass Books, an imprint of Northern Illinois University Press

Published by Northern Illinois University Press, DeKalb, Illinois 60115

Manufactured in the United States using acid-free paper

Library of Congress Cataloging in Publication Data

Panning, Anne, 1966–

Butter / Anne Panning.

 p. cm.

ISBN 978-0-87580-681-5 (pbk. : acid free paper)

ISBN 978-1-60909-066-1 (electronic)

1. Self realization Fiction. 2. Minnesota Fiction. I. Title.

PS3566.A577B88 2012

813'.54 dc23

2012019741

In memory of my mother,

Barbara Panning

(1945–2007)

BUTTER

Chapter One

Memory: I am eight, going on nine. I wear high, tight ponytails, the part white and crooked down the back of my head like a crack of lightning. I hold my father's hand. It is dry and worn smooth. I imagine he has no fingerprints because of the smoothness. "This is where the butter is folded, Iris," he tells me, pointing to a large silver machine. He flicks off a panel of switches, and the humming stops; the large door opens up like a mouth. It is full of butter— soft pale yellow, beautiful tons of butter. It's shiny. I rush up to it, peer in, and smell: salt, cream, the scent of my father's white uniform hanging on the banister—bitter, almost like urine, but sweeter.

"We'd like to talk to you about something, Iris," my mother, Marilyn, said. She passed the bowl of mashed potatoes to me, and I scooped some onto my plate and made a deep wide hole in the center for gravy. She looked unusually dressed up in a white blouse with pearls around her neck and in her ears.

"Yes, Iris," my father said. He locked eyes with my mother and dished a small piece of stringy roast beef onto my plate. "Gravy?"

I nodded. It was a big dinner, and my favorite part was the green beans cooked in fresh cream with lots of butter. My father had made this cream and brought it home for us in an old mayonnaise jar. I salted and peppered everything, wondering what they were going to say.

"Iris," my mother said, looking down at her plate. Her eyelashes were long and dark and pointed. She looked up at my father again, and I began to wonder what I'd done. "You know we love you very much, don't you?"

"Yeah," I said, accidentally kicking the cat under the table. I reached down and tried to rub her head, but she got away.

My father poured me a big glass of milk, but it was the thick kind from the creamery, and I didn't think I could drink it all because it made me so full and my mouth so gummy. "We love you dearly, Iris," my father said, stabbing into his clump of beef. It had a clingy piece of yellow fat hanging to the side. "So we want to tell you something that's very important, because we feel you should know and never have to wonder."

I looked up at my mother. "What?"

She set her fork and knife down and folded her hands. I was beginning to think somebody had died, maybe my Grandma Laura, and I shut my eyes. "Have you ever heard of children being adopted?" my mother said, blinking. Her face was powdered and pale, her lipstick strong and red. "It's when a married couple who can't have any children takes in a child who has no parents."

My father cleared his throat, as if it was time for his part. "You're our adopted daughter, Iris. We want you to know that, so in case anyone ever mentions it, you can say you know." His hair was combed back in little greasy stripes, and his eyes were bright under high pointed eyebrows.

My mother picked up her fork and fluffed her potatoes. "We love you as our daughter, Iris. Nothing changes. We always have and always will. Someday, when you're older, we'll talk more about it, okay?"

"Okay," I said, then sat quietly. Then it made sense how my eyes were so round and big and brown and didn't match her pinched green ones or my father's see-through blue. I wasn't really theirs. I pulled up my knee-highs through my jeans, and peeked under the table. My mother's bony ankles and my father's thick black shoes met and cuddled down there, and I wondered whose I was.

WE LIVED IN A BIG HOUSE on the side of Wishbone by my school. Our house was old and painted tan on the top and brown on the bottom, with a big porch where I liked to read books and draw. My room was upstairs at the end of the hallway. It was light purple with all maple furniture. My mother said that was a good combination, because then I'd still like it when I was older and it wouldn't seem juvenile. I had built-in bookshelves full of stuffed animals and miniature dolls sitting at tiny tables, but my mother said I could fill them with books when I was older.

My favorite thing to do at the time was to lie under my bed and pretend I was dead. I'd put my pillow down there and lie with my hands crossed over my chest, listening to noises. The pipes thumped on and off as my mother washed and rinsed each dish, and sometimes in winter I could hear the snow fingernailing against my window, or my father's car door muffle shut and his boots stamp off snow in the doorway. When he called up the stairs, "Iris?" I didn't answer. I'd lie there, my eyelids fluttering, trying hard to be still. I liked to make them worry a little, but they never thought it was funny. Usually, after about four calls for me, my father took the carpeted stairs by twos and slowly opened the door to my dark bedroom.

The first time was the funniest. I was hardly even breathing as I watched his feet circle the room. He looked in the closet, then walked out into the hallway; he then came back, pulled up my bedspread and found me.

"Iris, what are you doing under there?" he asked, pulling me out by the legs. My butt slid out, and I sat up.

"I'm playing I'm dead."

He sat down on my bed, still wearing his white creamery work clothes, smelling that musty butter smell. "Why are you playing dead?" he said, scratching his fingers through his hair.

"I just like to," I said, and sat in his lap.

"Well, I brought you a bag of chocolate malted ice-cream cups. They're in the freezer."

I hugged him around the neck. I loved chocolate malted cups. We already had a whole strip of tiny wooden spoons wrapped in white paper hanging from the cupboard, and I tore one off like a movie ticket whenever I wanted.

"But don't play dead anymore, Iris," my father said as we walked down the stairs together. "It's not a very nice thing to do."

ON A SNOW DAY IN JANUARY when school got canceled, I called up my friend Sylvie and asked her if she wanted to come over. She lived five houses down from mine, the last one on the block. Her house had chipped white paint with black trim and looked tall and spooky next to our big fat one. Once, when I'd asked why the glass in their windows was wavy and a little blurry to see through, she said it was because their house was an antique. Her mother had told her that, and to be proud that everything was old and unique, even the wood floor, which curved and rolled like waves on a lake in the dining room.

I met her at the front door in my stocking feet. She was wearing a bright red hat, a red scarf, red mittens, and blue zip-up coat. She didn't have boots on, like my mother would make me wear, but tennies. "No school!" she said, holding her fists up in the air. She was like that. She got very excited about every little thing. I took her coat and laid it nicely on the plaid couch.

My mother was somewhere in the house. As Sylvie followed me upstairs, I could hear the click of her fingernails on the adding machine in her little office off the kitchen. Sometimes she did books for the creamery at home instead of going up there. She said it was better because then she could be with me, drink tea, play records, bake, or even take a nap if she wanted to. I liked her to be home, even if I didn't see her for hours. She was also writing a book, she said, and had a big blue electric typewriter in her office. I didn't know what it was about, but I hoped she'd let me read it.

"So what do you want to do?" I asked Sylvie.

She lay down on my bed and rested her feet up on the wall. "I don't care," she said. "Whatever."

I hated when a friend said "whatever," because then I had to decide everything. "I know," I said, and rushed over to my closet. For Christmas I'd gotten a Barbie Beauty Shop, which was a giant Barbie head on a stand, with a built-in tray around her neck for holding makeup and bobby pins and stuff. It came with little cotton balls for removing the makeup, and small pink combs and brushes for doing her hair. There was eye shadow you had to wet with a little sponge on a stick. I dragged it out and set it on the floor.

"No way—I didn't know you got that!" Sylvie said, coming over. "Why didn't you tell me?" Sylvie's jeans were faded in big patches at the knees.

We both started going to work on a hairdo, wetting down the plastic hair with a cup of warm water from the bathroom. I knew Sylvie's family didn't have much money because Sylvie never seemed to get what she asked for for Christmas. Plus, they had a whole bunch of kids in their family—six, actually, Sylvie being the fourth. But I thought she was lucky. At least she knew that her mother and father were her real parents. They all had small noses, and this special pointed chin that was really elegant and made all the girls and their mother look pretty.

I was still wondering about my real family.

"Hey, Sylvie," I said, "guess what?" I got up to stretch my legs out and sat back down in a new way.

"What?" She didn't look up.

"My mother and father told me I was adopted," I said. "Can you believe it?"

"You're kidding!" Sylvie said, putting a hand over her mouth. "Tell me what they said exactly." She crawled over closer to me on her knees.

By this time we were sick of the big Barbie head, so we went to the bathroom, where we had mint-green twin sinks. We both liked to just mess around in there, sit up on the counter with our feet in the sinks, and look in the mirror, talking.

I told her everything and didn't realize how upset I was until I started crying. I watched myself in the mirror; ugly red blotches splattered across my forehead and neck. My lips looked shiny and maroon and puffy.

Sylvie leaned over from her sink and patted me on the back. "It's okay," she said, which only made me cry harder. "It doesn't matter if you're adopted, as long as you have good parents. Your parents are nice, Iris! And you get free ice cream and chocolate milk from your dad's store, and lots of cute clothes. Huh? Think of that." She rubbed my knee like my father would. Her skin was all washed-out from the bright lights around the mirror.

"And when you get older you can go to a church somewhere and find out your real mom." She reached over and handed me a tissue. "I know because one of my cousins—Vicki, she's older— she did that once, and then she went out and found her mom in California. You can do that, too, if you want."

I looked up at Sylvie in the mirror and nodded. My French braids were fuzzy and falling out, and I just wanted to be alone.

THAT NIGHT SUPPER WAS SPECIAL for some reason, because we got to eat TV dinners in the living room. I loved the pale yellow butter that flooded over the square of mashed potatoes, and the little nugget of chocolate cake, which was so flat it was really a brownie. My mother and father were very quiet, and my mother wore jeans with slippers. Her glasses were pushed up on top of her head like in the movies. I watched as she ate, and after only a couple chews, she stopped and stared off. Was she going to cry? It looked like it.

My father was still in his white creamery clothes, and as usual, they were all stained with grease spots. The sanitary paper cap he had to wear was tossed on the floor like trash. Something was wrong; I could feel it. Nobody talked, and we watched the news, chewing. Maybe something bad had happened in our country, but when I asked, my mother said, "No, honey, just eat your chicken."

Later that night, when I went downstairs for a drink of water, I saw the warm yellow light on in my mother's office. I walked as quietly as I could, barefoot, holding my nightgown up above my knees. I crawled under the kitchen table and peeked around the corner. The door was open a crack, and she was in there, her body all folded up in the chair like when I did a cannonball off the diving board at the pool. There was a bottle of beer sitting on the desk, but it looked full, and she hardly ever drank beer except on Fourth of July picnics and New Year's with their friends. She stared at the brown bottle, crying a little, then put her hands up to her forehead and cried a lot. It made me want to get out of there, so I ran upstairs and dove into my bed, the sheets cold and whispery on my legs. The last thing she needed was me to give her more problems, but it was so hard to sleep. I watched the tree's shadows on my wall for a long time. They looked like bony witch hands pinching.

AT THE END OF THAT WEEK, Friday, I walked up to the creamery after school like I did sometimes. I carried my books in a flat red canvas bag with blue buckles, and I swung it to the rhythm of my walk. I liked to see my father marching around the place, operating all the machines and selling milk by the crate to farm families when they came into town. He told me he was one of the few left, a dying breed, and even though I wasn't sure what he meant, I always smiled.

I walked slowly down the sidewalk and noticed how everything was so black and white in winter. The trees were black, the roads, the cars seemed black, but the grass was white, the sky was white, my boots were white with white fur trim. I saw my father through the glass door, swinging a bucket of vanilla ice cream out of the big cooler for a lady. My mother was there, too; she sat on a wooden stool with one skinny leg stretched out in front of her and her arms crossed. She was really beautiful with dark red hair. "Let's not call it red, Iris," she always said. "It's really more of an auburn." She was wearing her blue stretch pants that I loved with a white blouse out loose. I could see her mouth opening and closing, and laughing, but she still didn't look very happy.

"Hi," I said, and ran to my mother. I hugged her around the legs, then my father picked me up, even though I was way too big for that.

"So, what did you learn today?" he said, patting my back like I was a baby.

I shrugged my shoulders. "Vocabulary words," I said. "Types of trees." When he let me down, I went over to the small cooler and picked out a Creamsicle. My mother watched me with her cheeks sucked in, thinking.

"Come here, Iris," she said, pulling over a stool. I sat next to her, tearing open the Cresthaven wrapper.

She rubbed a warm flat hand on my back. "Sweetie," she said, and I looked over without turning my head. The creamy vanilla ice cream and orange sherbet mixed in my mouth so sweet. "How would you like to spend the weekend at Grandma Laura's?"

My father talked on the black wall phone, nodding his head, laughing so hard his shoulders shook. His back was to us. Before I even answered, she went on, rubbing my back so softly it made me sleepy. "You see, your father and I need some time alone together. We have to take a little trip. I haven't been feeling well, and there's been some problems."

When I asked what problems, she raised her hand, then pushed back my bangs, fluffing them. "It's nothing for you to worry about, honey. It's adult problems that we'll take care of. But I talked to Grandma Laura, and she said she'd love to have you come stay. Your father and I will drive you over after we close up here, okay?"

"Okay," I said, but something felt off. I looked out at the street through the glass door and suddenly got scared that maybe they'd decided to take me back. Maybe they didn't want me anymore. I chewed on the wooden Creamsicle stick until it gave me little splinters in my tongue.

ON THE WAY HOME, my mother let me stop at Ben Franklin to pick out a little something to take to my grandma's. Inside, it smelled like popcorn and chocolate and fresh clean rubber from the white Keds in back. I picked out a package of Shrinky Dinks, which the girls in my class had been raving about and wearing as necklaces with little holes punched in them, then strung on yarn. My mother had never heard of them and thought they sounded complicated and messy, but she let me get them anyway. She was still in her faraway staring-off mood and looked right through me. I probably could've picked anything, and she'd have said, "All right, fine, let's just go."

On the car ride, my parents let me sit between them in the front seat. The green dashboard lights glowed up onto our faces and made me feel cozy and safe. I closed my eyes and wished they weren't going away without me. The heater blew onto my legs, and I unzipped my coat. In the backseat, milk bottles clanked around in the full crate we were bringing for my Grandma Laura. I worried they'd break, but my father said, "No, they're very thick glass, honey," and rubbed my head.

Grandma Laura lived in Mankato, which was much bigger and better than Wishbone because it had a mall and buses and McDonald's, and usually Grandma Laura took me to the movies when I came. I also had all kinds of cousins there, who sometimes came over with my aunts when I stayed. DeeDee and Melanie were my favorites, but it was also fun to play with the boys—Noel, David, and Carter were all boys belonging to another family, the Nelsons. They were a little older than me, but they always dragged me around on their shoulders or gave me piggyback rides, even though other times they could be kind of mean.

My father didn't come in with us, which was odd. He gave me a one-armed hug as my mother and I slid out the door. Grandma Laura lived in a small brick house up on the hill with white awnings over the windows with gold *M*s painted on them, for her last name, Morgan. Our last name was Kauffman, from my father, but I wished it was Morgan. Iris Morgan sounded more elegant than Iris Kauffman.

My grandma's eyes lit up when we walked through the side door from the garage. She bent down to hug and kiss me, then took my mother in her arms and held her for a long time. They rocked back and forth, and I could smell the powdery perfume of my grandma mix with my mother's strong flowery one. Grandma Laura ran her hand over my mother's shiny hair, and I stood there with my small blue suitcase and book bag, watching.

"I'm so sorry, honey," Grandma Laura said. She held my mother's face in her hands and wiped away tears with her thumbs. They both tried to cover when they remembered me, though.

"Have a fun weekend, you two," my mother called as she ran out to the car, which was still running. She wore a black fur-collared coat and tall boots. From the living room window, I watched the red taillights disappear.

WHILE MY GRANDMA MADE DINNER, I went into the TV room with the matching soft blue chairs. One chair was for my grandpa, who had died a few years ago, and now you could tell which was my grandma's because it was wrinkled and smashed down and had a heating pad over the top. All I remembered of my grandpa was his long, thin face, like a dog's, and the white hairs that grew out of his nose and ears. He never really talked to me much. I liked it now, with just my grandma here alone with me.

I watched the last half of *Gentle Ben* and wondered about the boy with the big teeth and plaid short-sleeved shirts who hugged the bear like it was a cat or a dog. I liked when they went zooming off in their pontoon boat through the reeds and the bear roared up on its hind legs. It was so far from my life, and yet I could identify with the boy's loneliness. Grandma Laura brought in a frozen pizza and told me to spread newspaper on the shag carpet and sit on the floor. Grandma Laura sat beside me, but it took her a long time to get down to the floor. I could actually hear her bones crack and pop like they might break. She fanned her legs out to one side and leaned a hand on the carpet.

We used heavy paper plates with Christmas trees on them. The pizza was cut into tiny squares, and I tried to avoid the dry corner triangles. The sauce tasted sweet and delicious.

"So, how's everything going, Iris?" she asked, reaching to change the TV channel to the news. "How's school?"

I shrugged my shoulders like I always did when people asked me that. "Fine. Good. I got moved to the top spelling group in our class, so I get to go way faster than the rest of the class. Me and two other kids." I crunched into my pizza and got crumbs all over the carpet. I rubbed them in with my hand.

"Well, that's pretty nice," she said. "You know, your mother was always good at spelling. So was I. It's something I never had to study—I just knew by imagining each word." She got herself off the floor by pushing up on the couch. It took her a long time. "Do you want any more?" she asked, pointing to the checkerboard of pizza on the cookie sheet.

"No, thanks."

"Here, hand it to me, would you?" I followed her into the kitchen, which was painted warm yellow and had dark wooden cupboards with glass panes. The only light on was a fluorescent stick above the sink, which made everything seem clean and taken care of.

"Grandma, what's wrong with my mother? Why are they going away?" I sat on the counter by the sink where she poured me a glass of milk and let me have Nestlé's Quik in it. I stirred and stirred it to bubbles.

She stood in front of me, pushing my hair back from my face. There was a smell from her, like cabbage and onions—not exactly a good smell, but I loved her. She had stars of wrinkles at the corners of her eyes and smooth flat cheeks. "It's nothing, Iris," she said. "Sometimes older people just need a vacation." She helped me jump down to the floor. "Do you want me to wash your hair? Would you like that?"

I nodded, my favorite thing. I ran and got two towels from the hall closet, one for me to lie on and one for my wet hair when I was done. Grandma Laura pulled off my sweater and turtleneck, and I was down to my T-shirt with little blue rosebuds on it. I lay on the counter, my head propped up by the sink with a towel. There was a tangled green plant above me, and I listened to her turn the spray hose on and test it on her hand. I closed my eyes, and soft warm water sprayed down my hair, spritzing onto my forehead. My grandma's hands swept it down in a bunch at the nape of my neck and squeezed the water out. She sudsed the Herbal Essence in, scratching lightly with her polished fingernails, and then she sprayed again. The soft warm threads of water on my head rinsing, my grandma's hands stroking, cupping my skull, soothed me. I never wanted it to stop. I could've fallen asleep.

WE SLEPT THAT NIGHT in her big four-poster bed. I wore one of my grandpa's white T-shirts, which went down to my knees and was so worn out it was see-through. The ends of my hair were still wet when we lay on the big feather pillows, facing each other, talking. The smell of Ben-Gay and her perfume made me sneeze three times in a row.

She reached over and touched my nose. "Want Melanie and DeeDee to come over tomorrow?" she asked, thinking I'd probably like that, even though I sometimes preferred just the two of us.

"I don't care," I said. "Sure. Maybe the boys, too."

She closed her eyes, and all her wrinkles stretched out and disappeared. "All right. Good night, sweetheart," she whispered, and kissed me on the forehead. I turned over on my side and clicked off the light but stayed awake for a long time after, worrying about things. Grandma Laura snorted and trembled in her sleep.

MELANIE AND DEEDEE WORE the same everything. When they came over with their mom, my aunt Patty, they both had on butterfly shirts, same style, different colors. Melanie's was light blue, DeeDee's was light green, and both had flowers on them. I called them butterfly shirts because the sleeves were big wing shapes and the armholes went practically all the way down to your stomach so that you could see in. In winter everyone wore them with turtle-necks underneath.

Without even discussing it, we headed to the back bedroom, which had become the playroom. It was painted a sick old green and had all Grandma Laura's broken and unused things in it. There was a Presto Burger machine, which we always smashed our peanut butter sandwiches in and pretended to cook. There was a whole laundry basket full of purses and an entire ice cream pail full of jewelry, and in the closet, a cardboard box with plastic flowers, hats, calendars, scarves, and old Monopoly and Candyland games with missing pieces and wrinkled cards.

DeeDee was ten, like me, and Melanie was three years older and loved to boss us. Melanie flopped on the bed and put her hands behind her head. "What should we do?" she said. "Want to play school? I get to be the teacher, though, because I'm the oldest." She already looked like a teacher with her pink glasses and bright staring eyes and long hair parted down the middle with no bangs, pulled back.

DeeDee and I shrugged our shoulders and wandered around the room, digging through everything. DeeDee looked like an exact miniature of her dad, my uncle Robert. They were both short with wide heads and blondish-red wavy hair. DeeDee had blue eyes, just like him, but Melanie was tall and thin and brown-eyed like Aunt Patty. They were each an exact copy of one parent. I wished I had someone to look like.

"Hey, Iris," Melanie called from the bed. She sat up now, stretching her fingers to her toes. "I'm sorry about what happened to your mom. I bet she's really sad."

DeeDee and I had crushed-down hats on, mine black with a misty veil and velvet prongs to keep it stuck on your head. DeeDee threw her pink hat at Melanie on the bed. "Mom said you weren't supposed to say anything!" she said. "You're gonna get it! Hey, Mom!"

"Shut up, you stupid idiot," Melanie said, throwing the hat back at DeeDee. I stood there at the end of the bed with a lump in my throat. I knew something bad had happened, but I still didn't know exactly what. I made Melanie promise to tell me, after DeeDee went out to the hall to check for privacy and closed the door.

We all sat in a circle up on the bed, serious. I was cross-legged with my hands folded in my lap, scared to know. "See, I heard our moms on the phone," Melanie began, "and what happened was your mom got pregnant two months ago. You knew she was going to have a baby, right?" Melanie pushed up her glasses and nodded at us, as if to reinforce it was the truth. "Well,"—she leaned closer, talking more quietly—"the baby died inside her. It was a miscarriage with lots of bleeding, and now they don't know what they're going to do. This is all from the phone call, because you know how my mom repeats everything anyone says on the phone? I hate that." She shook her head, then leaned back, finished. "Yeah. So that was it. I guess you're still going to be an only child, Iris."

I couldn't move or say anything, but I nodded like I got it. Inside, my stomach was shaking, and I needed to talk to my mother. I needed that more than anything. DeeDee just twirled away and started acting like it was nothing. I walked quietly to the door and left the room, my footsteps echoing down the hallway like rain.

ON SATURDAY AFTERNOON, Grandma Laura, who loved the movies and used to be an actress in the theaters in Minneapolis a long, long time ago, decided it would be a treat to drag us all— me, DeeDee, Melanie, and the three boys—to see *Benji*. I'd been wanting to see it, but now there were too many people and I was worried about my mother. Where had my father taken her? Why hadn't they told me? When had this bleeding happened? I felt as if I was another person from the one who hid under my bed and scared my father—someone new now, without anyone.

We pulled into the driveway of the Nelsons' house. Theirs was small like Grandma Laura's, not big like our old house. It was one story, painted watermelon pink with white trim and a pale brick wall around half of it. I could see the boys fussing with their jackets through the big picture window and my aunt Deb hurrying them. DeeDee put her arm around me in the backseat and smiled. I looked out the window and watched the pale puffs of car exhaust rise up into the air and stay, it was so cold.

The movie theater had a long slanting aisle with a runner of big-flowered carpet, pink on brown. I tried to end up between Grandma Laura and DeeDee, but Noel and Melanie sat on either side of me. We took up a whole row. The seats were scratchy rough green velvet with smooth metal bottoms stuck full of gum. The place smelled musty like a cabin closed up over the winter.

Before the real movie started, there were ads for restaurants, insurance companies, and carpet places in Mankato. They were just slides with rounded edges like we saw in school about the formation of rock or branches of the government. They stayed on for just a second, then another one flashed up, faded and spotty, and another. A tape-recorded voice told what you could buy at the snack counter.

I cried through the last part of the movie, not because of Benji, but because I was afraid. Noel, who was just a little older than me, reached over and grabbed my hand. He was dark-skinned and dark-eyed like a Mexican, even though he always said he was not, he was Italian and Irish. The snot rolled down my nose and onto my lips, itching, but I let it run and sat tightly on my other hand, waiting for the movie and the whole day to be over. Noel rubbed the back of my hand with his fingers, and they felt dusty, like there was flour on them.

AFTER MY PARENTS BROUGHT me home the next day, things seemed better. The house had the usual Sunday night quiet where all you could hear was the refrigerator humming, very few lights on, no traffic on the streets. My mother and father sat reading sections of the Sunday paper, then tossed them to each other when they were done. I got the funnies and lay back reading in the recliner. They were playing Elvis records, and it was snowing just a little, and I had to think everything was better because it was so nice, so peaceful, my mother humming and jiggling her foot up and down.

When my mother and father were in Wisconsin, they'd bought me a flat hunk of cheddar cheese in the shape of a cow. It was coated in wax with black blotches for the eyes and feet. Even though we had hot lunch, I was going to bring it to school the next day with a Baggie of Ritz crackers and share it with Sylvie. I had it sitting beside me on the coffee table so I wouldn't forget it.

"Ready for bed?" my mother asked me, yawning. She stacked up the newspaper and set it at the end of the couch. My father sat with his hands crossed over his stomach and smiled.

"I guess," I said, and went over to kiss my father good night. "I have school pictures tomorrow," I said, looking back at my mother. "You told me to remind you." I watched as she and my father gave each other the eye, then started laughing.

My father pulled me close and sat me on his lap. "Let's tell her, Marilyn," he said. "I can't wait."

"Tell me what. What?" I said in a panic. I was ready for it. I'd been waiting for the time when they told me I had to go back to where I came from, but I didn't think it would be so soon.

My mother sat on the arm of the couch. She was wearing a red sweatshirt and baggy brown corduroys and looked so young and pretty. Her hair was pulled back at the sides with two barrettes and flipped under by the ears. I would hate to lose her. Oh, I couldn't lose her. I almost started to cry, but held back. Maybe if I acted stronger they'd change their minds. "Well, Iris," my mother said, looking more at my father than at me. She raised her eyebrows at him. He was wearing a gray sweatshirt and khakis, his weekend clothes, and it was strange not to see him in white. He swung his eyeglasses around in circles.

"Iris," my father said, hugging me around the shoulders, "you're going to get a brother soon. Adam."

I looked at my mother to check if this was true. She nodded several times, smiled, and came to hug me. We were all three crammed up on one chair, but I wasn't sure I understood.

"How?" I asked. "How are we getting him?" I thought of the bleeding Melanie had told me about, how there had already been a baby inside my mother that had died.

"We're adopting him, just like you," my mother said. "It'll take a while, but we're so lucky, all of us. Aren't we lucky, Iris? It's going to be so much fun."

I nodded. She took my hand, and we climbed the stairs while my father turned out all the lights behind us.

On my rocking chair, my mother laid out a red cardigan, a white blouse, and a black plaid skirt for school pictures the next day. Two red ribbons hung on the doorknob for ponytails, and they almost blew off when my mother whished out of the room on her toes.

THAT NIGHT I THREW UP off the side of my bed like a waterfall. My head burned in hot waves, then the next minute I was sweaty cold. My mother rushed in, tying her robe tightly around the waist. "Iris? Iris, honey," she said, and her cool smooth palm rested on my forehead. "What is it? Did you eat lots of junk out at Grandma Laura's this weekend with the kids?"

I half nodded and half shrugged. I couldn't remember. There had been a giant box of Good & Plenty, movie popcorn with fake oily butter, Dr Pepper with crushed ice, then spaghetti for supper with whole milk and garlic toast.

"Bill, come in here, would you?" my mother called out into the hallway. "Iris is sick. Can you grab an ice cream pail from downstairs, too? I think she might throw up again."

Suddenly, lights started popping on all over the house, and I heard my father fumbling for his glasses. He padded down the stairs, came back with the empty plastic bucket, and set it on the floor.

"Could you . . . Bill, would you mind getting a rag or an old towel or something, too?" my mother asked, turning toward him. She reached for his arm and squeezed it, smiling as if she was sorry. "Please. We've got a mess over here."

My father looked dazed and had a tall coned hairdo from sleep. He wore boxer shorts and a flannel shirt, open loose. The room smelled like old hacked-up rotten pizza, and then I remembered the frozen pizza my Grandma Laura and I had had. The sheet where I threw up was wet and flappy with little pieces of food on it, and it was all I could do to squirm out of it.

My mother carried me into the bathroom as my father cleaned up. She set me by the toilet, and I just stood there, looking in. There was a warm wet washcloth, and my mother cleaned me up, then smeared a little Crest on my toothbrush and said, "Brush now, you'll feel better."

I got to wear my summer pajamas because they were all I had clean, and I flapped my arms up and down because they felt so light and cool on my shoulders. My mother and father let me sleep between them, even though I knew I was too old. But it felt good! Oh! I twirled my head down between the canyon of their two fluffy pillows and lay flat on my back, feeling the warmth from both of them radiating into me. It was already almost light out. A pale Easter-egg blue crept in behind the shades, and I closed my eyes, not wanting morning yet.

Chapter Two

Memory: I am ten years old. I sit on the bathtub's edge and watch my mother get ready. The face powder compact is hard green plastic. She pats circles over her nose and cheeks. Black liner rims around her eyes like an animal. Finally, the lipstick: a dark cardinal red. She spreads it on, puckers, presses a tissue to her mouth, then sends the tissue floating into the toilet bowl. I rush up, stand, and watch the red kiss spinning atop clear water. "Is that my kiss?" I ask. "Or Adam's?"

My mother shushes me. "You're so excitable," she says. "Just stay calm."

She flushes. The lipstick kiss disintegrates, is gone.

After many, many trips to the Open Hope Adoption Agency in Rochester and over a year later, my mother and father brought Adam home. The biggest surprise of all was that he was not a bundle of a baby, but my age, or close: he was twelve and I was eleven. Although I'd known this beforehand, it seemed easier to deal with in theory than in actuality. My parents and I had discussed it over and over, how I was to act with a new brother, how it would not affect their love for me, how Adam had come from a family who hadn't loved him enough, so he would probably be hard to get along with at first.

When I asked why they picked a boy older than me, my father had said, "Oh, it takes too long to get a little baby nowadays, and we wanted you to have someone your own age to play with." But it seemed strange, and I wasn't sure I liked the idea of someone being so close in age.

To make it easier on Adam, they decided I should stay home and have Sylvie over while they picked him up, plus have Grandma Laura come to stay with us. Sylvie was very excited and said that if Adam was cute, he might become her boyfriend. She had a new clipped haircut that year, blunt to the chin, like so many of the girls, but I'd kept mine long, with bangs, so I could do braids or ponytails or curls or a bun. There was a big square purple comb sticking out of her back jeans pocket that said COOL in red-and-white checkered letters. I had a blue one with colored hearts on it, but it always poked me in the back when I sat down, so I kept it in my book bag.

Sylvie and I had dish towels wrapped tightly around us, thanks to Grandma Laura, and we were making brownies out of a box. The picture showed a big walnut pressed into each brownie, and I told Grandma Laura that I didn't want that; I hated nuts.

"That's fine, Iris," she said. "We have no walnuts anyway." She had WCCO on the radio and scratched at an itch with the handle of a measuring cup. Her hair was gray, and with her brown eyes, it looked wrong somehow, like pennies and nickels. She smelled slightly of sauerkraut.

"Well, all I can say," Sylvie said, stirring the batter, "is I wonder what he looks like." Her eyes got big as she scraped the dry mix off the side of the bowl and into the dark, wet batter. "Where did he live before? Do you know? I wonder who his mom and dad were."

I shrugged my shoulders, wondering who my own real parents were, not caring about Adam's yet. Sylvie slid the brownie pan into the oven, and Grandma Laura turned the white kitchen timer to thirty. It ticked loudly. I hooked arms with Sylvie, and we danced around the room like we'd learned in school. "Skip, skip, skip to my lou / skip, skip, skip to my lou / skip, skip, skip to my lou / skip to my lou, my darling." That was the part when you changed partners and got to hook arms with a new boy.

When we heard the car pull up outside, we grabbed each other's arms and screamed, then ran to the living room window. Grandma Laura was right behind us and pulled the curtain back. There was still snow in some places, even though it was supposed to be spring now. Dark dirty patches of it rimmed our yard like a tiny mountain chain. My parents got out of the big red station wagon and slammed their doors. Where was Adam? My mother opened up the back door, and he walked out slowly, holding a beat-up blue duffel bag over his arm. He had a perfect round haircut like someone had put a bowl over his head and cut right around it. His eyes were dark, from what I could see, and he had very red lips. My father reached down and rubbed his head as they came up the sidewalk.

Adam wore a jean jacket with a red hooded sweatshirt underneath it and Toughskins. He didn't really look older than me. Suddenly, Sylvie grabbed me around the waist and said, "Cute!" She leaned over and whispered to me, "But he needs to get a different haircut." We both jumped up and down, excited and nervous to meet him. Grandma Laura opened the heavy front door, and the cold came sucking in. I looked down at my stocking feet and wished I had gotten myself more ready.

"Hello, hello, everybody," my father said. He led Adam inside with his hand, and we all clustered around the door, awkward. Nobody else said anything.

"Well, why don't we all go into the living room," Grandma Laura said, and she led the way. We had a new piano along one wall, which I'd started taking lessons on, and I sat on the slippery polished bench. Sylvie rushed over and slid her butt over next to me. That way we left the good couches and chairs for the adults, and for Adam. I swung my legs back and forth and took a quick look at him while he was turned away. He seemed okay and smaller than I thought he'd be.

My father and Adam sat side by side on the plaid couch, and Grandma Laura took the rocker. My mother walked in, still unraveling the scarf from around her neck, the scarf I'd given her for Christmas. It was fuzzy gray with white snowflakes knit into it and long tassels. After she'd taken her things off, she sat on the plaid love seat, facing my father and Adam. She clasped her hands around one knee and smiled.

"So," she said, and looked around the room at each of us, one by one. "I think we should introduce ourselves to Adam." She paused for a second, thinking. "And of course, Adam, we want you to know how welcome you are here in our family. You can call us Mom and Dad, and you can think of Iris, here, as your sister."

Everyone turned to look at me, so I smiled. "Hi, Adam," I said, looking over at him quickly. "It's nice to meet you." Then, in a nervous way to take attention off of me, I said, "This is my best friend, Sylvie. She comes over a lot, and we can all do things together sometimes if you want."

Adam nodded, and I could see how really dark brown his eyes were. They were almost black. Maybe he didn't want to hang out with us, I didn't know, but I said it anyway to be nice. He looked over at Sylvie, then stared out the window at the front yard. Grandma Laura went over and gave him a big hug, and I could see how stiffly he took it, but he patted her back a little, too. He stayed sitting down.

"It's so nice to have another lovely grandson," Grandma Laura said, hobbling back over to the rocker, "and with such pretty eyes." She sat down, out of breath, and smiled.

I nudged Sylvie. We both knew you weren't supposed to say to a boy that he was pretty or he'd feel stupid. My father was smiling wide and hooked an arm over the back of the couch where Adam sat. My mother looked happier than I'd seen her in months. When she smiled, her dark lipstick made her teeth look shiny white and perfect.

"Iris," my mother said, "don't you have a present for Adam? Remember . . ." She gave me the eye to go get it, because I honestly had forgotten. I nodded, and ran to get it out of the entryway closet. It was wrapped in an old cowboy boot box and looked bigger than what was really inside. I set it on Adam's lap.

"Wow," he said, before he even opened it. The wrapping paper had footballs, basketballs, tennis rackets, and hockey sticks floating on blue clouds.

"Go ahead," my father said, tapping him on the knee. "It's just a little something. No big deal."

I sat back on the piano bench and knew that if it were me, I would have hated to open a present in front of people, especially strange people I had only just met. Adam tore at the wrapping paper carefully and politely, and folded it into quarters to give back to my mother. Then he lifted the lid and found the Twins baseball helmet.

"Neat," he said, and put it on his bowl haircut. "It's nice. I like it." Everybody smiled at him, and almost like he'd forgotten, he said quickly, "Thank you."

Just then the timer went off in the kitchen, and the warm sweet smell of brownies drifted in. We all got up in a panic to turn the thing off, and soon everyone was moving around except Adam, who stayed sitting on the couch. He looked out the window again, and I couldn't tell from the doorway if he looked happy or sad. I thought sad.

THAT NIGHT, AS MY MOTHER and I had discussed, I waited to talk to Adam a little bit alone, to get to know him better and make him feel at home. I sat on my bed, still dressed in my jeans and turtle-neck, and listened for him to finish brushing his teeth in the bathroom. The whole house was already closed up for the night. My parents were in bed, reading. Adam's room was at the end by the stairs, next to mine and two doors away from my parents.

I heard the water turn off in the bathroom, then the toilet flushed. I was nervous and thought maybe I should've waited until morning when we left for school. I couldn't decide. But he might've felt lonely and sad in our big old house with all of us sitting in rooms with doors closed. I stepped out into the hallway and found him just standing there, between the bathroom and his room. He wore blue pajamas that looked like long underwear, but they weren't waffly like long underwear but smooth.

"Hey," he said in a half whisper. "What're you doing up?" His bare feet looked bony, and the toes were long, like fingers.

"I like to stay up," I said, leaning against the wall. "Want to go downstairs for a brownie and talk?" I rocked back and forth against the wall.

He motioned with his head for me to follow him, and I did, even though I thought I should be the one leading him around our house. The kitchen was extra clean and organized like my mother loved it. I flicked on the light above the stove so it wasn't so bright, and Adam grabbed the brownie pan sitting on the counter. We sat up at the barlike counter on wicker stools, and I slid the pan cover back. I wasn't even hungry, but I ate one anyway, holding a paper towel underneath it so I didn't make a mess.

"You know I'm adopted, too," I said to Adam, who ate the brownie by pinching off little chunks. He seemed to be nice, I thought, but maybe a little shy.

"I know," he said, shrugging his skinny shoulders. "But you're spoiled." His thick hair swung around when he tossed his head.

I looked down at the counter and stopped chewing. For a second I was stunned into silence. Why had he said such a thing? "I'm not spoiled," I replied.

"Mmm-hmm," he said. He kicked underneath his stool with his bare feet, *thump, thump, thump,* over and over.

I went to get myself a glass of water and almost ran upstairs to my parents' bedroom to tell them what he was really like.

He sat back, balled up his paper towel, then crossed his arms. "Is it always like this with your family? It's like TV."

I shrugged and stood shifting my weight from one foot to the other. I gulped down the tap water. "Who were your parents before?" I asked, setting the glass down. "Do you know?"

He jumped down from his stool, swung his arm around in the air in big circles like he was winding up for a pitch, then dropped it at his side. "Who cares?" he said, yawning. "Let's go back up."

I turned out the kitchen light, and we started toward the stairs, but he stopped me by the dining room table. The streetlights shone through the windows like moonlight. We were both giant black shadows against the wallpaper. Even the teacups and plates in the corner hutch made shadows.

He held out his hand for me to shake like an adult, and I decided I had to, to be nice. We were about the same height, and I could see his eyes shining. "Well, good night," he said, and headed upstairs again. I followed.

"Good night." I shut my door and leaned against it. Having a brother so fast like this was confusing and hard, and it was only the first day.

ADAM WAS ALREADY HARD TO LIVE WITH, and I could tell my mother was frustrated because her voice sounded high and tight like it only did when she was upset. It was Monday morning, and Adam said he wasn't going to school. I was in my room with the door open, pulling on my knee-highs, and I could hear them talking.

"Adam, you have to go to school," my mother said quietly. "It's not a choice. You just have to. Iris is going. You can walk with her."

"I can't," he said in a mumbling voice. "I don't feel good. I have to stay here."

My mother sighed loudly, and I heard her get up and walk around his room. My father was already at the creamery. He got up way before the sun because he said he had to be there when the farmers brought the milk in. He sometimes got up about four-thirty in the morning, and I wouldn't see him until suppertime. "Adam, please," my mother said, and I heard the shade being pulled up in his room. "Let's not argue about this. You're not ill, and you know it. Now come on. Let's get going."

"No!" Adam barked at her, and I began to wish we'd waited to have a nice baby boy instead of all this trouble.

"Well, suit yourself," my mother said, out in the hallway now. "But this isn't a very good way to start out here. In our house, the children have to go to school, or they'll be punished." She ended up at my door and poked her head in. She rolled her eyes and grabbed for my hairbrush on the dresser. The bed sunk down where she sat behind me, then she started brushing my hair, pulling it all up into a high ponytail. I didn't have a binder, so we sort of danced across the floor with her holding the hair and me grabbing for a binder, until finally it was done. It was a tall skinny ponytail that pulled tightly on my head and made my eyes burn until I loosened it.

Adam ended up going at the last minute. My mother sat in her office, typing, and let him make the decision. I stood out in the yard waiting for him with Sylvie, mad that we were probably going to be late. He came running out with three new Mead notebooks my mother had bought for him—red, blue, and yellow—and just a red hooded sweatshirt for a coat. Sylvie and I still wore our winter coats because of the cold wind.

"Come *on*," Sylvie said, stamping her foot. "It's already almost eight-thirty."

"I know," Adam said, and he started walking fast down the sidewalk. We had to run to catch up. "School is for retards anyway."

"It is not," Sylvie said, holding her books tight to her chest. "I like it. Me and Iris both do."

I nodded, but had to walk behind them because there wasn't room for us all on the sidewalk.

"You would," Adam said, kicking at hardened clumps of black snow. "I suppose you both get As and kiss the teacher's ass, too."

"Ick!" Sylvie said, and slapped him on the arm. "That's gross! Don't talk like that." She slowed down and walked beside me, leaving Adam in front of us. We whispered about him and rolled our eyes.

"I thought he was going to be nice," Sylvie whispered. "I don't want him to be my boyfriend, I guess. Not if he acts like this."

We were so close to school we could hear the bell ring; we ran across the street, forgetting to look for cars. As we rushed up the slushy sidewalk to the big maroon doors, I saw Adam turn off down the street, away from the school.

I pointed him out to Sylvie, but we both just shrugged our shoulders. There was nothing we could do. Maybe if my mother and father found all of this out, they'd send him back. I kind of hoped they would.

THE WEEK WENT BY, AND SOMEHOW Adam got forced into going to school and didn't make too much fuss. I was in sixth grade, in Mrs. Scholhauser's class, and Adam was in seventh, with Mr. Hudson as his homeroom teacher, who had a reputation for being hard and strict, even though he was young and handsome and spent an hour each day reading novels out loud to the class. I kind of hoped I'd get him next year, because Sylvie's older sister Janelle said he turned out the lights when he read and everyone could put their heads down to listen. It sounded nice. He'd already read them *A Tree Grows in Brooklyn* and *Where the Red Fern Grows*.

My teacher, Mrs. Scholhauser, was older and less interesting. She was married to Wishbone's chief of police, wore big black glasses, had huge breasts, and always snuck diet candies into her mouth during class. Sometimes if you asked a question, you could catch her just chewing and chewing and it took her a while to answer. She'd divided our class into committees for everything from current events to windowsill decorating to health and safety reports to sports. She said kids needed to be more well-rounded nowadays and made us report in front of the class every week.

I was thrilled when Sylvie and I got asked to be in charge of the holiday committee. We got to take some of the class treasury funds and go up to Ben Franklin to buy little decorations of chicks and Easter eggs to hang up in our room and tape onto the door that faced the hallway. We bought three rolls of crepe paper— lavender, yellow, and pink—and twirled it around the blackboard and bulletin boards. We even got to pick out treats for the class, so we bought bright pink and yellow Peeps, which made everyone's desk a sticky mess.

The town of Wishbone wasn't big enough to have separate kindergarten, grade school and high school, so they were all lumped together in one—Wishbone Public School. It was a long two-story brick building that used to have huge tall windows that went up to the ceiling, but some parts had been replaced with colored insulated squares to save on heat. You couldn't see out as much now, just cars and the lawn instead of up into the big oak trees like before.

Mrs. Scholhauser's room was on the second floor, next to the fifth grade classroom and the band room, which had recently been painted with big blue elephants and giraffes playing drums and cellos. Mr. Hudson's room was on the first floor, directly below me, and when we went down to the gym for P.E., I sometimes peeked in to see Adam. He usually sat tapping his feet really fast and looking out the window. He always acted as if he couldn't wait to be let out, to be free, as if he was being held against his will.

On Friday afternoon, he and I met up outside by the carport, where my mother picked us up because it was raining. I could see our big red station wagon in line with all the other cars, and my mother leaned forward and waved. Adam and I ran over with notebooks over our heads since it was a bad windy rain. Inside, the car's windows were steamed up, and my mother rubbed at the windshield with a Kleenex.

"Hi, you two," she said, then steered the car out of the line. Adam was in the backseat, and I was in front. My mother turned onto Main Street and stopped at the only stoplight in town. There she took a left, went a block down, and slid to a stop in front of the creamery. "Kauffman's Dairy," it said in blue block letters on the white sign. "Your father might need a little help," she said. "Come on." We all got out of the car and ran for the door. The rain came down in long sideways needles and stung my cheeks. I felt glad that it was the weekend, even though the weather was so bad.

Nobody was in the creamery, and my mother had to call back to the sterilizing room for my father. Adam scuffed around the wooden floor, peering into the ice cream cooler full of treats.

"You can have something if you like, Adam," my mother said, placing a hand on his shoulder. "But just pick one thing so you don't spoil your appetite for dinner. Okay?"

"Okay," he said, without looking. He shrugged her hand off his shoulder, and my mother stepped away, looking hurt. She crossed her arms across her chest and pulled her sweater around her.

"Me, too," I said, and ran over to pick something out. It was always a hard choice. Did I want a Popsicle or something creamy like a Fudgsicle or Creamsicle? Adam grabbed a Drumstick, and I thought of how good that last little bit of chocolate was at the very tip of the sugar cone. I took one, too.

My mother went to the cash register and rang it open. She ruffled through the bills, muttering numbers out loud quietly, probably to see how much money we'd made. Lots of kids usually came in after school for a treat, but today, because of the rainstorm, it was quiet. I could hear the Coca-Cola clock buzz up on the wall. Cars drove by and made long splashes. "Damn," my mother said, and closed the register drawer. She bumped her elbow on the counter. "Ouch!"

"What's the matter?" I asked.

"Nothing, just nothing." She went back into my father's office with him and closed the door.

I could tell something was the matter. Maybe she'd decided it was too expensive raising two kids, so now they had to pick only one, me or Adam. Adam had been better lately, quiet. Quieter than me, so they'd probably pick him. Maybe it wouldn't be so bad, I thought, to get sent back to my real mom. She probably missed me, whoever she was. Maybe she'd never wanted to give me away in the first place, but she was forced into it. Maybe she was really young and pretty and wore big colored scarves tied in her hair and sparkly lipstick. Maybe we'd be like girlfriends.

"Hey," Adam said, shoving the last of his Drumstick into his mouth. He pointed to the cash register. "Do you know how to open that?" He talked with his mouth full, like I'd been taught never to do.

"Yeah. Why?"

"Show me how," he said, and hurried over to it. A big gust of wind spattered rain against the glass door. "I just want to try it."

I walked over to him, hands on my hips. "Why? Do you want to steal from us?" I felt like I was his mother.

"No," he said, using the same mocking voice he always did. "Just show me."

"I'm not going to." I checked for my parents, but the door was still shut. In fact, when I got closer, I could hear their voices, and my mother sounded angry and upset.

"Come on," Adam said.

I climbed up on the wooden stool and sat on my knees. "Okay, I'll show you, but you don't get to touch it. Even I'm not supposed to." I checked over the buttons, trying to remember. "It's this one, No Sale." I punched the button, and the drawer rolled open with a ding. Then I slammed it back closed so Adam couldn't do anything and so my parents wouldn't catch me.

"Neat," he said. "Let me try." Before I could stop him, he punched the button and the drawer rang open again. He elbowed me away and grabbed a ten dollar bill, one of only three in there.

"Hey," I said, "you can't do that! It's stealing. I'm going to tell. I will." I tried to say it all loud enough so maybe my parents would hear and come running out, but they didn't.

"You would tell," he said, jumping away. "Spoiled." Then he ran out the door, into the rain, his longish hair swinging in strings.

I TOLD MY PARENTS RIGHT AWAY, and my father went running off down the street to try and catch him. My father was still wearing his white creamery uniform with clear plastic gloves and a clear plastic apron tied around him, kind of like a slicker in the rain. But Adam was gone.

The three of us sat around the counter, wondering what to do. "Well," my mother said, running her hands through her hair, "for only being in seventh grade, he sure has big problems." She stared out the window, twirling the ends of her hair. "But then, we knew all of this when we got him. I mean, it's not really his fault. The awful parents he had were just—oh, I'd like to . . . I don't know. I guess we just have to be patient. We just have to." She sighed.

My father was less nice. "I don't care what problems he's had," he said. "We can't just sit by while he robs us. We can't be stupid."

"Well, I'm not being stupid, Bill."

"I know, I know," my father said.

"But we can't be too hard on him either. We might make it worse."

"I suppose we should talk to him," my father said. "Let him try to explain what happened or why he thought he needed that money."

"I suppose." My mother looked far away again, and I didn't want to lose her. She twirled her tiny earrings around and around.

I listened to them back and forth, my chin on the counter.

Just then Mrs. Scholhauser, my teacher, came in. I rushed around like I was busy helping my father stack butter in the cooler.

"Iris!" she said, spotting me immediately. "How nice that you can help your parents out here."

I nodded and forced a smile, but got back to my fake work. My father kept stacking butter and clear plastic tubs of sour cream and winked at me.

"Hi, Doris," my mother said to her. "What can we do for you?"

I just about died of embarrassment as Mrs. Scholhauser shook out her umbrella and pulled a folded-up list out of her purse. I followed my father into the back and stayed there until I was sure she was gone. I put on one of the sanitary paper hats and watched the heavy cream being separated from the milk. It was warm and wet in the room, and this time it smelled in a strange way like peaches.

THAT NIGHT ADAM SAID HE WAS SORRY and gave back five of the dollars. At the supper table, he said he'd bought baseball cards, Twinkies, and a small tin game of Chinese checkers with the other five. I didn't believe he'd bought any of that, because where was the game? I hadn't seen it. He said he hadn't meant to steal, but thought since we all owned the store together like a family, he could take a little. I knew he knew better and glanced at him as I ate a forkful of corn. I knew he really meant to steal. His dark eyes flashed at me as if I'd better not say anything.

My parents practically cheered about his apology and said that they forgave him. "Just don't ever do it again without asking," my father said, pointing at Adam. "You have to ask. The dairy is a business I run. It's not my personal wallet. Understand?" He stared at Adam for awhile to see that he understood, then went back to eating. "Honey, would you pass me the butter?"

He'd brought us home some fresh Grade AA, which was the palest and sweetest butter he made. There was a fist-sized glob on a little sheet of wax paper, and my mother slid it over to him with her fingers. When it was finished, I liked to lick the paper. Sometimes I ate butter by the stick like a candy bar, but it felt heavy as a rock in my stomach, like when I ate raw cookie dough. My mother said it was sick, and snatched it right out of my hand when she caught me. "Never, never do that again," she'd said to me last time. "Do you want to grow up and be fat? Do you want no one to like you? Because that's what'll happen if you keep eating this butter." I hardly ever did it anymore, but I did try to lick the paper in secret.

Since it was Friday night and there was no school the next day, my parents told us we could stay up late. "Can I ask Sylvie overnight?" I asked. "Please?"

My mother looked at my father, and he shrugged. He pushed his plate away, then lit up a cigarette and blew smoke off to the side. "All right," he said. "But don't you and Adam want to do something together? Does it always have to be Sylvie, too?"

I didn't answer, but my mother stuck up for me. "Oh, Bill. They're best friends. Sylvie can stay, Iris," she said. "The three of you can all spend some time together."

Adam rolled his eyes, but didn't let my mother and father see. He'd ripped his paper napkin into shreds and was balling the pieces up into little pellets. I could hear his feet tapping underneath the chair, like always. The cat, who'd been purring by my legs, ran away scared.

After the dishes were cleared and we'd had our chocolate pudding in Tupperware cups, the kind of pudding with skin on it, which I pulled off and stuck in my father's cup, Adam and I went into the family room. I lay on the footstool on my stomach and watched TV. Adam sat on the floor, his back against the couch.

"Don't have Sylvie over," Adam said, not looking at me.

I was practicing my crawl stroke on the footstool, but stopped and sat up. "What? Why not?"

"She doesn't like me," Adam said. "She's a snot." He wiped at his nose and reached across the carpet to change channels. There was nothing good on.

"She is not," I said. "You're just jealous." I took one of the couch pillows and threw it at him.

We started pillow fighting until I got smacked a little too hard in the face and called quits. My eye was watering, but I didn't cry. We were both out of breath and sat up on the couch. "I know," Adam said. "Let's just you and me have a slumber party down here tonight. We can stay up and watch Carol Burnett and have sleeping bags down here and everything. Yeah, let's do it." His dark brown eyes shone. He pushed back his bangs with his fingers.

"But why can't Sylvie come, too? She would be fun."

"Nah. Just us. Okay? You want to?"

My mother and father came in to watch the news with steaming cups of coffee. "Want to what?" my mother asked, sitting beside me. She folded her legs up under her and pulled the afghan over both of us. She set the coffee cup on her knee carefully. "What are you planning now?"

I looked at Adam and made him be the one to tell them. Of course they'd like it if it was his idea. Anything he did was okay because of all the problems he'd had; that was what it seemed like. He moved to the soft blue chair. "We want to have a slumber party down here, me and Iris," he said. "Do you have any sleeping bags?"

My father looked up from his coffee, interested. "Hey, sounds like fun. Maybe we should join them, Marilyn." He looked over at my mother and winked, and they both shared a sparkly look.

"You can," I said. "It's not really a *party* party anyway."

"It's okay," she said. "We're just teasing." She put her warm hand on my leg and rubbed up and down. I leaned my head against her arm and breathed in the soft sweet smell of her talcum powder, which she dusted on after her baths with a big pink puff.

It ended up that Sylvie couldn't come over anyway because she was sick with the flu and so were two of her brothers. After *Columbo* my parents said good night and headed up to bed. They left me and Adam with a whole stack of fresh cool pillows and two sleeping bags from the cedar closet and a big bowl of popcorn with butter. We turned out all the lamps and only had the TV's jumping colors as a light. It did seem fun, and Adam was being nicer to me than usual.

After awhile, though, my eyelids started to get heavy, and I could barely stay awake. Adam and I had our sleeping bags right next to each other, facing the TV at an angle. When I was just about asleep, I noticed Adam crawling out of his sleeping bag to turn off the TV. The family room was an added-on room in the back of the house my father and grandfather had built, and was shaded in the summer by big maple trees. At night it never got completely dark in the family room, though, because our neighbor's bright yard light was always on, spreading over their yard and right into our windows.

I nuzzled down into my pillow and curled my legs up under my nightgown like a cocoon. I was so tired I didn't even say good night to Adam. I could hear him breathing though, and it didn't sound like he was asleep.

"Iris?"

"Hmm."

"Are you asleep?" I heard the crunchy fabric of his sleeping bag as he turned over. I'd let him have the new green one, which was the same material as a winter coat. I opened my eyes, which felt glued shut, and saw him propped up on his elbow, looking at me.

"Yes. I'm asleep." I closed my eyes again.

"Hey." He reached over and shook my arm. "I said, hey."

I turned over flat on my back and stretched out, my bare feet cold against the empty end of the sleeping bag. "What? What do you want?"

"Want to play Truth or Dare?"

"No."

"Why not?" he asked, sitting all the way up now, out of his sleeping bag.

"Because, it's a stupid game. And I'm sleeping." But then I sneezed twice in a row, deep hard sneezes. My sleeping bag was the old brown one with duck-hunting scenes on the inside flannel, and it smelled like mold and must. I rubbed my nose really hard.

"Can I come in your sleeping bag with you?" Adam asked.

I squirmed down deeper into mine. "No. There's no room."

Adam tapped his feet up and down on the carpet. "But I hate sleeping alone. I'm used to sleeping with my mom. It's too cold to sleep alone."

"You slept with your mom even when you were this old?" I turned over, interested. The itch in my nose wouldn't go away.

"Just sometimes," he said, crawling back into his sleeping bag.

My eyes were wide open in the dark. The wind started to blow outside, and small ticks of rain hit the windows. I could see them cling to the glass and shake, then go drizzling down. I made no sound, and finally Adam settled back and put his hands behind his head.

It was a long time before either of us said anything. "You're my sister now," Adam whispered, and I didn't say anything back. I lay still, thinking about my new life, about Adam for a brother, about being adopted.

I must've finally fallen asleep, because when I woke up, my mother was humming by the piano in the living room in her robe. She glanced over at me and smiled. A coffee cup sat beside her on the bench, steaming up in curling clouds. I looked over, and Adam was gone. He was already up, his green sleeping bag tied tightly in a bundle like a pot roast with strings.

Chapter Three

Memory: An early Easter morning; the daffodils are blooming fresh. My father takes me aside and places a pink plastic egg in my hand. I shake it. It rattles with something secret inside. When I try to open it, he says, "No, take this to your mother. Tell her the Easter bunny brought it. See what she says." He winks. I want whatever's inside. I don't want to give it up.

My mother splits the egg in half, and a string of pearls spills out. She drapes them between her fingers. My father mouths, "I'm sorry." My mother shrugs her shoulders. She places me squarely in front of her like a shield.

All I want is candy, but there's a bitterness I'm tasting.

Adam and I woke up very early Easter morning, and I was surprised to find both my parents already up. They sat in the kitchen with cups of coffee, pouring over manila folders from the creamery, stacks of wrinkled pink and yellow forms fluttering inside. An adding machine on the table ribboned out a long receipt of purple numbers. The sun streamed in through the windows and onto the floor in big bright squares, and it made me have to blink to see through the dark spots in front of me.

My mother had her forehead cupped in the palm of her hand and her other hand wrapped around the coffee cup. Her hair looked coppery like new pennies from the bank. There was a burning cigarette hanging between my father's lips, and he blinked away the smoke as he punched at the numbers and leafed through papers. "Damn," he said, before he saw me or Adam in the doorway. "Dammit."

"What?" I asked. I wore my quilted pink robe with silver flowers running down it, and the hand-knit slippers my mother made me every year. They were pink-and-purple checkerboard with pink pom-poms.

"Well, hello there. Happy Easter," my mother said, turning to us. "You're up so early." She looked pointedly at my father so that he shut off the humming machine and pushed the paperwork away. His hair was slicked back in perfectly combed stripes, although one or two fell down near his left eye and caught in his eyelashes. My father stubbed out the cigarette in the big green-and-orange ceramic ashtray I'd made in school. The edges were pinched crumbly with thumbprints like piecrust. His eyebrows shot up, and I noticed how red his eyes looked around the blue. "I think I heard the rabbit down here last night," he said. "Did anyone else hear it?"

Adam sat on a wicker stool at the counter and made a snorting sound. "Oh, yeah, the Easter bunny, right?" He was being sarcastic and mean again, but I didn't care. I'd decided to ignore him and stay as far away from him as I could. Of course I didn't believe in the Easter bunny anymore, but it was fun to pretend with my parents.

My father scratched his nose with his thick red thumb. "I think he left something for you two around here."

My parents followed me as I took off and started looking behind chairs, behind the magazine rack, under the coffee table. They usually hid it in really easy places, and finally I saw the twisted colored straw handle shoved between the piano and the wall. It was full of pastel malted milk balls, stuck-together rows of marshmallow Peeps, jelly beans, Reese's peanut butter eggs, and a few of the real eggs we'd dyed the day before. There was also a pack of plastic headbands in all pastel colors and a whole package of white anklets with lace trim.

Adam's was right next to the TV. His plain-colored round basket had all the same candy as mine, except he got white tube socks and a new tightly stitched baseball. He dug around in the basket, munching on the jelly beans, then pushed it off to the side.

My mother and father settled back on the couch and smiled. They looked happy in a way that I knew wouldn't last. My mother chewed at the inside of her mouth. She was looking at me, but really looking right through me; I could feel her cloudy stare enter me in front and leave out the back.

When my father put his arm around her shoulder, she moved away and lay on the couch, her head leaning on the arm of it, her hands tucked under her cheek. She looked like a young girl. My father slid a hand up over her hip, and I couldn't help noticing how curved it was, her body, like a beautiful guitar.

EASTER WAS AT GRANDMA LAURA'S that year, which it was every year. She refused to go anywhere else because she was too old, she said, and it was tradition to have all of us crammed in her little brick box house with nowhere to sit or stand. Every year, she and my uncle Robert, who was short and energetic and a lawyer, hid colored eggs all around her yard for us to find, and one of them was always wrapped in tinfoil with a ten dollar bill taped around it. Last year I'd found it, and the year before that, Melanie had. This year, though, there were still patches of dirty icy snow in the back, where no sun reached, and the ground was spongy and soft so that I wasn't able to wear the white sandals my mother had bought specially for me at Penney's. I had to wear my brown lace-ups, which were dark and scuffed and not very Easterlike, but I got to wear my new socks so it wasn't too bad. It'd been a very long winter.

For some reason, we didn't go to church that Easter, one of the few times we usually went, so we were the first ones to arrive at Grandma Laura's in Mankato. We walked in, all of us holding ridged glass bottles of milk with pleated foil tops, jelly jars of cream, uneven wedges of butter in sealed Tupperware, and a big gallon pail of vanilla ice cream, which was frosted up on the outside.

"Oh, you!" my Grandma Laura shouted, placing a hand to her mouth, as if it was still a surprise that we would bring dairy foods. "What is this? All of this! You shouldn't have."

"Hi, Mom." My mother kissed her lightly on the cheek and pushed past her to the refrigerator. We all followed and handed over the things that needed chilling.

"Hi, Laura," my father said, squeezing her arm. He was the last one in and carried a grocery bag full of food and fruit and rolls in one hand, and a beautiful blooming Easter lily wrapped in pink foil in the other.

"Iris!" Grandma Laura swept down and pulled me to her. "So pretty! And Adam!" She made room in her other arm to take him in, but Adam shifted away to the TV room. He lurked in the doorway, doing one of his favorite tricks. You stood in the doorway and pushed the outsides of your hands against the frame until they hurt so bad you could hardly stand it. Then you stepped away, and magically, as if they were wings, your arms floated up without your even trying.

He did that now, over and over, grinning when it worked. He didn't even say hello to Grandma Laura or how are you. Grandma Laura hugged me closer and whispered in my ear. "He's a tough nut, isn't he, that one?" I nodded into her hair, and she patted me on the behind, letting me go.

Soon Aunt Patty and Uncle Robert showed up with the girls, Melanie and DeeDee. They brought in more grocery bags of food and a coconut-sprinkled white-frosted cake shaped like a bunny. It had a pink gumdrop for a nose and black licorice eyelashes. I could tell it was a store-bought cake, which was just like them. They were richer than everyone else, and the girls always had the best of everything.

DeeDee, Melanie, and I sprawled out on the living room carpet, which was a deep brown marbled pattern. It was the only big room in the tiny house, and soon everyone wandered in, filling up all the chairs and the couch. It smelled like coffee and rich roasting turkey meat. DeeDee and I entertained everyone by doing the splits in the center of the room, then holding up our arms in *V*s. We were practicing to eventually be cheerleaders.

Then the side door opened, and Aunt Deb and the boys came in. Aunt Deb and my uncle Wayne were separated, and now Uncle Wayne lived in an apartment in Minneapolis where he worked in a factory and had a girlfriend who was a stripper. That's what I'd overheard from my mother throughout these past months. Nobody talked about it in the open.

The boys—Noel, David, and Carter—came into the living room, filling it up even more. To be funny, David, the middle brother, pretended to rev up a motorcycle, then made like he wiped out and slid across the room on the side of his leg. Noel, the youngest, started wailing like an ambulance and pretended to pick David up in a stretcher. They were always showing off.

"David! Noel!" Aunt Deb yelled from the kitchen. "Lay off. Now." They didn't listen to her though, and she continued to unload all the relish trays and other foods she'd brought. Everybody talked louder and louder, all the kids bouncing and bending around, making more noise. Coffee was served, and cans of Orange Crush and root beer were opened for us kids. Uncle Robert and my father talked loudly about business and smoked cigarettes by the front door. My father was almost a whole head taller than him.

Suddenly, in the middle of everything, Carter, the oldest grandchild, looked around and asked, "Where's Adam? Didn't he come with you?"

We all stopped talking and looked around.

"I'll go get him," I said, popping up from the floor. "He's in the TV room, I think." I stuck my head in and found him there, watching an old black-and-white movie. He sat in my grandpa's old recliner, the one that was still velvety and new.

"What're you doing?" I asked, not sitting down. "Why don't you come out and see everyone?"

He wouldn't look at me, even when I walked over in front of the TV. His eyes were dark and watery, and the outfit my mother made him wear, dark brown pants with a striped button-up shirt, made him look old and formal. "Just leave me alone," he said, and waved me away with his hand. His long hair was combed over to the side and split at the forehead into a part.

"What's wrong?" I asked. I could tell something was.

He finally turned to face me. His long lashes made his eyes look pretty and soft, and his skin was a warm color, like he was suntanned. But then I noticed there were small brown scars in tiny circles on the back of his right hand. I tried not to stare, but felt so awful, remembering my mother telling me about how his first family wasn't good to him. I tried not to act like anything was unusual, though he didn't seem to notice that I'd seen.

"I just don't feel like it," Adam said. "Everyone's so loud." He put his hands over his ears and jiggled his feet up and down. "Hmm–hm–hmm–hm–hmm. Blah, blah, blah." Then he hummed loudly, hands still over his ears, to drown me out.

LATER IN THE AFTERNOON, the sun came out, and it was finally warm enough to play outside, barely. All of us kids zipped up our coats and went out to the backyard. The adults didn't even care anymore what we did. Dinner was long finished, and the big jug of Mogen David was almost gone. Bottles of beer were being drawn out of the refrigerator. My father and Uncle Robert, the only men, were talking really hard and serious and smoking one cigarette after another. They sat in the TV room, away from the women, rubbing their brown-stockinged feet back and forth, relaxed.

Grandma Laura had an attached garage, and Melanie and Carter, who were the oldest and acted like they were too cool to play with us anyway, decided we were going to play Annie Annie Over. Carter started looking for a ball.

"No, let's play Seven Steps Around the House," DeeDee whined. She was wearing a hilarious green jumpsuit with a zip-up collar and a macramé stretch belt around the waist. Aunt Patty thought her girls were always in high fashion, but I didn't. They never just wore jeans and sweatshirts, but always wore something inappropriate and gaudy.

"I can't find a ball," Carter said. He was the tallest and seemed to try to shrink down his size by slouching his skinny shoulders and hanging his head. He was starting to get raised yellowish pimples that I would've just taken between my fingernails and popped open to let out all the pressure if it were me. I felt kind of sorry for him, though, because his father had left the family, and now Carter had to act like the man of the house because Aunt Deb was always hysterical about something and a nervous wreck, according to my mother.

"We can play Truth or Dare," Adam said. He sat on the cement stoop, hands in his pockets. "You don't need anything to play that. And there's so many of us, it would work good." No one wanted to argue because we'd been told to be extra nice to Adam lately because he was new to our family.

"Okay," Melanie said, pushing up her pink glasses that seemed to always sit crookedly on her face. She held up her hands and waved everyone over with her fingers, just like a teacher did when recess was done. "Into the garage."

The garage had a greasy, metal smell, and circles of grainy oil were all over the cement floor, so no one wanted to sit down. Noel got the idea for each of us to pull a clean garbage bag out of the box to sit on. It was cold on my bare legs, so I clutched my knees up to my chest and pulled my dress around so no one could see my underwear. The cold from the cement floor crept up through the garbage bag and my clothes and to my butt. All my grandpa's tools still hung off the Peg-Board in perfect order, and above us, the summer patio furniture was held up by the wooden ceiling beams. Even a mattress was up there, and a red canoe, and I was beginning to worry that it all might collapse and kill us.

"Okay, who's first?" asked Melanie, who was the obvious leader of the game. She held up a pointy finger. "But no rotten stuff. I swear I'll tell if anyone tries to pull anything." She reminded me of a squirrel who was excited about a big batch of nuts it'd just found and was hoarding them away from all the other squirrels. "Carter, you start. Ask anyone you want."

Carter sat with his long skinny legs bent up to his elbows. He was really too old to be playing with any of us, but he went along with it in his good-natured way. He was nice like that. He wore a white hooded sweatshirt over his good dress-up clothes and black high-tops. "Okay, okay," he said, rocking back and forth. "Ah, let's see." He looked around, and everyone looked away. "Okay, Iris, Truth or Dare."

Before I could answer, Melanie piped in. She spread her hands out in the air. "Hey, let's say you can also add Double-Dare, Promise, or Repeat, okay? Okay." She nodded in answer to her own question, and thinking that we all agreed, she sat back.

All eyes were on me. Cars drove by on the slushy street, and as the sun disappeared, a cold darkness settled in the air. "I'll pick Dare." Usually Dare was easier because then you didn't have to tell any of your worst secrets but just went running around screaming something stupid.

"Dare, hmm," Carter said, drumming his fingers against his lips. "Let me think." The rule was also that no one could help the person think up the Dare or Truth.

DeeDee and Noel were kicking each other with muddy shoes, already sick of the game. I looked at Carter so he wouldn't give me anything too bad and so he'd hurry.

"Okay," he said, snapping his fingers. "You have to go inside and say that Melanie just got hit by a car and they better call an ambulance. Yeah."

"No way!" Melanie said. She shoved her long stringy hair behind her ears. "That's too much. Everyone will worry and have a heart attack and then get mad. Something else." She crossed her arms.

"Okay, okay," Carter said, laughing. "Umm, why don't you go lie out in the middle of the street until a car comes and wait until the last possible second before getting up."

Melanie lowered her eyebrows. "Carter," she said. "You know better." She sounded just like our mothers.

Adam nudged me on the elbow. "Do it. You won't get in trouble. She has to do it. It's a dare. You can't just say no to everything, Melanie, or it's not a game." Adam got up and started pulling me to my feet. "And if she gets killed, we'll just say it was a car accident." He snickered into his sleeve, and swung the hair out of his eyes.

"That's not very nice," DeeDee said, sticking up for me. Her thick golden hair was bound up in a bun, and pieces stuck out all over where the bobby pins had gotten loose. She kept cupping the bun with her hand.

I just shrugged and got up. Mainly, I knew I was going to get my good clothes all dirty, and my mother would sigh and act like we were all a bunch of brats. "Why you turn into an absolute monster when you spend time with your cousins, I'll never know," she always said. "You all bring out the beast in one another."

I walked out into the street, which was paved but kind of pebbly. It was very wet, and I had a dress on, but I pulled my jacket down over my butt, sat, then lay back. They were all watching from inside the garage, but no cars came by. The pavement was very hard on the back of my head. I put my hands over my chest and thought it was not so different from playing dead under my bed, except I hadn't done that since Adam had moved in with us. I closed my eyes, then opened them. There was a fine mist in the air that made my cheeks feel dewy. I could feel the backs of my bare legs get cold and wet. The sky was gray and dull and rumbled with faraway thunder or an airplane—I couldn't tell.

"Hey, you can come back now," Carter called. "It's been long enough!"

"No, stay until a car comes!" Adam called back. "You haven't done the whole dare yet!" I could hear him and Carter fake-fighting about it and pretending to kickbox or something.

I closed my eyes and smiled. I could've stayed there forever. I could've taken a nap. But then I heard the slush on the road separating as a car took a corner and came up the hill. I began to panic, thinking the driver might not see me until the car was all the way up the hill, and then it would be too late. The engine sounded closer and closer. At the last minute, I sat up, hands still crossed in position over my chest. The car was a big dark green one with its headlights on. I felt like a trapped mouse, frozen, unable to move. It was impossible for me to get up and run. Then the horn beeped loudly, and the car stopped.

The driver got out of the car and hurried over to me. It was an old man in a long navy-blue coat and a gray hat. I looked down, and saw my Windbreaker was all mucked up and soggy with dirt and gravel. My legs were stretched straight out in front of me. "Honey, what's the matter? Are you all right?" He gently put his hands under my armpits and eased me up. "Did you get hurt?" He spun me all the way around to see that I was all right, then stood back, scowling.

"Iris Lucille!" my mother yelled, hanging out the front door. "Get in here right now! Come on!" She waved her hands at us, then came running out in her high heels and no coat. "I'm sorry," she apologized to the man. "They were just playing a foolish game." Her thin flowered dress rippled in the wind and separated between her legs.

The man muttered something, waddled over to his car, then started driving slowly up and over the hill. When he was safely gone, my mother bent down to my level and grabbed me by the shoulders. "Iris," she said, and her breath smelled like alcohol, "do you know that I was just getting up to get a glass of water and looked out the window, and do you know what I saw?" She shook me. "Do you?"

I didn't say anything, but hung my head.

"I saw my daughter lying in the middle of the road! I thought you'd been hit by a car and were dead! Dead, Iris!" Her green eyes were wild and watery in the cold wind. "I thought my little girl was dead!" She bit her lip, and tears streamed out of her eyes. "Do you know what that did to me? Do you?" Another harder shake. "It destroyed me, Iris! It absolutely destroyed me! Oh, god." She put her head against my chest and cried freely now. I put my arms around her. No one was left in the garage anymore, and the street was empty except for us in the middle of it.

My mother finally pulled herself together and inhaled deeply. She sighed. "Oh, Iris, what am I going to do with you? You don't— it's so hard—your father and I . . ." She stared off down the street at nothing. "Well, I don't want to talk about it now. Come on, let's get you home and into a hot bath." She grabbed my hand, and we ran across the street, onto the spongy yard, up the cement stoop. I noticed a petal-pink Easter egg shoved behind the old geranium pot and tried to reach for it, but was pulled into the house by my mother. The door closed with a sucking sound, and the steamy warmth of the house curled around my bare legs and up through my clothes.

I was cold and chilled to the very center and could not stop shaking.

ONE HOT TUESDAY AFTERNOON in May, I came home from school and found everything stirred up. My Grandma Laura's white car was in the driveway, and so was our red station wagon, which my father almost always took up to the creamery for the whole day. Sylvie and I stopped and looked at each other.

"What's going on?" she said. "Isn't that your grandma's car?" She swung her book bag in the air, pointing at the Cadillac.

"I better go see," I said. "It's probably Adam again. Stealing or something."

Sylvie started down the sidewalk, her skinny legs in white knee-highs looking like pencils. She waved back at me. "Call if it's something good!" Her dark hair was shiny in the sun like a horse's, like Black Beauty.

Inside the house felt wonderfully cool and quiet. I threw my books down on the stairs and tried the living room, but no one was there. The clock buzzed in the kitchen, and there was no note. Sun spilled through the family room windows in wide dusty beams, but nobody was in there, either.

"Hey!" I hollered, walking back through the kitchen and dining room. "I'm home! It's me, Iris!" Since I was starving to death, I reached into the pantry and grabbed the Cap'n Crunch, peanut butter flavor. I loved to eat it out of the box, even more than with milk in a bowl. As I was crunching, I made one last check in my mother's office, but it was dark and unusually tidy. The typewriter was turned off and fitted perfectly with its gray plastic IBM cover.

"We're up here," my father said, coming down the stairs and into the dining room. "But we have to be a little quiet." He put his finger to his lips. "Come here a minute and sit down."

I slid out a heavy dining room chair with a woven seat and half sat on it. My father did the same. "What's wrong?" I asked, getting cereal crumbs on the good wine-colored tablecloth. "Did Adam do something wrong again?"

My father shook his head slowly and looked down at the floor. "No, Adam's fine," he said. "It's your mother."

She's dead, was all I could think. She's dead.

My father picked at things on his pant legs, and I noticed in the middle of the day like this, he didn't even have his creamery clothes on. He wore soft gray corduroy pants with a plaid shirt, like he'd gotten dressed up, but not too dressed up.

He folded his hands and set them firmly on the table, rolling the thumbs back and forth over each other. "I guess I might as well tell you what happened." His bright blue eyes looked smaller than usual, and the skin seemed hooded over them like an old person's. "She was going to have a baby. You see, she was pregnant, and since she's had trouble with this in the past, it was kind of touch and go. We didn't want to tell you until things were safe."

Again? My eyes must've widened and looked scared because he smiled and placed a big hand over my small one. "She's all right, Iris. She's fine." He took away his hand and sat back, chuckling a little. Then the sick look came across his face again. "But the baby came out early, by accident. It was a miscarriage. Have you ever heard of that?"

I nodded, thanks to Melanie and DeeDee, but really I didn't understand how it all happened, where, what it looked like. My father cleared his throat and looked out the window, irritated, as a loud car without a muffler blasted by. "Your mother is very sad, Iris. And I am, too." He put his fingers up to his chest gently. "She's going to need you and Adam to be very good and helpful around here, and to try to cheer her up. It won't be easy for awhile, and even if your mother seems to not want to talk, she isn't mad at you. She's just hurting inside."

I took all this in by nodding and agreeing to be good, and wondered if Adam knew. Could this be the second time she'd lost a baby? Then I wondered why she kept trying to have more babies in the first place when she already had me and now Adam. It seemed like she wasn't happy with us, and wanted more or better, or kids who were really, truly her own and looked like her instead of just being adopted.

GRANDMA LAURA WAS GOOD at making the house feel cozy even without my mother being around. She put on a Bing Crosby record as she was fixing supper and left all the shades up so that I could see myself twirling around in the black window reflections. My mother never would've left the shades up at night. My mother would've also never cooked asparagus with lemon sauce and served it over fish. We were more used to eating meat and potatoes, or hamburgers with chips, or tuna hotdish. My father probably wouldn't like this food.

It was suppertime, and Adam was still not home from school. Who knew what he did all the time, though now that daylight lasted longer, my father said he'd probably be out playing ball or bike riding with his friends. I didn't know and I didn't much care either.

I hadn't seen my mother yet, since she'd been sleeping when I got home. My father was up there now, so it was just me and Grandma Laura in the steamed-up kitchen. Grandma Laura had a tight bunched-up look on her face as she moved from stove to cupboard and back again, to sink, to stove, to oven. There was a green, earthy smell in the air from the asparagus, which I was sure I'd hate.

"Grandma?" I sat up on the counter, away from the stove so I wasn't in the way.

"Yes?" She went about her business.

"Umm . . ." I didn't know how to ask what I needed to ask. "Well, what happens when you have a miscarriage? Does the baby come out?"

I could sense a tightening in my Grandma's back, and she answered without facing me. "Yes, it does. It comes out a little too early. And that's what happened to your mother."

"But, how does it come out? Didn't she have to go to the hospital?"

"Why yes, she did," Grandma Laura said, sliding the clear glass pan out of the oven. The white fish bubbled with buttery lemon juice. It was sprinkled with coarse black pepper, and the asparagus lay over it like limp, dead people. "But she only went for a little while. She had the miscarriage at home, and then she just went in for a checkup to see if she was all right." She folded the faded blue potholder in half and closed the oven with it. "Now, we should get your father." She set her hands on her wide hips and checked the table in the dining room, which was set and ready with four places.

I stayed on the counter. "But what happens to the baby now?"

Grandma Laura looked me in the eye, first hard, then softer. Her dark brown eyes looked full and sad. She scratched her sharp flaky fingernails up and down her arms. "The baby's already in heaven, Iris." She came over and patted her warm hands on my thighs. "Let's just not talk about it for now. Let's just stay quiet." I put my arms around her neck, and let her lift me up, then down.

THAT NIGHT IT WAS WARM enough to lie in my bed with the windows open. I could hear crickets out in the yard and leaves rustling in the breeze. My white dotted swiss curtains blew lightly open, and I had the covers pulled only halfway up, to my waist. My mother and father were already in bed for the night, although I still hadn't seen my mother since she'd been given medicine to make her sleep and relax. I'd heard Adam come home while I was taking a bath, but I hadn't seen him, either. Grandma Laura said he was next in line for a bath since he'd been out roughing around with his friends, but she made me go to bed because it was a school night. She would sleep downstairs on the Hide–A–Bed in the family room, since she'd had to drive all the way from Mankato this afternoon and didn't like to drive in the dark. She told my father at supper that she would stay and help out for a few days, until my mother felt better.

Everything was very quiet and dead feeling, and the thought of going to school the next day seemed hard. I clasped my hands underneath my head and wondered if there would be a funeral for the baby or not. I imagined myself at the grave site where all the red clay dirt had been dug up around a little rectangle of a hole; I was wearing a black straw hat with a long ribbon fluttering off the back. How would I cry when I'd never even seen the baby and it had never seemed alive to me in the first place? I wondered if it was a boy or a girl, and what they were going to name it. Jennifer? Mary Beth? Brian? There would've been three of us then, and I would've loved to have had a sister.

There was a quiet knock on my door, which was open a tiny crack to let in some of the night light from the hall. Adam slipped in. "Hi," he said, and I could smell the nice shampoo clean of his hair and the scrubbed soap smell from the bath. He sat on the end of my bed and pulled his knees up to his chest. "You asleep?"

"No." I shoved my two flat pillows up into a higher ledge for my head. "I was just thinking." I pulled my puffy white bedspread up to my chin and smoothed the edges tight over the sides.

He wiggled his feet, and picked at his toenails. "I heard about the baby," he said, whispering. "Dad told me."

I had never heard Adam call my father Dad, and it seemed upsetting and wrong. He wasn't his dad. He wasn't even *my* dad; he was my father. Adam should've called him his father, too.

"I know," I said. "I wish they would've told us she was going to have a baby before now. It's just like last time."

The wind suddenly brought the pale curtains flying high up into the air, then sucked them down again with a snap. There was a heaviness in the breeze, like it could rain or storm, and in the next second, a white flash lit up the sky, followed by a loud boom of faraway thunder that made me jump. The rain started almost instantly and sounded like a fine silvery prickle against the flat maple leaves. I could hear it plop down in bigger drops on the dry sidewalk.

"Are you scared of storms?" Adam said, going to the window to look out. The rain sounded like fizz against the house, and he pushed the window shut a little so my floor wouldn't get wet. "Because I can stay in here with you if you are."

"I'm not scared."

"You're not?"

I shook my head, then realized he couldn't see me in the dark. "No."

"Then why did you jump practically out of bed when it started to thunder?" He went over and sat in the rocking chair, which my mother'd picked up at an auction and painted white with red heart decals running along the top. The chair creaked, and the wooden joints groaned when he rocked back too far.

"I didn't."

"You did too." He stopped rocking and leaned his head back. "You know what my mom used to do when she couldn't pay the heat bills in winter and my dad never made any money?" He didn't wait for me to answer. "We'd get into bed together naked because that's the best way to get warm. Sleeping with someone else is really the best way to get warm." He started rocking again.

"You slept with your mom like that?"

It was hard to gauge his expression in the dim light, with the rain drizzling down the window, casting shadows across his face. He rocked in and out of the light. "And sometimes my dad would come home really late, because he was a bartender, and he'd come in really quiet and slide into bed, smelling like cigarettes and beer. I had to move over so I wouldn't get smashed."

A loud crash of thunder rumbled through the sky, and it sounded like it had traveled down the very middle of a nearby tree and cracked it to pieces. The rain sprayed against the house, and I could see it beading up on my windowpane, dripping to the floor. I got up and shut it, and suddenly the room had a muffled, too-quiet feeling. I dove back into my bed, bunched up the covers all around me, and felt Adam looking at me from the rocker. The storm no longer sounded so close and dangerous, and I wanted him to leave so I could go to sleep.

He slid onto the bed and lay next to me, on top of the covers. "I'm sleepy," he said.

I shrugged him off. "Why don't you go to your own room? I want to sleep now."

He leaned on one elbow. "But don't you hate sleeping alone?" He was stalling—I didn't know what for this time.

"No."

"Why not?"

"Because I just don't. I'm used to it because I'm the only kid."

Adam laughed and lay back down next to me. "But now you have a brother!"

"So?" I said. I kept my eyes on the window and the pale storm, which was moving away slowly. "You better go to bed."

Then, as easily, he leapt off the bed and padded across the hard wood floor in bare feet. "Good night," he whispered, then he shut the door.

I lay there, wishing I had a sister instead.

My mother was like a zombie the whole next week, and Grandma Laura moved around her carefully, as if watching over a small child with broken bones. Grandma Laura brought her cups of steaming Earl Grey tea, the paper tags fluttering in the air like little moths. Grandma Laura did our laundry, too, and it smelled different somehow, like candy mints. My T-shirts felt limp and heavy, as if they were wet, but they weren't. My mother barely ate, and when she did, it was slices of cheese with Ritz crackers. She drank clear tall glasses of water. I worried but tried not to get in the way. I didn't even know what to say to her anymore.

On my very last day of school, I emptied out my metal desk, which was full of silvery pencil shavings and dirty rubber bands. I threw three of my notebooks away, which were full of pictures and notes to Sylvie, and halfway listened to Mrs. Scholhauser give her Farewell to the Sixth Grade speech. "You will not forget this year," she said, crossing her arms over her huge breasts. "Seventh grade will be different, more a preparation for your adult life. But I hope I have instilled in you a sense of civic responsibility as heads of your committees in this class." Her mouth was hiding a diet candy. I could always tell by the way she rolled her tongue around her back upper teeth, to get out the stick. She kind of looked like a horse doing it.

I blew out the dirty dust at the bottom of my desk, and pushed the rest out through the little metal hole. At the very end of the day, we were given lengths of coarse brown paper towels and white cleaning powder, and were asked to scrub our desktops as hard as we could. Mine was clean from the beginning, but I did it anyway. The room smelled like a swimming pool and cherries, and I felt a small sadness as we filed out the glass-paned door for the last time.

Sylvie and I celebrated by hanging around downtown and taking our time browsing through all the stores. We looked at colored pens on strings with scented ink at Walt's Drugstore. We checked out the barrettes and Slinkys at Ben Franklin, and bought big full-size Charleston Chews, strawberry and chocolate. We even took our shoes off on the walk home and felt the warm grainy sidewalk so nice under our bare feet.

When I got home, my mother was on the couch in the family room watching the tail end of her soap opera, as usual. Even though it was a beautiful, sunny day, and I'd seen people kneeling in their gardens, pulling weeds, or out strolling their babies around, my mother wore the same outfit as every day—my father's gray cardigan, a white T-shirt, and Levi's—and sat in the same place at the end of the couch, barefoot. Her dark red hair had lost its shine from not being washed every day. Now she pulled it back in a small ponytail and used bobby pins to hold the bangs back. It looked greasy. She never spoke loudly or got excited about anything anymore. Everything now was separated into before or after the miscarriage, as if they were two entirely different lives.

My father popped in a couple times each day to have lunch with her, or a cup of coffee, since business at the creamery was down. I'd overheard my father talking to Grandma Laura one night after dinner, and he said he didn't know how he could possibly stay open beyond this year, since the new Pac 'n Save grocery had opened up in town with warehouse prices. Apparently, nobody wanted to go out of their way for a separate stop just to buy milk, butter, and ice cream, even if it was the best. Nobody had time, my father said. They all liked the huge new barnlike store with cereal boxes stacked up taller than our house and forklifts driving all over inside. Sylvie and I had seen it. We went there with her mother on Saturdays, but I didn't tell my father. He would've been enraged. He even got mad when we went to our relatives' houses and they had bright yellow margarine on the table and not butter. Real butter was pale, with no dyes; that was what he had always lectured me about. It looked more like cream than like sunflowers, he said, and that was how you knew.

SYLVIE'S FAMILY ACTED completely different than ours. Their house always had smells and projects and visitors, whereas our house was more settled and quiet and empty feeling. Sylvie was used to dealing with so many brothers and sisters and fighting for the shower or the phone, but I pretty much could do whatever I liked whenever. Sometimes I kind of envied Sylvie's busy, loud house, although after awhile, I got headaches from all the noise and commotion.

On the first Saturday morning after school let out, I went over there, and the place was a disaster. The rooms were all small and narrow because the house was old-fashioned, and furniture was crammed against the walls and in the middle of the room, so you could hardly walk through without bumping into things. There were six kids ranging in age from her youngest brother, Ryan, who was six, to her oldest brother, Kyle, who was twenty, lived in a trailer at the edge of town, and had two little babies of his own already.

Sylvie's mother, Elizabeth, was cleaning the oven when I came in. Janelle, Sylvie's older sister, was standing at the kitchen table with a cookbook spread open, making fudge. Clothes tumbled in the dryer next to the stove and made the room steamy and hot. "Hi, Iris," Sylvie's mother said to me with her head still halfway in the oven. She came out and sat straight up on her knees, wiping at her grayish hair that'd fallen into her eyes. "How's your mom?"

She knows? I thought. How did she know about my mother? "Okay. She's still a little—" and I stopped, not knowing what to say. "She still doesn't feel very good."

"Well, she'll be all right," she said, spraying more white foam into the dark oven. "You'll see."

Janelle stirred the pan of melted chocolate, and stood with one foot flat against her other leg. She wore a purple sweat suit, and her breasts looked heavy and loose in it, even though I saw the bumps of bra straps. "Sylvie's upstairs," she said. "You can go up."

I passed through the dark living room, which was no bigger than my bedroom and carpeted in green and brown shag stripes. The TV was on and newspapers littered the floor, but no one was in there. There was a plate with orange peelings on it in front of the couch and a glass half full of milk. "Sylvie?" I called up the stairs, which were stacked with schoolbooks, folded clothes, boxes of shotgun shells, and two belts.

"Come on up!" she hollered. There were baskets of dirty clothes lined up in the narrow hallway, and finally I stepped my way into Sylvie's room. It was painted plain white and was probably the brightest room in the house with three long windows right in a row that went almost all the way from the ceiling to the floor. Her floor was a swirly green-and-pink linoleum, and two of the walls were slanted down, like a barn. I loved her room.

"I'm just trying to get this stupid record player to work." One of her brothers had given her his old phonograph, which looked like a tiny brown suitcase. The speakers were each about the size of a fat paperback, and were covered with an old glittery gold fabric. We only owned about three or four records each, but had plans to go up to Jay's Hardware that afternoon and look for an Olivia Newton-John 45 or a Shaun Cassidy in the record bin.

"Is your mom doing better?"

I flopped down on Sylvie's unmade bed, after pulling up the loose blue blankets. "I don't know, not really. She doesn't talk anymore or *do* anything. She just sits and watches TV in the same clothes over and over."

Sylvie sat on the edge of her desk, fingering the phonograph needle. "Well, my mom said that can be really hard on a person and it takes a while to get over. But at least she has you and Adam. That's lucky."

"Yeah, well," I said. "I'm not sure that's what she thinks."

She couldn't say much to cheer me up, but just being around her always helped me shake things off.

When I finally walked home from Sylvie's at suppertime, it was still light out, beautiful and sunny, and I carried my new 45 in a plastic bag. It was Debby Boone's "You Light Up My Life," and Sylvie and I had listened to it over and over on the scratchy record player in her room. For some reason, it always made me cry at the end when she sang the refrain in slow half time. Sylvie and I had both just lain on her bed, side by side, listening, until her mom had called up the stairs that she needed Sylvie to help with something, which was my hint to go.

When I walked up the sidewalk to our house, I could already hear my mother's voice, piercing and loud, and my father's low mumbled answers. I didn't know where Grandma Laura was during this fight, but her big white car was still shining in the sun, parked in the street now to make way for our station wagon to go up and down the driveway.

I pulled open the front screen door and stepped in quietly. They hadn't heard me, obviously, because they kept shouting, or my mother did. I set the record carefully on the wooden bench, trying not to let the plastic bag crinkle, and sat down on the stairs to listen. I leaned on the big-flowered wallpaper, light blue on cream with green twirling stems.

"Just quit! Quit it, now! I don't want to talk about it anymore." My mother's voice sounded thick and blocked-up from crying.

I couldn't quite hear what my father said next, but my mother fired back at him. "You don't understand, Bill! You just don't, and you can't. I can't keep on like this."

There was a heavy silence, and I heard the coffeepot being taken off the stove, and a slow stream being poured into a cup. A chair was pulled out, and my father, I guessed, sat down. "Then what do you want, Marilyn? Just tell me what I can do, and I'll do it. If you have to leave, leave. But I can't live like this either." He took a sip of coffee. "And I don't think it's been easy on the kids, for that matter. Iris has been acting very strange lately. I worry about her."

I sat up, confused. I had? I always had the feeling that my father was too busy to notice anything, and this worry of his surprised me, made me feel more loved even.

"Iris always acts strange," my mother said, then blew her nose loudly. Hearing this stunned me, and I clutched my knees to my chest and held my breath. "Iris is a strange child. Even you used to say so when she always played dead under her bed and then laughed." Another chair was pulled out, and scraped the floor. "I think she's jealous of Adam. I really do. I think she needs . . . something."

"Look, Marilyn, we need to talk about us right now, not the kids." I heard his silver cigarette lighter grind up and light. He sucked on a cigarette. "I mean, what? You're hurting, I know. You've had a terrible loss again, I know. So have I. But this means you want to leave? Is that really going to make anything better? And what about the kids? Are you going to take them or what? Are you even capable of taking care of yourself right now?"

He left a space for her to answer, but there was only silence. A sound of a hand smacking down on the table echoed through the rooms, then my father exhaled cigarette smoke. I knew that tired, puffing sound so well I could see the exact look on his face as he did it.

"But money," my mother said. "I just don't see how we can make it with the creamery losing money now. I mean, what are we going to do? There's barely enough for groceries anymore. I got down to my last five dollars last week and realized it had to last until, well, until there was more. It's the damn creamery. You have to get out before it sinks us."

More cigarette smoking, the hum of the kitchen clock above the sink, fingers drumming on the plastic tablecloth.

"Do you want a divorce, Marilyn? Do you want a divorce so you can go out and marry some rich guy who can take good care of you and buy you anything you want? Because go ahead. Go right ahead."

I heard his chair pull back, and I got up, too, standing on the stairs, panicked. I could hear my father walk into the dining room, getting closer to me, but he stopped, went back to my mother. "You know what your problem is, Marilyn? You have no idea what you want. I mean, I can't help it the baby died. I can't help it that you can't be happy with the two children we have. That's it! There's nothing we can do! And I'm sad, too." He said that part in a mean mocking way, the way Adam sometimes talked to me. "But you still don't know what the hell you want. Do you?" He was almost around the corner, back in the dining room. "You wish you had never even married me."

I could hear my mother crying, and imagined her collapsing into her arms at the sticky kitchen table.

"Can you deny it, Marilyn? It's your number one regret, isn't it?" I heard him attempt a laugh. "I was stable. I was easy. I didn't cause you any grief. It was just *easier* to marry me than to say no, wasn't it?"

I couldn't hear the next thing my mother mumbled.

Just before my father could find me on the stairs, I ran them by twos all the way up and dove onto my bed, out of breath. I didn't know if he'd heard me or not.

The front door closed, but didn't slam. As soon as he'd gone, a loud cry came from my mother in the kitchen, so full of hurt it made me shiver.

Chapter Four

Memory: *It is the middle of the night. I cannot sleep. My mother sits in our new kitchen. In front of her, a plate of carrot sticks, a tub of dip. She slides them over to me. I crunch loudly. She crunches loudly. We both laugh.*

Above our heads, a fluorescent light buzzes. It washes my mother out. A white thigh escapes her satin robe. Her toenails are painted pink. "Never underestimate yourself," she says, then breaks into song. "'I am woman, hear me roar.'" She raises her fists up in the air, shakes them. I crinkle up my face, confused. "Girl to girl," she says. "You'll know what I mean someday."

A moth flies through the torn screen, flutters up against the awful buzzing light. My mother says, "How beautiful is that, hmm?"

Things happened quickly the summer between sixth and seventh. The creamery was only open four days a week instead of six, and my father started painting people's houses for extra money. I saw him sometimes when I walked around town with Sylvie or went bike riding. He stood high up on an aluminum ladder with its little feet dug into someone's soft yard, a drippy, messy paint bucket hanging in front of him. His clothes were frosted with little white flecks like snow. He'd wave or whistle, but never came down from his perch.

I kept hoping his extra job would be enough to keep him and my mother together and make it okay, but it clearly wasn't. My mother, a different person now who didn't fix up her hair or dress nice anymore, decided she was taking me and Adam and moving all three of us to a tiny apartment on Main Street above Dana's Clip & Curl Salon. Dana was a friend from her old bowling league, and had short permed hair, tiny lips, and wore dozens of colored bracelets banging around her wrists. We were going to move in that night, she said, after the other renters had moved out. My mother had tried explaining it to Adam and me, but it still didn't make any sense and seemed to me an overly dramatic reaction to a simple fight they'd had. I desperately didn't want to go, but couldn't say anything against it. All I knew was I was going to miss my father.

While my father was gone, Grandma Laura, who had stayed around to help longer than we'd thought she would, tried to talk my mother out of leaving. "Marilyn, what? What will this do?" Grandma Laura said. This time I was right there in the family room with them, watching TV. No one asked me to leave the room or tried to talk in code so that I wouldn't understand. The sun shone in golden and hazy and made me sleepy. I lay on the carpet with my head on the inside of my arm, staring into the orange fuzzy carpet pieces, dreading this new life that would strip me of a nice house and a real family.

"I know you don't understand, but it's something I have to do," my mother said, sounding better and stronger than before. "I need some time, and I'm going to get a job, at least part-time so I can be there for Adam and Iris."

Grandma Laura clucked her tongue, and rubbed her hands up and down her thick knit pants, pull-ons with long seams down the legs. "Well, you'll have to get a good job to afford an apartment, and this house, too. My gosh." She gestured around the room and sighed, then tried a different approach. "You see, when times are tough, you don't just run away. You have to stick together and help each other. That's what marriage is. And what about Bill? Now what will he do? He's got the whole creamery on his shoulders, and he's always relied on your help. Think about it hard now. Think."

My mother apparently didn't want to think. She squinted her eyes as the sun came right at her, and gripped the arms of the chair. "It's already settled. I've already paid the deposit." She got up and drew the shade down. "Like I said, I don't expect you to understand. Even *I* don't understand. But I can't stay here. Everything feels dead here. I need a change. My friend Dana belongs to a women's group and asked me to join. She said it's made a big difference in her life." She came and knelt beside me. "It'll be fun, Iris, won't it? Like a little vacation for us." She tapped me on the back.

"Don't get mixed up with all those women trying to be men," Grandma Laura said. "Because that's what they want, isn't it? They say equal rights, but they really just want to be the men." Grandma Laura shook her head and muttered in disapproval.

Just as my mother seemed about to go into her lecture about woman's equality (which we'd all heard before), Adam rode up on his bike in the backyard, tossed it onto the grass, and came through the sliding doors. "What?" he said, shrugging his shoulders. "How come nobody's talking?"

Grandma Laura left late that afternoon, still telling my mother she was doing the wrong thing. "This will drive you apart more than anything," she said, loading up her big car with soft flowered luggage and a grocery bag full of fresh butter, cream, milk, and cheese. "It won't fix anything like magic." Still, she hugged my mother tightly and held one hand protectively over her head, as if to keep her safe.

"Now come here and give Grandma a hug good-bye," she said to me, bending down. I threw my arms around her neck, and felt warm and safe in the soft shelf of her breasts and the bulge of her belly. "Here, take this and buy you and Adam a treat," she whispered, and slipped a ten dollar bill folded in half into my hand. I looked up at my mother to see if it was okay, but she was staring off down the street. Sometimes she made me try to give the money back to Grandma Laura, even though I always ended up keeping it.

"Thanks," I said. "Good-bye." I kissed her soft wrinkled cheek, which had a fruity makeup taste from the bottled blush I'd seen her rub on with a Kleenex. I waved as she drove off down the tree-lined street and turned the corner, and I kept waving until she was absolutely out of sight. My mother stood with her arms crossed and one foot on top of the other. It felt like my last hope was gone, and there was no one left to stop my mother from doing this.

WHILE MY FATHER WAS STILL AT WORK, my mother rounded up Adam and told him to get ready. "Now I want you to take all your clothes and really nothing else. We can come back later to get things if we need them." Adam stood at the top of the stairs, and my mother was down by the front door, digging through the hall closet. I sat on the couch, watching her. "You too, Iris," she said, and she ushered me to the stairs.

In less than an hour, we were all packed into the station wagon and ready to go. Sheets and fuzzy blankets pushed up against the back windows. My mother had her hair dryer, scarves, and clear plastic makeup bag shoved between the dashboard and the windshield. I could just imagine the lipsticks melting into a bright red waxy puddle. Adam and I barely fit in the front seat beside her and more soft tangled piles of clothes.

Wishbone had a pathetic downtown shopping district with only a single street where all the stores and businesses were. It only took about a half second to get there. There was diagonal parking on Main Street full of pickup trucks and big sedans, but my mother swung around the corner and turned into the alley. Our wide car barely fit. We had to squeeze by the backs of buildings and garbage cans and junky parked cars. I could imagine it all scraping the red paint off our car, leaving a thick gray line.

She parked in the one empty gravel space behind Dana's shop, and ran to get the key while Adam and I waited by the Dumpster. Adam and I hadn't been talking very much, and I didn't know if he was mad at me or what. He'd stopped coming into my room at night to talk.

"This'll be cool to live here," he said, and shoved his hands into his jeans pockets. "There'll be more happening." He looked up at the gray wooden stairs that led to the apartment. There was a small tar-papered balcony where you could maybe sit in the mornings on a lawn chair and read or have your breakfast, but the view would only be the back of another old building.

"Is it like where you used to live?" I asked, and realized how little I knew about Adam's life before Wishbone. I didn't even know if he was from Minnesota.

"Sort of," he said. He jumped up and sat on the hood of our car. "We used to live in Chicago, but then my dad owed some money, and we had to leave. It was kind of an apartment like this, above a store, but not a neighborhood like this. My mom worked at a gas station."

"Then where to?" I leaned against the stair railing and kicked my foot around in the gravel.

"Then we went to Milwaukee, and later to Minneapolis. But my dad started hitting my mom, and people would hear, and the police and social workers started coming to our house. Then I got put into foster care in St. Paul. It was a family of fatsos. The mom and dad and two kids were all huge and fat and never stopped eating. They were pigs."

My mother came out of the building dangling a key from her fingers, smiling. She had her sunglasses propped up on her head and looked young again. Adam and I followed her up the narrow wobbly stairs to the apartment. "Dana said we can paint it any color we want, and she'll pay for the paint, if we do the work." She tried the key but couldn't get it to turn in the lock.

I walked over to the tar-papered balcony, which had a skinny metal railing around it, and peeked in the window. I saw a kitchen with green tile walls and a small white stove that looked half the size of our big one at home. There was also a small refrigerator, and a black clock on the wall shaped like a cat with a long tail wagging off the end.

"Okay," she said finally, swinging open the door. "Here we are."

We entered the kitchen, not really a whole kitchen, but a small line of cupboards, a stove, and a refrigerator. There was a round table with metal legs and a red top that sat by the window. Next was the living room, which had dark wooden floors, a dark green couch, a brown chair, and a flowered love seat that was pretty threadbare and smelled like shrimp.

To the right was a hallway with a bathroom off to one side, and two bedrooms on the other. The doors were all open, and when I pulled the knob on one of the bedroom doors, it felt light and hollow. The bathroom had the same mint-green tiles as the kitchen, and was only big enough to stand in, not walk around. There was no bathtub, but a white shower unit with a wavy glass door.

The whole apartment was small and dim, but there was something about it I liked. It felt private and old-fashioned, and I could imagine myself lying on the couch reading with the windows open, cars driving by below and people walking on the sidewalk. I could have Sylvie over to people-watch out the windows or to sit out back on the balcony and suntan. Some nights maybe we'd go just down the street to the Ondov Theatre for a movie. "It's nice," I said to my mother, who was busy opening all the kitchen drawers and cabinets.

"Isn't it?" she said, brightening. "And no mice. Good." She slammed the drawer shut and dusted off her hands. "Did you see your bedroom? It's got two nice windows, and bunk beds for you and Adam. Come on," she said, swooping me along with her by the arm. "Do you think you want the top or the bottom bunk?"

I'd had no idea I'd be sharing a room with Adam, and instantly lost my little bit of excitement. There was no way I was going to share a room with him. No way. Where would I dress? How would I ever sleep? "I don't want to share a room," I mumbled.

"I call top," Adam said, climbing the ladder attached to the foot of the bed. He bounced on the upper mattress, which was covered with a dark red blanket that hung down over the bottom bunk like a stage curtain.

Before I could argue further, my mother ordered us down to the car to start bringing up loads of clothes and blankets. I wanted to talk to her about the bedroom, but she finally seemed perked up again like her old self, and if I complained too much I thought I might ruin it all.

THE NEXT MORNING MY MOTHER set up her typewriter on a small table in the corner of the living room. The apartment felt dark and old, with the sun still on the other side of town. There was a cold shadowy draft, and the faded flowered curtains blew lightly. I sat at the red kitchen table and drank water out of a thick glass I'd never seen before. Adam was still asleep in the upper bunk bed. We'd all been too tired to stay up past eight o'clock, and I barely remembered even putting my pajamas on and hitting the pillow.

"What are you going to do today?" I asked my mother, who acted like she had a plan. She had already showered and put on makeup, and wore a light blue dress with sandals.

"Well, first I'm going to type a couple of letters for some jobs in town." She poured herself a cup of coffee and sat beside me at the table. "Then I'm going to fix this place up a little bit. Maybe look at paint samples for the walls in here." She turned and looked around the living room. "What do you think—light green or maybe a pale yellow to cheer things up?"

"I like yellow."

"Yes. Me, too." She put one arm back against her chair and leaned into her hand. "And later on I'm going to send you and Adam down to help your father in the creamery. Then I'm going to write." She nodded over at the typewriter and looked back at me. "By the way, how are you and Adam getting along? You seem to really hit it off, huh? He can be sweet if you just give him a chance. Considering what he's been through, you know." She clicked her perfect oval fingernails against her coffee cup.

I swallowed and tried very hard to agree. "I guess," I said, sitting on my hands. "He's all right. I mean, for the most part."

"That's good," my mother said. "Whenever I see the two of you together, it makes me so glad. I think we really did the right thing." But then a dark troubled look came over her face, and she stared out the window, into the alley. A big white garbage truck slowly drove through, making a loud beeping sound, and lifted up a big overflowing Dumpster. We could hear it shake all the junk out, and watched it crash back down, empty.

I tried to change the subject. "So what do you write about at your typewriter? Are you writing stories?" I went to check in the refrigerator for some juice, but it was empty except for a box of Arm & Hammer.

My mother smiled shyly and held the coffee cup against her cheek. "Well, maybe writing *a* story, I guess. I'm writing about my life growing up in Mankato, before I met your father. There's definitely a story there. I'm just getting the details down before I forget."

Before I could ask more questions, Adam came out of the bedroom, yawning. He wore a Chicago Bears jersey and red gym shorts. His lips always looked deeply red to me, as if he had lipstick on. Luckily, he had gotten a new haircut and didn't have the bowl cut anymore. The new short hairstyle made his dark eyes look big and flashy, and his cheeks stand out.

"Adam, you better hep to, because you have to go help your father in the creamery," my mother said, then finished up her coffee. She leaned her head back to get the very last drop, as if it were a precious last drink of water in the desert.

"Hep to," Adam said. "Nobody says hep to." He sat at the table with us. "I better *hep to.*"

Just when my mother was saying how sweet Adam could be, he had to act like a snot and make fun of her. My mother stiffened and pulled her chair back from the table.

"I'm hungry," Adam said, leaning on his hand and practically lying on the table. "Isn't there anything to eat? I am starving to death! Help me!"

I glanced at my mother and knew she had already seen me looking into the empty refrigerator, although I'd tried not to let her notice.

My mother pressed her fingers up to her temples. "Look, I'm sorry! I haven't gotten around to shopping yet. Do you think you can survive? Do you think you can just hold on for two seconds while I try to figure this out?" She walked into the living room and looked out the window. "I mean, we only just got here last night. God, Adam."

He's ruined it, I thought. Now she'll go back to her staring, faraway self like before. Now the apartment won't seem good, and she won't want to write her story. Adam could ruin everything so quickly.

Instead of losing it, though, she ordered Adam to take a shower, and told him to make it snappy. I sat there waiting for him to make fun of that, too, but he had the good sense not to.

"So where do you think you'll be able to get a job?" I asked. I couldn't imagine her anywhere but her little office at home, tucked behind the kitchen, cozy and lit with small lamps and a flat flowered pillow on her chair. I could see her bent over the adding machine, flipping over one yellow form after another, punching in numbers on the clicking keys like animal claws on glass.

"Iris, I don't know. Somewhere. Can't you be a little more supportive? Can't you say, 'I know you'll get a job somewhere, Mom. I know you can do it'? I mean, I don't know if I'll get a job *any*where, but I have to try." She sat in front of the typewriter on one of the kitchen chairs, and rolled a piece of paper into the machine. "Look, honey. I'm sorry. It's just, this is hard on me right now." She exhaled loudly and set her fingers down on the keyboard. "Anyway, Dana said they're hiring a bank teller across the street. I'm going to try that first." Adam seemed to bring out the worst in her, but then again, so did I. It didn't take much anymore to send her over the edge.

I went and got dressed and listened to her type, stop, swear, fix things, type some more. Soon Adam was ready, and we headed down the stairs to the alley, leaving my mother alone, for which she seemed grateful.

"Bye," she called after us when we were almost halfway down the stairs. "Say hello to your father for me." Then she got up and ran to the window. "Oh, and tell him you haven't eaten! He can feed you!"

Maybe she didn't realize how loud she was being. I supposed the whole town could hear her.

THE CREAMERY WAS ACTUALLY BUSY when we walked in, which made me relieved. Maybe my father would make enough money to have me, Adam, and my mother back at home. I loved the rich musty smell of the butter being folded in back, and could smell it instantly. I could almost taste it fresh and melting on my fingertips, and realized how hungry I was. The ice cream coolers hummed and gave off a cool white light, and Adam and I rushed over to look at the white paper wrappers, hiding chocolate or orange or grape underneath. I was so hungry I could feel the juices channeling and squirming in my stomach when I even looked at the food.

"Go ahead, kids," my father said, nodding at the cooler. "Although isn't it a little early for ice cream? Didn't you just have breakfast?" He rang up one crate of milk, handed out change, and smiled until the customer was gone. "Go on, kids, go ahead." Even though it was our own store, I always felt shy about taking things, as if I were stealing.

I was so hungry I took two things: a chocolate malted cup and an ice-cream sandwich. I ripped into the ice-cream sandwich right away and felt my mouth water as I bit into it. Adam took a Drumstick like always, and I followed his eyes to the door. A tall, thin woman I'd never seen before stepped in, wearing a pink flowered sundress with a crinkled elastic top that accentuated the circles of her small breasts. She had dirty white tennies on with no shoelaces, and her thin brown hair was held up in back by a leather and stick bun holder.

"Adam Christopher Riley!" she shouted, and we all swirled around in surprise. "Come here." She pointed to a spot on the floor in front of where she stood. Her skin looked dark and sooty, yet there was something pretty about her in a delicate bony way, like a model. It seemed her wrists might snap off if you grabbed her too hard.

Adam's dark eyes flashed first at her, then at my father and me. This woman had the same jet-black eyes as Adam. She also had the same pointed cheekbones that made her look skinny and dramatic, just like Adam.

"Adam Christopher. Here. Right now." She clapped her hands at him like a dog, and I noticed the purse slung under her arm, which looked as if it was made from a hammock—and a dirty one at that.

"Can I help you with something?" my father said. He stood smoothing his grease-spotted white apron. "I'm his father. What do you need?"

The woman looked puzzled and sad. She walked over to the ice cream cooler, where Adam stood dead still. She put her arms around his shoulders from behind. "I'm his *real* mom, aren't I, Adam?" She nudged him with her knee, but he stayed silent. "He shouldn't have been taken away from me. It was all a mistake."

My father scratched behind his ear, something he always did when he was nervous or worried. He made a move toward her, and the old stained floorboards creaked. I could see the blue veins protruding from his arms. "Just a minute here. You're Adam's mother? Adam, is this true? Is she? This is important, so speak up. Now." My father rubbed his hands together and waited, an eye on the door.

People constantly turned into new people right in front of my eyes. It had happened with my mother, when she'd stare off and leave me cold, then the next minute cuddle and love me. It'd happened with Sylvie when she became snotty and sickening around our other friend, Carla Holbrook, and then was the same nice best friend when it was just the two of us. Suddenly the Adam I knew, who swore and teased me, was gone, and now there was this new, shy, scared person, who stood looking at me as if I could help him somehow. I shrugged my shoulders and started to say that I thought we should call someone.

My father spun around and shouted at me. "Iris, stay out of this! Just keep quiet!" I did. I vowed not to say a word, no matter what happened, only I wondered if this could happen to me one day. A strange woman would show up as my real mother and take me away. Why couldn't this happen to me? My father had never yelled at me like this before.

The woman held out her long, thin hand. "My name's Lavanda Riley. I should have introduced myself before, but Adam here—"

She raised her eyebrows and gestured toward him. "I just saw him, and *bam!* immediately I lost my senses." She slapped her forehead with the palm of her hand.

My father stepped back, rubbing his chin. I was pretty sure he must've seen the real life resemblance between Adam and the woman, especially the way they both stood holding their hands on their hips, their heads tilted just a little to the side. It was pretty hard to miss.

"And you are . . . ?" She tried to meet my father's eyes.

"I'm Bill Kauffman."

"Nice to meet you, Bill." She nodded and looked around at the coolers. "And this is your store?"

"I own the creamery." My father never liked it when people called it a store. It always had to be the creamery. A store was where you bought dog food and toilet paper, he used to say. Here we sold homemade butter and fresh cream, which was why it was a creamery. A *creamery*—the very word sounded delicious to me. He even had trophies for his prizewinning butter sitting on shelves in the basement at home—little gold-plated cows held up by fat wooden pillars.

My father crossed his arms and tucked his hands underneath his armpits. "Look, I don't know what you're doing here or what you want, but I think it would probably be best for everyone if you left right away."

She came rushing up to him, as if she was going to hug him or kiss him. Instead she stood in front of him, gesturing wildly with her arms. "Look, I just want to talk to you a little about Adam. He's my son! And I know you all have adopted him and everything by now, but you don't even know the whole story. He got taken away from me unfairly! It was all his father's fault, and—"

I could tell my father was not taken in by her, and he motioned for me and Adam to come over behind the counter. Adam, who always seemed to be jiggling his feet and drumming fingertips against tables, was now stunned into stillness. I threw away our ice cream wrappers and leaned on the wooden counter. My hands were sticky and hot, and I wanted more than anything to wash them off in the bathroom with the blue pump soap that smelled like cherries.

"I want you to leave now," my father said. "All you're doing is upsetting the children."

"Wait! Just wait! I've left my husband, and I just wanted to work out some sort of deal where I could visit Adam. That's all I want to do is visit with him, say, maybe every other weekend, or even once a month, or whatever you want. He's my son. You know about that. You have a daughter, I see." She smiled at me, revealing jumbled gray teeth. "Adam? Tell him you want to see me, too. Tell him that."

"I'm asking you to leave now," my father said, and just as he walked over to open the door for her, there was a customer. It was the owner of the Ondov movie theater, Mr. Blundell, and his three little boys. Two of them were identical twins with hair so blond it was white. "Hi there," my father said, as if he were there just to greet them. "Nice day out there."

Mr. Blundell agreed and picked up a small metal basket. The three boys ran to the ice cream cooler and tried to peer in, but they were too short. Mr. Blundell chose cheddar and Havarti cheeses, and my father took the big rectangular blocks and cut thin slices that fell softly onto the waxed paper. The Havarti left greasy orange streaks from the rind.

"Adam, run!" the woman called when my father was busy behind the counter. It was just like a movie, and we all turned, stared, the cheese cutter blade spinning like a big silver wheel. The woman rushed out the door, Adam followed her, my father followed them, and the cheese cutter blade spun and spun. Mr. Blundell and his boys stood back, confused.

I worried about the cheese cutter hurting someone, or chopping off fingers, so I crawled behind the counter and pulled the plug. A tiny blue spark leapt up. The machine stopped with a slow grinding sound, and silence fell around us like snow. It hit me that I might never see Adam again, and I realized that I would miss him in a way.

The three Blundell boys hung out the doorway, watching the chase scene. "That lady must have been a robber!" one of the twins said, and he pretended he had a gun in his hand. He made shooting sounds and chased his two brothers around until they were all three screaming.

"Quiet, boys," Mr. Blundell said calmly, and they listened to him. He turned to me, touching his mustache. "I suppose we'll have to come back for these things. I see you have a few problems on your hands."

I must've looked at him kind of strangely, because he came over and patted me on the shoulder. "It's all right. It's not your fault." He looked up at the big Coca-Cola clock, and rubbed a hand over his balding head. "Maybe you ought to call your mother up and have her look after the store. All right? Can you do that?"

I nodded and said that I would, then watched them leave, all with their blond hair. I turned the lock on the glass door and ran behind the counter so no one could see me. When the coast was clear, I reached up for the black wall phone, but remembered that we had no telephone yet in the new apartment. There was no way to reach my mother, so I decided I'd just have to hide and wait for my father to return.

I heard the butter machine in back click into a new cycle, and wondered how I would know when the batch was done. Would I have to add anything? And how about all the milk in the sterilizing room? What if everything spoiled? There was so much to take care of, and I wished I wasn't always the responsible one.

AS IT HAPPENED, MY FATHER RETURNED with Adam and my mother. My father knocked on the glass door with one knuckle, and I made no rush opening it for them, angry that they'd all left me. "Come on, Iris," my father said impatiently. I saw him light up a cigarette and toss the match on the sidewalk. "Come *on.*"

I let them in, but didn't say anything. Adam and I gave each other looks that said: We'll talk about it later, just the two of us. I knew there would be another big family meeting, deciding what to do about the woman who said she was Adam's real mother.

My mother paced back and forth, her arms crossed. My father plugged in the cheese cutter, finished slicing, then wrapped the pieces in white paper and wrote BLUNDELL across it. He stuck it in the cooler, looked up at the clock, and sighed. "I don't know how she found out where he was," my mother said. "It doesn't make sense." She sat on the tall stool behind the counter. "They told us in Rochester she'd have no way of knowing. No way." She got up again. "This is just great."

"That's easy," Adam said. "I called her." He turned his back to my mother and stood looking out the door.

"Adam, you're kidding," my father said. We all looked at one another in disbelief.

"I called her up one night because I missed her. It was no big deal. I didn't tell her exactly where we lived, though. I just told her you ran a creamery in this little town by Mankato."

"Jesus Christ," my mother said, hands on her temples. "Adam, do you know what kind of position that puts us in?" She paced again, then stopped to grab his shoulders. She didn't shake him, but let him go. "Stupid! That was a very stupid thing to do."

"Marilyn," my father said, "calm down."

"But that woman! She's terrible." My mother walked over to me and, surprisingly, set her hand on my head gently. "She does *not* want what is best for Adam. She's proven that already. She just wants to screw everything all up for him again. I don't know why you didn't call the police. You know you should've, don't you?"

My father's face was red and splotchy like when he exercised, which was rarely anymore. He slicked his hair back and shook his head. "I already told you, Marilyn. She agreed to leave and promised not to bother us again. If she comes back, yes, all right, I'll get the police involved, but I just don't think we need to take it that far, all right?"

My mother frowned, and her forehead wrinkled. "And you believe her? You believe what she said?"

"Yes, I do. I have to."

"You have to?"

My father shook his head. My mother chewed on her lip.

There was silence between them. The clock hummed; the milk bottles went through the last hot-water spray rinse in back, and it sounded like rain. My mother grabbed my hand, grabbed Adam's, and pulled us to the door. "Let's get out of here," she said, pushing us out to the red station wagon. As we drove away, I saw my father watching out the window, blue cigarette smoke curling up around him like fog.

At first my mother didn't tell us where we were going, and I was too afraid to ask, but as the miles built up and it was clear we were headed far out of Wishbone, I started to get tired and hungry. Adam was sprawled out in back, his bare feet hanging out the open window, and I was stuck in front with my mother, who was clearly on some sort of rampage. I could see it in the way her delicate nostrils flared.

I sat with my ankles crossed and my head back against the vinyl seat, watching the scenery flash by. I could tell we were heading into Mankato by the tall jagged clay cliffs, the wide glassy river, and the little dug-out caves that my Grandma Laura said used to be the Indians' houses. When we passed one, I sat up and tried to get a better look, tried to imagine what it would be like to sit inside the cool earth on an animal-skin rug, cooking corn or getting my hair braided. Some of the little cave openings had wooden door frames around them, but no doors. I would've loved to go inside and see if there were secret writings on the walls.

The big road sign said Mankato and North Mankato, and had one white arrow going straight and one curving off in a different direction. I looked hopefully at the row of McDonald's, Burger King, and the big white Happy Chef statue, but my mother didn't stop or even glance that way. She gripped the steering wheel with both hands and blinked into the sun.

I figured we were going to Grandma Laura's, but it didn't seem right somehow. We didn't go up the hill, past the big church, but kept on down the highway and got off in a neighborhood by a school. It felt familiar, but I couldn't be sure.

"Iris, stop biting your fingernails," my mother said, turning down a street of small square houses with perfectly mowed lawns. "Don't you want them to get long and keep them nice like mine?" She dangled a hand over the seat and fluttered her fingers. "Then you can buy bottles of polish in all kinds of colors. Like this I have on now is, I think, peaches and cream." She set her warm hand on my bare leg. "See? Isn't it pretty?"

"Yes." I rubbed the shiny smooth ovals with my finger, but she had to pull her hand away to make a turn. When I looked up, I saw my cousins Noel and David outside on their bikes, only it wasn't their same watermelon-colored house, but a plain white one with two front doors. "Hey, it's Noel and David!"

Adam sat up, awake for the first time since the trip. "Where are we?" he asked. He stretched with a loud grunting noise. His face had a deep red checkerboard pattern on one side from the vinyl seat. He hung over the front to see what was going on.

My mother turned off the car and checked herself in the mirror. She fluffed her hair back and removed a barrette, held it in her teeth, then clipped it back into place. "This is Aunt Deb's new place. They live on the right side there." She pointed to the side where the grass hadn't been mowed and where the windows were bare without curtains. There were empty cardboard boxes stacked up by the crumbling cement stairs. "Now don't smart off to the kids about this place," my mother warned us. "They had to move because she couldn't afford the old house without Uncle Wayne there. Now behave." Noel and David must have recognized our big red car, because they dropped their bikes in the grass and came running over.

Aunt Deb was talking on the telephone when we went inside, and held up a finger to us that she'd be just a minute. Their house was even smaller than our new apartment, with fewer windows and only one bedroom. The whole place was covered with puffy brown carpeting, and it felt moist and squirmy under bare feet. I peeked in the bedroom and saw there were three beds, one big and two small. I wondered about the arrangements.

The bathroom had a rusty toilet bowl that was constantly trickling water and a tiny flowered dresser made of cardboard to hold soap and washcloths and toothpaste. Everything felt cold and clammy from the big air conditioner in the living room window. It streamed wetness into the air.

Aunt Deb and my mother sat down at the kitchen table to drink coffee and talk. The two boys were outside, but I didn't know where Carter, the oldest, was. Maybe he had a job already. I sat at the table next to my mother and listened to them talk about Uncle Wayne and his new girlfriend. For being sisters, they didn't look that much alike except for their mouths. They both had wide full lips that broke into smiles instantly and nice straight white teeth. Aunt Deb wasn't as pretty as my mother. She was just a shade less in every way. Her hair was mousy brown next to my mother's deep auburn. Aunt Deb's eyes were an "indistinct hazel" (according to my mother), whereas hers were a deep swirly green, like a lake.

My mother was also thinner and able to wear short shorts and sleeveless dresses, but Aunt Deb always stayed with pants and T-shirts. The thing that was the same was they both didn't live with their husbands anymore.

I got bored when they started talking about everyone in the family, so I went outside to look for the boys. They were in the backyard, taking a bird's nest out of a small apple tree. Noel held it like it was a real live baby, and when I got closer, I saw that there were eggs in it—tiny, white, with brown speckles. I knew that you weren't supposed to take nests out of trees, especially with eggs in them, but Adam touched my arm and said, "It's okay. We won't hurt them."

Later I found them smashed.

We spent all day there, and I was so bored I finally pushed some clothes off the couch and fell asleep watching TV. When I woke up, it was almost dark, and there was a strange man in the house, who I heard my mother call Mike. My mother picked me up and carried me out to the car. She told me in the car that he was Aunt Deb's new boyfriend.

"Boyfriend?" I said. "Why does she have a boyfriend?"

"I don't know," my mother said, switching on her headlights. "It's good for her, I think, to have somebody around. Divorced women always lose in the end, you know? I like to see her having a little fun." She shrugged her shoulders, as if not quite convinced herself.

Instead of turning onto the highway and going back to Wishbone, my mother turned the other way, past the Madison East shopping center where I got my school clothes, until we finally took the hill up to Grandma Laura's. The car windows were all rolled down, and the sweet smell of lilacs blew in around us. Even though it was almost dark, kids were still out riding bikes, adults were out walking or sitting on lawn chairs in their yards, and I wished we were back at our big house with my father. I could've been spinning cartwheels with Sylvie or just sitting on the stoop, talking, watching the cars go by.

Grandma Laura seemed completely confused as to why we were there without calling her first. She welcomed us in, but her house already looked like it'd been closed up for her to go to sleep. It was dark and quiet, and only a small light from her bedroom could be seen. "Are you staying the night? What, Marilyn? Tell me what you're doing." Grandma Laura wore a short nightgown that snapped up the front and pink terry cloth slippers. I hardly ever saw her bare legs, and now, in the small kitchen light, the veins looked dark purple and raised and tangled up in knots.

"You can stay, yes, yes," Grandma Laura said, turning on lights in the living room. "But you can't run away forever. This is probably not your answer."

My mother sat down on the couch, setting her purse on the floor. "Well, can the kids just stay for awhile? I'll explain later, but I have to go back and get some of their things."

Adam was on the floor with his feet up on one of the good velvet chairs. His hands were folded behind his head, and I couldn't tell if he was asleep. Usually if his fingers or feet weren't drumming or wiggling, he was asleep.

"Marilyn, why? What will this do?"

"Mom, please don't. Not now. We can talk tomorrow when I come back."

My grandma threw her hands up in the air and rocked back in her chair. "All right, all right. You go, but try to settle this soon. You can't always take the children running. They need their own beds, too. They need to be home."

My mother stepped over to her and kissed her on the cheek. "Thanks. I'll be back tomorrow morning, and we'll talk. We will." Next she hugged and kissed me, then Adam. "Bye-bye. See you tomorrow. Be good." She blew us a kiss from the doorway and left.

I didn't know why we were visiting everyone like this out of the blue, why we weren't in our real house or even our new apartment. Maybe my mother was scared Adam would be stolen. Maybe she wanted to go catch the woman who claimed she was his real mother. Or maybe she just couldn't stand being with us anymore.

Grandma Laura was too tired to stay up and didn't hide it. She kissed us each and gave us two of Grandpa's old white T-shirts to sleep in. Adam and I settled into the double bed in the green playroom. The headboard and footboard were huge curved half circles of wood, and made me feel protected, as if I were on a little ship at sea. Adam put his arm around my waist, as if he was scared I'd get away, too. It didn't exactly feel bad.

Chapter Five

Memory: Fourth of July. My father takes me for a ride in my uncle's boat. I sit behind him, watch his pale bare back crisp in the sun. Something about the slope of his shoulders alerts me to the fact that I am losing him.

He asks me not to take sides. I cannot see his eyes through the sunglasses.

"What do you mean?" I say.

"Things can get ugly." We circle the lake where everyone but us seems to be having a riot. I notice a girl my age dancing on a dock. The chicken dance. In a flowered bikini. She's cracking her family up.

My father laughs. "Well, live it up while you can, I guess."

I wait for the next part, but that's it.

Over a week passed, and my mother still hadn't come back to get us. She hadn't even been back to bring us our things or our clothes, and finally Grandma Laura had to call Aunt Patty to bring over some of Melanie and DeeDee's things for me to wear. It was embarrassing by then, as if we'd been abandoned, and I couldn't help but think it reflected on Adam and me. When it got dark and we could hear Grandma Laura's loud snoring that sounded more like snorting, I tried to sleep but couldn't. I didn't know where my mother was, or my father. I didn't know what was going on. Nobody told us anything.

We spent the days at Grandma Laura's quietly and slowly. In the mornings, there were big breakfasts with little juice glasses and small separate plates for toast, and our choice of eggs, French toast, pancakes, or waffles. She made bacon in the oven so the fat leaked out into the broiler pan. Afterwards, I'd stand on a chair and help her dry the dishes, but I never knew where anything belonged and had to stack it all up on the counter. Adam sat at the table and watched, or sometimes snuck outside to shoot baskets in the driveway.

In the afternoons, we rode around in her big white car with soft maroon seats to do errands. We went to the bank, where they gave out free Dum Dums, as if everyone didn't know they only cost a penny each. We went to the drugstore in the mall to pick up her prescriptions, which were given out in tiny white paper bags, stapled at the top. I liked to hold the crunchy little packages, which seemed like they held great secrets inside. Sometimes we stopped to see her friend Trudi, who lived in an old folk's home, Sunset Terrace Care Center. I hated it. It was up on a hill with nothing around it but empty dry fields of grass. It smelled exactly like old candy mints and pee, and there were always people crying out from their rooms and rolling around in wheelchairs with wobbling heads right by the front door.

Trudi had heart problems and had to wear a clear tube that piped oxygen up her nose. She was tiny and shrunken like a dried-apple doll and stayed in bed with her blue hands resting on the covers. Adam and I sat quiet and still in the big vinyl chairs while Grandma Laura sat on the bed and combed Trudi's hair. They talked about little things or they didn't talk at all, and pretty soon it'd be time to go. Poor Trudi, Grandma Laura always said, as she backed out of the parking lot. I knew they were the same age and guessed it must scare her to imagine she could end up just like her.

In the evenings we got interesting colorful suppers. Corkscrew noodles with vegetables and cheese sauce and black olives thrown in. Pigs in a blanket with fresh carrot sticks cut in zigzags. Spaghetti noodles with a white sauce instead of red, and bright green spinach blended in. I liked most of it, but I missed my mother's fried chicken and pitchers of iced tea with lots of sugar and an orange squeezed in.

After eating, we turned out the lights and settled into the TV room, although we were limited to one hour of TV after the news. Adam and I usually argued about *Happy Days, Shazam!, Charlie's Angels,* and *The Wonderful World of Disney,* which was on only on Sundays, though. Grandma Laura liked to turn off the TV early and listen to the crickets, read, play solitaire, or just sit in her La-Z-Boy, wiggling her feet, hands crossed over her belly, watching us play Sorry! or checkers.

It was the hot, humid part of summer, when it acted like it might rain and the sky went purple and dark, but then it wouldn't. There was nothing going on and nothing much to do, except I worried about what'd happened to my mother and father. I worried about never seeing them again. Were we really that bad?

ANOTHER WEEK WENT BY, then another. Grandma Laura's patience started to wear out, and she sent us off to take naps every afternoon after lunch like we were toddlers. Surprisingly, I kind of grew to like it. Sometimes I'd lie on the couch just before our forced nap time and pretend that I was already asleep. That way she walked over, looked down at me, and let me stay there. I'd lie there with my eyes pinched shut and listen to her pad through the house, pulling down shades to keep out the sun's bright hotness. When she left, the living room had a golden buttery light, darker than sun, like syrup. I could hear Adam saying he wasn't tired, that he wanted to go outside, but Grandma Laura insisted he at least rest, and she closed the bedroom door on him.

The phone hung on a wall in the kitchen, and one afternoon Grandma Laura picked it up and dialed, sitting at the kitchen table.

"Hello, Bill? This is Laura." I could hear the conversation perfectly. "Have you heard from Marilyn yet? Mm-hmm. Mm-hmm. Yes, well I was wondering about the children. I think they're starting to get anxious." She paused, listening, and I could imagine my father in his creamery uniform, stained with dark greasy splotches, standing by the cash register in the creamery.

My grandma's voice rose up in excitement. "Really? That same woman? Uh-huh." She listened for a long time without saying anything. I tried to piece it together, and finally guessed that it must've been the woman who said she was Adam's real mother. She must've been back looking for him again. "No! My garsh," my grandma said, then tried to temper her voice. She whispered. "No, I won't tell them. It's better left alone, at least for now. You leave it alone, too, now. You need to sit down with Marilyn and talk." She listened quietly again. "Well, if you do talk to her, tell her to phone me. Mm-hmm. I will do that, sure. Bye-bye now."

I pretended that I was dead, for old time's sake, to relax me. I crossed my hands over my chest and breathed so that my stomach didn't rise up too much. I tried to empty my head to black. What would happen if I left the world? What if I never grew up or had a baby or got a job? It wouldn't matter a whole lot, it didn't seem. What if I wasn't in this room but really inside a coffin, with cool satin lining the color of coffee with cream? The idea of dying excited me and made me feel hopeful in a semisick, feel-sorry-for-me way. Everyone would be so sad. They would say, "But she was such a sweet child. It's so unfair."

ON OUR THIRD WEEKEND at Grandma Laura's, she decided it would be good for us all to get away since it was the Fourth of July. I had a feeling something big was going on between my mother and father, and that we'd have to be here until they worked things out, if that ever happened. Grandma Laura told us on Friday morning that we were going to go up to Aunt Patty and Uncle Robert's cabin on Lake Wakina.

"DeeDee and Melanie will be there," she said, pushing her chair back from the table. "That'll be good fun for you kids."

I nodded and swung my legs back and forth, chewing. Grandma Laura had made me a three-minute egg, which had just the right soft, warm, golden yolk. She gave it to me in a tiny silver cup, and more than anything, I liked to look at how beautiful it sat there like a moon man. After I peeled it, I liked to take a bite, then also take a bite of toast so it was blended together. I was glad to be going somewhere else, because Adam was starting to get on my nerves. He talked on and on while we lay in the big sleigh bed at night, and I listened but didn't answer anything back. I'd lie there and wait until he fell asleep. Then I could feel hot, tight tears trying to come out of my eyes, but I'd swallow them back and pound my head back on the pillow until I was okay.

We spent the day going on more errands with Grandma Laura—to the grocery store, where we got to buy special things like Doritos, strawberry pop, squirt cheese in a can, and Triscuits, and for my own treat I picked out a Banana Flip. Sylvie and I always bought them at the grocery store in Wishbone and walked down the sidewalk licking the sweet sugary foam that oozed out the sides of the taco-shaped sponge cake. My mother raised her voice the time she caught us eating them. "Iris! Do you realize that what you're eating is perfect junk? It's terrible for you, and it's going to make you fat. I can promise you that. Do you want to be fat? Really, now, throw it away, will you? You'll get sick." Sylvie and I hid them while she wasn't looking, and brought them up to my room. I missed Sylvie a lot lately. She was good at imitating our moms when they were mad—how they'd put their hands on their hips and talk through their teeth.

After our "naps," Aunt Patty called and said they were ready, that Uncle Robert was finally home from work. We'd been waiting so long that now it didn't even seem much fun anymore. We piled into the car, which was already packed with big blue coolers, folded lawn chairs, stacks of towels, boxes of groceries, twelve-packs of pop, and headed over to their house in the rich part of town where the houses all had decks and were painted beige or gray. We pulled into Aunt Patty's driveway to wait for her, Melanie, and DeeDee. Uncle Robert was driving his red convertible over alone because he had to stop and get some things for the boat, plus he had to work a little bit tomorrow, even though it was a Saturday.

The girls smelled sweet, like strawberry essence shampoo and Juicy Fruit. Melanie had a Judy Blume library book with her and said she had to sit by the door for light, even though it was only about an hour to get there. DeeDee didn't care and got the middle with the hump in the floor. I looked back and tapped her knee with my fingers, and she smiled. She looked chubbier than when I'd last seen her and had even more thick red freckles all over her face and arms. In the rearview mirror, I could see Uncle Robert's little red car behind us, his hair blowing. Once in awhile, we all waved back at him, and he beeped the horn to answer and waved up high.

The cabin was painted dark green with white trim and looked like a cottage in a kid's book. It wasn't very big, but had a nice-size screen porch in the front with two rollaway beds draped with checkered tablecloths. That was where I'd sleep, hopefully with DeeDee and Melanie and not Adam. There were trees all around the cabin, and the lawn stretched right out to the lake where there was a little sandy beach and an L-shaped dock. When we got out of the car, I could see the lake twinkling and sparkling in the sun, and finally I could breathe and relax a little.

After all the food was unpacked and the suitcases hauled in, we put on our swimsuits (mine was borrowed from Melanie and droopy in the butt) and ran down to the dock. Boats were driving around everywhere, and Melanie grabbed the big inner tube and air mattresses out of the shed for us to play with. The water was olive green with small balls of yellow floating in it, which Uncle Robert kept telling me were turtle eggs but I knew they were just algae blooming. He wore bright orange-and-yellow tropical swim trunks and had a blue life jacket buckled around him. Orange chest hairs curled out by the neck and at the bottom, where his fat belly showed. He was short and pudgy, not tall and thin and handsome like my father, who I wished was here with us. I felt like the extra kids everyone had to haul around and feel sorry for.

"Anyone want to go for a boat ride?" Uncle Robert asked, and we all shouted, "Yes!" He uncapped a bottle of beer and wiped around the rim with his thumb. "Good. Let's go. But you have to wear your life jackets. No one allowed without a life jacket." Adam ran into the boathouse and grabbed a bunch of the orange old-fashioned kind that you pulled over your head and buckled with a white strap around your middle. When I put mine on, it felt like a big hard loaf of bread was holding up my neck, and I couldn't move my head freely.

The big blue-and-white speedboat had built-in seats and hard blue carpet all over the bottom. We all stood on the dock while Uncle Robert unsnapped the thick plastic window covers and folded them away in a secret compartment. Finally we all got in— me, Adam, Melanie, and DeeDee—then Uncle Robert pushed us off and jumped on at the last minute. Soon we were slapping across the water, zigzagging to avoid all the other boats. Some people were just sitting quietly in rowboats trying to fish, and I felt bad when we drove by and made huge waves that practically tipped them over.

Uncle Robert stopped the engine and dropped the anchor, and the boat rocked back and forth. "Anyone want to jump in for a swim?" The sun was starting to set, but it was still warm enough. I thought I might do it, if anyone else did. Before discussing it, Adam ripped off his life jacket, pointed his two hands together, and dove in. Melanie followed, only after tying her hair back tightly with a binder and storing her pink glasses in the glove box. DeeDee and I held hands, pinched our noses shut, and jumped in screaming. The water was over our heads, and I wished I would've kept my life jacket on. DeeDee and I did a back float and a dead man's float, but then I felt something tugging at my leg. I got pulled under and almost swallowed a whole mouthful of lake water. It must've been Adam goofing around, but when I came up for air, it happened again and I started to choke. "Quit it!" I tried to yell, but I went down again and again and started to panic that maybe no one would notice and I'd drown. My death wish come true, I thought, but finally I kicked Adam off and grabbed on to the boat. I could hardly breathe, and the water made its way through my lungs and nose, burning. I realized I was crying and choking at the same time.

Uncle Robert swam up to me like a big walrus and asked if I was all right. His reddish hair was so thick on his head and his beard that the water was dripping off instead of soaking in. He and DeeDee put their arms around me and helped me back into the boat, where Adam and Melanie sat wrapped in towels. The sun had just about set now, and most of the boats were heading back to shore. Still coughing, I sat up front by Uncle Robert and felt the air cold on my wet skin. "You all right?" he shouted over the loud motor and slapping water. "You had me a little scared. I thought you knew how to swim."

I looked up at him, mad. "I do know how to swim!" I shouted back. "Adam kept pulling me under!" I hoped Adam could hear me. I wiped my runny nose with the corner of the striped beach towel and couldn't believe it when Uncle Robert laughed. He slapped a hand down on my leg.

"Oh, he was just having fun with you, I'm sure. Boys'll be boys, you know?" Uncle Robert stood behind the steering wheel with one knee on the seat and slowed the boat down. He glided us in at an angle to the dock, and before it could bump, he jumped out and eased the boat in, then tied it up. He cracked open another beer from the cooler, and I realized he wasn't my favorite uncle anymore.

FOR DINNER, UNCLE ROBERT INSISTED that we have barbecued ribs and chicken on the grill, even though Aunt Patty and Grandma Laura were simply going to boil up some hot dogs because they were tired. "Then you go ahead and make them, Robert—I'm not making all that at this hour," Aunt Patty said, flopping down into a recliner. She looked young in a loose flowered sundress with straps that made an X on her back, her curly red hair twisted and held up in a barrette. Grandma Laura tried not to get involved, though she talked him into just grilling the hot dogs along with some hamburger patties soaked in Worcestershire sauce and garlic salt. It was better that way, because Uncle Robert always got excited about a big project, but midway through he fizzled out and wouldn't finish. Like last Christmas he got everyone excited to build a snow kingdom in Grandma Laura's backyard, but then quit right in the middle and never made the tower like he'd promised. All of us kids were mad, and our toes nearly frostbitten with cold.

I had decided not to talk to Adam until he apologized to me, and if he never apologized to me, then I'd never talk to him. He sat at the kitchen table, watching Uncle Robert grill outside—the only one out there because of the mosquitoes. Instead, we all sat inside and watched TV, except for Melanie, who was still absorbed in her Judy Blume book. I didn't see what the big deal was about those books.

After eating hot dogs so burned the skin broke apart in flakes, everyone seemed tired and sat around, listening to the crickets. We all had to line up for baths, except for Grandma Laura, who got to go first since she was the oldest. She took forever. All of us kids sat on the scratchy orange couch and watched *Star Trek*, a show I'd never liked because it all happened in that claustrophobic spaceship and they never got to go outside. My eyes started to close, but I fought it. Sometimes a boat cruised slowly by with green or blue lights on it; we could hear it out the open windows and always had to peek out just to see. Uncle Robert was sound asleep in the green recliner, his face pointed straight up, his tiny mouth open in an *O*. He still had his swim trunks on, and a white V-neck T-shirt that showed those red chest hairs again that kind of creeped me out.

After Melanie and then Adam had had their baths, and it was just me and DeeDee on the couch, trying desperately not to fall asleep, Aunt Patty came over and rubbed her hands up and down Uncle Robert's shoulders. You could tell they were in love because of how he stretched awake, but didn't get mad that she'd woken him up. He pulled her close to him and kissed her behind the ear. "Bob," she said softly, "come to bed now." Listening to them gave me the saddest feeling for my own parents, who seemed to have abandoned Adam and me. I felt so left out, even with all our relatives, even with Grandma Laura and Adam. I knew I must've failed them somehow, or not have been enough, but I couldn't figure out what I'd done or not done or how to make it up to them. Especially if I didn't even know where they were.

JUST AS MELANIE, DEEDEE, AND I were settling into the big rollaway bed with Adam in his own across the porch, we heard a car pull up behind the cabin. Nobody ever came driving up at night, and Uncle Robert got up to see what was going on. Grandma Laura got up and seemed scared, standing at the sink with a glass of water in her hand, her stiff gray hair bunched up in back where she'd been lying down. I could hear the sound of people walking and swishing through the weeds and grass, and soft voices that floated through the screens. The footsteps stopped, and my mother and father peeked in the door at us. The moonlight was so bright I could see them clearly.

Uncle Robert unlatched the door. "Bill and Marilyn! What a surprise! We sure weren't expecting you two." He let them in, and right away my mother came over to my bed and sat down softly. Melanie was asleep, and I thought DeeDee was pretending to be for some reason. My mother put her hand on my forehead, as if I was sick, then slid it down my cheek. "Honey," she whispered, "how are you?"

"Pretty good," I replied. I saw my father checking on Adam, who was obviously asleep because of the little snore he had that drove me crazy. I wanted to shout to my father, "Adam tried to drown me today!" and get him in trouble finally, but I couldn't. A thousand questions rushed through my mind about where my mother had been, why she'd left us for so long, what was going on, but she shushed me before I even had time to ask them.

"Just go back to sleep," my mother said, and she pulled the soft white sheet up over my shoulders. She put a finger over her lips as my father came over and stared down at me. I had no idea what they were doing here so late, and together on top of everything, but I closed my eyes slowly and loved how they both bent down and softly kissed the top of my head.

For the next few minutes, I lay there, listening to all the adult things going on in the kitchen. Aunt Patty was magically awake and perked up again, and she brought out a bag of pretzels while she and my mother chattered. Bottles of beer were uncapped, Uncle Robert told stupid jokes, they started playing cards, laughing, trying to keep their voices down but always forgetting. Not once did anyone say, "Where have you two been? What about your kids?" They didn't talk about it, but from the way my mother's voice sounded, and how softly my father talked, it seemed they must've been back together. I turned over on my side and felt the cool lake breeze blow across me. I could see the whole yard outside under the moonlight and the water lapping against the dock, silver. Someone had wind chimes a couple cabins away, and I heard them tinkle and ding softly, like glass. My mother's voice, my father's, close to me at last, and I fell asleep, trying to hold on to it all.

THE NEXT DAY WAS THE FOURTH, and I woke up to the sound of firecrackers popping off all over. Uncle Robert gave us some little gray pellets that turned into squirmy puffy snakes when you lit them with a match, but there was nothing that exploded or made lots of noise. Grandma Laura said it wasn't worth the risk of having her grandchildren's hands and faces blown off, and Adam, brat that he was, pouted when she said that. I waited impatiently for my mother and father to get up, hoping they'd explain what'd been going on, but they slept late, and by the time they were up and dressed, we were all outside on the dock already.

My mother finally came out of the cabin, squinting and clutching a cup of coffee. She was changing again, somehow—I could feel it. She was softer and gentler, with a secret look in her eye. The white sundress she wore looked loose and baggy, and her hair, longish now, flipped and curled like it never had before. It took everything I had not to run up and grab on to her, fall at her feet, and beg her not to leave me alone with Adam again. Instead, I watched her sit quietly on the dock with her toes in the green water, smiling at things everyone said, but not talking.

My father came out soon, coffee in hand, and stood behind her, his knees bumping against her back playfully. She grabbed his bare feet and squeezed, and seeing this bit of love between them made me almost crack with happiness. We all stood and watched Uncle Robert's boat blaze around the lake with Aunt Patty trailing behind on a bright yellow rope, waterskiing. She dropped down on purpose right in front of the dock, sinking slowly like quicksand.

Melanie clapped and jumped up and down. "I want to go next!" she hollered. "Can I go now? Can I? I never get to go."

"Hang on!" Uncle Robert called across the water, and steered the boat slowly toward the dock. "I need a break." He pointed to my father and laughed. "Are we hanging one on this morning or what? How about you, Marilyn? Need a little hair of the dog?"

"We're doing all right," my mother said. "Just fine." She held up her coffee, then took a sip.

My father nodded, but didn't look fine to me. His forehead was pinched and full of deep worry wrinkles, his skin pink and tender-looking. He'd never been good at staying out in the sun, but burned a bright cheeky pink.

Before we went up to the house to change, I caught Grandma Laura looking at the two of them with deep concern, as if she'd just found out they were dying with only a month to live. Grandma Laura looked very 1940s in a big straw hat with a pink scarf tie, a light blue zip-up dress, and wide cork-bottomed sandals. I got up, ran to the cool shade by the cabin, and waited to see what was next.

After a big breakfast of pancakes and bacon, made for everybody by Uncle Robert, who pretended he was a waiter as he served us, my mother and father said it was time we went home. Before it had barely started, our cabin trip was over. My only question was, which home—the apartment above Dana's or the house?

To MY SURPRISE, our living situation seemed even more compli-cated than before. My father stayed at the house, and my mother, Adam, and I went back to the hot little apartment on Main Street. Just when it seemed they were back together, I'd been fooled, only this time my father and mother still got together and talked on the phone, even slept together in the apartment sometimes, but my father always left eventually. It was impossible to ask my mother about any of this without making her mad. Plus, she'd gotten the job working at the bank across the street, so every day from noon to five she wasn't home, and when she did come home, she pulled off her bra through her sleeve holes, threw it across the room, and needed to lie on the couch with an arm over her head, resting. I'd take her pumps and set them quietly in the closet, then wait for her to wake up and feel like talking. Much of the summer passed like that, with Adam and me alone in the apartment, waiting for her. We ate cold macaroni salad and crackers almost every day of the week. I missed our old life.

During one of those long slow afternoons I went to the library down the street, which was really just a paneled back room of the police station. You could hear the static of their walkie-talkies while you were browsing through yellowed paperbacks, and sometimes you ran into one of the cops, since the library and police station shared bathrooms. The librarian, Vivian VonAhren, was an older lady with short dyed-blond hair and blue-tinted glasses, who did the work on a volunteer basis and always let you know that when you asked for help. The whole library was no bigger than our living room at home, and didn't have the greatest selection, but there was a corner in back with an old pink couch where I liked to sit and leaf through the magazines. I liked the shots of models wearing bright yellow or red tennis shoes that matched their sweatshirts and hair barrettes. Their hair was always thick shiny blond or brunette that seemed to barely fit inside the ponytail holder but came spilling out in glossy waves around their shoulders. I never left without a book, and was right in the middle of the Nancy Drew series, which I loved. I could read a whole Nancy Drew in a day, so I always checked out two or three, even though Vivian VonAhren tried to get me not to. "Do you think you'll be able to read all of these before the due date? Maybe someone else might like to check them out," she asked me from behind the plain wooden table with no drawers that was her desk. Everything was piled up on it. "These are due by August third."

"I know," I said. "But I read fast."

She sighed and spent at least a minute lining up the rubber date stamp on the card. The date came out in fuzzy purple numbers. "August third," she reminded me.

"Right." I got out of there before she could say it again and pinched my nose because of the stinky aftershave smell coming from the police office down the hall. I could see them in there biting into sandwiches and drinking Dr Pepper. Not a lot of crime happened in Wishbone.

When I got back to the apartment, Adam was on the couch, looking out the window, his back to me. Lately he'd been sprouting up much taller, and his face had gotten a sharper older look. I set the Nancy Drew books on the table and thought about what to eat. My mother wasn't exactly good about keeping a stocked refrigerator, but I found an apple and some Kraft cheese slices.

"I'm bored," Adam said, flopping down on the couch, his hands behind his head. "There's nothing to do around here."

"Mrs. Scholhauser told us there's no reason for anyone to ever be bored," I said with my mouth full of apple. "She said you have to use your inner resources."

Adam wandered over and sat across from me at the table. He put his chin in his hands, sulking. "Well, I don't have any. It's just hot and stuffy around here. I hate it. I might just run away one of these days. I really might." He drummed his long fingers on the table and gazed out the window at the squirrels running over the tar-papered balcony. I was always afraid they were going to get inside, like they had at my aunt Deb's house once. There was a tiny hole in the window screen above the kitchen sink that had grown bigger and bigger. Finally one summer a couple of squirrels got in, ran all over the house, and chewed up food on the counters and some newspapers. That was why I was careful to keep the doors and windows closed here so they didn't scamper in while I was in bed. My mother thought I was crazy and too much of a worrywart, but I couldn't help thinking about these things.

I bit into a piece of cheese and looked up at Adam. "You won't run away. Where would you go? How would you eat?" I twirled the apple core between my fingers, then got up to throw it in the silver garbage can with the foot pedal. We never had such a fun garbage can in our old house. My mother'd bought all kinds of weird things for our apartment like colored plastic plates with molded compartments for different foods, plastic glasses with gold glitter in them, and a shower curtain with a world map on it. That was her new way.

"I could figure things out," Adam said, and he grabbed a cheese slice from my plate. He bit around the shiny square in a star pattern, then flopped it around in the air. "I could always go back to my real mom's. She's in the Twin Cities somewhere. She wants me back anyway." He sat up straight and pounded a fist on the table. "Hey! She'd probably let you stay with us, too, if you wanted to leave. You wanna?"

"No!" I looked at him like he was sick. "Of course I don't want to run away to your other mom's. Why would I want to?" I knew he'd never just run off. Even though he acted tough, I thought he was scared of his real mom. Still, I envied him that he even had the option of a real mom. I threw away the wrappers from my cheese slices and was about to call Sylvie, but decided to change into shorts first since it'd gotten so hot. I deliberately slammed the bedroom door and started digging around in the dresser, but nothing was clean. The flowered shorts I'd worn yesterday were on the floor, so I pulled them on. Who cared? They looked all right, and I wasn't going anywhere anyway. A pink tank top was also on the floor, so I wore that, too. Just as I was about to go back out to the living room, Adam came in without knocking.

"I told you to knock!" I said, hands on my hips. "I was getting dressed!"

"So? Doesn't matter to me." He stepped around piles of his dirty clothes and pushed the window open. Hot sun poured in along with noises from the street. You could see the dark brick of the bank perfectly from here, and I thought I saw our mother through the bank's glass front. I wasn't sure if it was her, though.

"Do you want to play a game?" Adam asked, then sat on the edge of the bottom bunk.

"No, and besides," I said, heading toward the door, "I was just going to call Sylvie. I haven't seen her for awhile, and I thought maybe she'd like to come over and suntan on the balcony."

Adam got up and blocked my way to the door. "Oh," he said. "Big fun to sit out in the sun and burn." He looked messy and ratty with a black T-shirt, cutoffs, bare feet. His dark eyes flashed.

I tried to step around him, but he moved in front of me. "Well, me and Sylvie like it. We like to sit and talk. Now I'm going to make some iced tea. Come on. Get out of the way."

When I called Sylvie, she wasn't home. I let the phone ring and ring and ring.

LATER, I WATCHED MY MOTHER walk across the street from the bank. Her hair was twisted up in back, and she wore a light pink skirt suit. I listened to her footsteps on the front stairs. She came in and immediately raised her hands, palms to us. "Please don't anyone ask anything of me until I've had a minute. It's not been the best day for me." She slipped out of her white pumps, unhooked her bra through the back of her blouse, and pulled it out, as usual, through an armhole. "And please pick up this mess, Adam—now." She pointed to papers and books on the floor and some of Adam's clothes. It was really not much of a mess, but Adam obeyed her anyway.

I stood by the couch, where she stretched out and stuck a pillow behind her head. She pulled off her clip-on pearl earrings and tossed them onto the coffee table. I still stood nearby, chewing on a fingernail. She settled herself, closed her eyes, then, as if she sensed me still there, opened them. "Iris? Yes? Is there something you want or do you just like watching me?"

"Nothing," I said. "I was just thinking of something."

Instead of asking what I was thinking about, she settled back and put her arms up over her eyes to rest.

When my mother woke up later, she went right to the shower and told us she almost forgot that she was having company over. I stood outside the bathroom door and listened to the water spritz on. I supposed my father was coming over for dinner like he did sometimes, even though she usually didn't call him company. She called him "your father," with a rough sound in her voice.

When she was done, my mother came out of the steamy bathroom in a peach terry bathrobe and a towel wound around her head. I stood in her bedroom doorway and watched her put makeup on and comb her hair out in long stripes. Her face looked fresh and soft, but she rubbed lotion into it anyway, and patted off the extra with a tissue.

"Is our father coming over tonight?" I asked, and picked up a bottle of CoverGirl liquid foundation. It was the exact color of coffee with cream, and I couldn't imagine spreading it all over my face, which was exactly what my mother did. Then she blued her eyelids, reddened her lips, and pinkened her cheeks.

My mother brushed the back of her hair up into a ponytail, then let it fall around her face. "Well, actually I was going to talk to you about it. It's a friend of Aunt Deb's boyfriend. Do you remember her boyfriend, Mike? He was there the night we stopped in for a visit?" She talked to me in the mirror. "Maybe you were asleep. Anyway, he has a friend, Blake, who just got a divorce from his wife and needs a friend. So he's coming over for dinner tonight."

I leaned my elbows on the table, thinking this over. There was no food in the house, plus I wondered if me and Adam were supposed to be a part of the dinner or if she wanted to be alone with him. "Are me and Adam going to be here for dinner?"

"Of course," she said, clipping on deep green earrings with black polka dots on them. "He likes kids." She put scented lotion on her arms and hands, then stood up in her bra and underwear to pick out a dress. Her hip bones stuck out like something dangerous. "Oh, don't mention anything about your father, okay? I mean, Blake knows about your father, but it's better not to talk about it, to be polite. Oh, and especially don't say your father still lives here in Wishbone in our house. You know?" She stepped into black flats, pulled a sea-green dress over her head, then buckled a thick black belt around her waist.

Something seemed odd about the company she was having, and then it hit me that it was a date.

"Well, does our father know Blake is coming over?" I had to ask.

My mother stopped what she was doing and put her hands on her hips. "Iris, it's okay. He doesn't need to know everything we do here. We each have separate lives. But, no, it's better if you not tell him." She took my chin in her hand and gave me a tiny kiss on the nose. Then, just when it seemed like old times between us, there was Adam, brooding in the doorway.

"Someone's here," he said, yawning and looking bored.

I WOKE UP IN THE MIDDLE of the night to go to the bathroom like I often did and heard noises. I slowly pushed open our bedroom door, looked out, and saw the lights were still on in the living room. Before I peed, I slid quietly along the hallway and peeked around the corner. My mother and Blake sat on the couch, drinking red wine and whispering. My mother's feet were in his lap, and she brushed his cheek with the back of her hand.

I kept wondering what my father would think, but before they could see me, I snuck into the bathroom as quietly as I could.

Secrets were starting to pile up inside me. My own, my mother's, Adam's. I made a promise to call Sylvie up first thing tomorrow. She'd know what to do, and maybe we could play records and talk about it.

Chapter Six

Memory: My mother is driving us home from school after meeting my teacher, who has told her my academic skills are exceptional. The station wagon smells like fried chicken from the takeout box in back. "She's one of those women's libbers," my mother says, and she lights up a cigarette. "She's a type, Iris—dime a dozen." We drive through town with the windows open. I stick my elbow out like my father. She flicks ashes out the window, then tosses the whole cigarette out. I watch it bounce, the tip glowing orange.

"Isn't that littering?" I say. I remember the commercial with the crying Indian on the highway.

"Isn't that my business?" she says.

Something turns inside: trust, fleeing. But she swoops in to save it.

"You are very smart, Iris," she says. "Smarter than you know."

The day after Blake came over for dinner, I went to the kitchen and picked up the small tan phone with the lit-up numbers right inside the receiver. Somebody was always awake at Sylvie's, but this time nobody answered. Since I was the only one up, I poured myself a glass of orange juice and sat down to watch TV in the living room. The morning felt cool and fresh, and since none of the stores were open downtown yet, the streets were quiet and calm. Robins sang; the wind blew through the curtains. I put my feet up on the coffee table and thought about Blake. It seemed wrong, I knew it was wrong, and yet, how could I know? What could I do?

I turned the volume down on Sylvester and Tweety Bird, put my glass in the sink, and tried calling Sylvie's house again. This time, after just two rings, her mom, Elizabeth, answered. "Hello?" Her voice always sounded completely surprised when she answered the telephone.

"Hi, it's Iris. Can I talk to Sylvie?"

"Well, you're sure up early, Iris. How are you? How's your mother doing?"

"Good. She's good. She has a job at the bank now."

"I know, that's wonderful," Sylvie's mom said. "How come we haven't seen you around here for so long?"

"I don't know. Just been busy."

She paused. "Well, just a second. I think Sylvie's awake. I'll holler up for her."

"Okay. Thanks." I brought the phone over to the kitchen table, and waited. It seemed to take a long time, so I browsed through a grocery store flyer.

"Hello?"

"Hi, it's me. You weren't sleeping, were you?"

Sylvie yawned long and loud. "Yeah, kind of. What's going on? Why are you up so early?"

I looked at the clock and realized that it wasn't even seven.

"I don't know. Hey, what are you doing later? You want to come over while my mom's at work and tan on the balcony?"

"Mmm, I don't know. Carla was going to come over, and we're supposed to help my mom in the flower garden. I have to call her later."

"Oh," was all I could think to say. *I* was the one who always went over to Sylvie's and helped her mom out with chores. That was *my* job. "Well, can you call me later? I'd kind of like to talk to you." I cupped my hand around the phone so she could hear me whispering. "It's about my mom."

"Oh," she said. "Well, me and Carla—"

"Anyway," I said, "I have to go. Call me later, okay?"

"All right. I'll talk to Carla later to see what she wants to do, but if she's busy, maybe I'll come over."

The words stung. After we hung up, I sat at the table, feeling like someone had socked me. Carla hung out with the popular girls who all wore Levi's and striped turtlenecks and sparkly studded pierced earrings. Now all I had left was Adam.

MY MOTHER SAW MORE AND MORE of Blake as the summer stretched on, and he started to seem more like my father than my *real* father, or maybe I should say my adopted father. It was okay because I liked Blake. He was tall and thin and wore tight jeans and tucked-in T-shirts in all colors of the rainbow, always with a pocket on the chest. Unlike my father, who was pale and had clear blue eyes, Blake had black hair, dark brown eyes, and a mustache that completely hid his upper lip. If I hadn't known him and saw him walking down the street, I might've thought he was from a different country. He also had a great laugh where he grabbed his knees with his hands and threw his head way back and sort of exploded, even about stupid little things I'd tell him—he'd laugh that hard. He got amazed easily, and I'd always been drawn to people like that.

Usually he came over after work, and what he did, from what I knew, was build houses in Mankato. My mother said he was in construction, but when I asked him about his job he said a lot of the time he was up on roofs all day, laying shingles and hammering them on. He said there were a couple of two-by-fours nailed onto the roof so he wouldn't slip and fall off. He'd come over smelling like fresh sawdust, a smell I loved, and by that time my mother would be back from the bank, out of her dress-up clothes and wearing shorts and tennis shoes. They cooked dinner together while Adam and I watched TV in the living room, or sometimes I sat at the table pretending to read when I was really just watching and listening to them.

My mother was different around Blake. Sometimes she sang along to songs on the radio, and they bumped butts with each other while they were boiling noodles for hamburger stroganoff. I *loved* hamburger stroganoff. A lot of times they'd set the canned things on the table for me to open—the cream of mushroom soup, a tiny can of mushrooms—or let me chop things up. It smelled so good with the hamburger browning on the stove, the onions sizzling, that I'd get impatient. We ate better since Blake had been coming over, but the only problem was he and Adam didn't really get along. Or it wasn't exactly that they didn't get along, but Adam didn't like Blake—not really a surprise. He'd told me so, and he'd told my mother, who only rolled her eyes, crossed her arms, and said, "Adam, don't even start. I do not want to hear this. I don't want you to say any more." But it was always sort of a problem now. I thought Adam did it just for the attention, especially because Blake and I got along so well.

At first Blake never stayed overnight, but would leave after the ten o'clock news. From the bathroom window, I'd watch him walk down the back balcony stairs in the dark and get into his green-and-white truck, which had tall racks and compartments in the back. My mother would blow him a kiss from the balcony, and on would pop the white headlights, then the crunch of gravel under his tires. I would dash back into bed before my mother came in, and lie there imagining his long trip back to Mankato alone. Where did he live? I would wonder. What kind of kitchen did he have? Did he sing in the truck on the way home?

LATER, ONE HOT, SWEATY NIGHT in August, I got up in the middle of the night to go to the bathroom, and heard voices—theirs—Blake's and my mother's. They were in her bedroom with the door closed, and I knew then he was probably staying over since it was so late it was almost light out. I thought of my father at home in our big house, in their old bedroom with yellow painted walls and a canopy bed, maple leaves clicking against the window, and felt sorry for him. He was probably asleep, but I thought of how unfair it was for my mother to have someone but not him. I could imagine him there, curled up like an old man or a baby, trying to shrink the big space of the mattress by putting himself in the middle.

On the last Saturday in August before school started, my mother took me and Adam school clothes shopping in Mankato. I'd been campaigning to go to Madison East Mall, which had a County Seat and a Dayton's, but when we finally got to Mankato my mother passed it and pulled into the big Kmart parking lot. Adam was in the front seat with his bare feet curled over the cracked maroon dashboard.

"Why can't we go to the mall?" I asked. "It's just over there." I looked longingly out the window at the huge gray building across the road.

My mother unzipped her purse, pulled out a comb, and cranked the rearview mirror over so she could see herself. She fluffed back her bangs and pulled sections of hair apart with her fingers. "Because," she said, looking not at me but in the mirror, "Kmart's just as good. They have a good sale on."

From the backseat, I watched her pull out a gold tube of lipstick and cover her bottom lip with a deep line of red, then smack to smooth it out. She swung the mirror back into position, grabbed a Kleenex from the box, and dabbed at her mouth.

I sat back, fuming. I was about to start seventh grade and didn't have any good clothes. How could I even go if I didn't have anything to wear? Before, it was bad enough when my mother wouldn't buy me Levi's but made me get JCPenney plain pockets, but now all I got was Kmart. Even Sylvie, whose family didn't have much money, had two pairs of Levi's cords, and I knew Carla had all Levi's because her family was rich. I wanted to go to the County Seat and at least look. All those perfectly folded stacks of dark jeans, with the Levi's-tag pocket on the top. And the corduroy colors were so good this year, with dark red like cranberries and light blue like the sky. I almost started crying, but bit my lip and told myself to get a grip.

"Come on," my mother said, and unfolded herself from the car. She clicked her door shut and waited for us to get out. Adam scuffed along behind her, and I stayed even farther behind. I used to think my mother understood me, but lately all she cared about was her new boyfriend. She probably would've rather spent her money on him instead of us. Or even herself—she was so selfish.

The store was bright white and red, and smelled like movie popcorn and hot dogs. I looked over at the snack bar and eyed the glass case full of big fat doughy pretzels, but my mother steered me away and grabbed a big red shopping cart.

"Here, I'll push it," Adam said, and took it from her, racing off down the aisle by the notebooks and crayons. Apparently everyone else had waited to do their school shopping until the very last minute like us, because there were all kinds of parents dragging around whiny kids, holding up ugly blouses and stiff colored pants that the kids shook their heads at and pouted over.

My mother was acting very cheerful and even humming. "Okay, Iris," she said, folding a piece of Juicy Fruit into her mouth. "Want a piece?" I shook my head. "Well, we better do you first. Girls are always harder. I think you can probably start with two pairs of pants and maybe three tops. That should be enough, right? Oh, and you need some new underwear and socks."

I didn't say anything, but followed her down the crowded aisle up to a round rack of girls' tops. They were long-sleeved shirts with colored buildings on them and a tiny satin bow at the neckline. "These are cute," my mother said, holding up one in shades of peach and dark green. She looked inside for the tag. "And it's your size." She turned it around, back to front, looking. I couldn't help but notice the big black-and-red sign above it: CLEARANCE SALE $4.99. People were crowded all around, and I worried that someone I knew would appear. She held it up to my chest. "Do you like it?"

"Not really." I fingered the stiff fabric, which felt cheap and rough, like it'd been dipped in glue and dried in the hot sun.

My mother frowned. "Why not? It'd be cute on you."

"I just think it's—" I could feel myself making a face against my will.

My mother sighed, and got the old faraway look on her face that I used to be afraid of. She put the shirt back on the rack, grabbed me by the arm, and leaned over, whispering. "Okay, then you tell me what you want. We don't have all day." She squeezed my arm once to let me know she was getting mad. I pulled away and started browsing through the racks of ugly matching clothes. It all looked cheap, like the stuff Margie Warren, a girl in my class, wore. The material was kind of see-through and stiff, and the buttons looked like they might fall off, and the hems in her pants and skirts were always unraveling and trailing pastel threads to the floor. No one liked her very much either, and I actually felt sorry for her.

I went through the whole girls' section while my mother went to find me big jumbo packs of cotton underwear and socks. When she came back, I handed her a plain white turtleneck, just to make her happy. I didn't think anyone would be able to tell it was only from Kmart. I could wear it under sweaters or just with jeans I already had. Besides, Sylvie told me she was starting a collection of all different colored turtlenecks this year, even some striped and with little prints on them.

"That's all you want?" my mother asked, gripping the hanger underneath her arm.

I nodded.

"You're too young to be this fussy, Iris," she said, stalking away, "but if that's all you want, then fine." She turned and waited for me to catch up to her. "My god, you're acting like I'm asking you to wear rags! I just won't put up with it. If your father were here—" she started to say, but didn't finish.

If my father were here, what? I wanted to ask, but didn't. My mother stood in the middle of a busy aisle, blocking traffic.

"Excuse me," another mom said, jammed behind my mother with a whole shopping cart full of kids' underwear and notebooks and glue and even one of those girls' shirts with the buildings and bow on it. A little baby girl stood inside the cart, and three other kids followed behind her.

"Oh, sorry," my mother said, moving out of the way, into a small row of alarm clocks and calculators. For a second we had peace and quiet, and my mother tried to pull herself together. Her green eyes looked tired and sad. "Iris," she said, putting her hand to my cheek, "it'll be all right, honey, it will." I looked up at her and smiled, hoping she couldn't see my real feelings.

We met up with Adam by the checkout counter. He had the cart filled with clothes for himself—striped T-shirts, two flannel shirts, three pairs of jeans, two turtlenecks, bunches of socks, a blue Windbreaker. "Quite the shopper!" my mother said, sorting through the cart and checking tags. "We better see what we have here." But before we knew it, it was our turn in line, and the clerk was ringing up our stuff quickly. My mother turned her back to the clerk and opened her wallet, furiously counting her money.

"Eighty-seven eighty-nine," the clerk said, after hitting the Total button. My mother looked at the register and asked to see the receipt. She scanned it up and down with wide eyes, then shook her head. Me and Adam stood behind her, staring at the rows of candy bars.

"Well, I guess I don't have enough cash on me," my mother said, opening up compartments in her wallet, as if she'd find a secret stash.

"We take checks," the clerk, Steve, said. He wore a red vest over a white T-shirt and looked like he was probably in high school.

"I don't have my checkbook on me," my mother said. I was ready to melt into a puddle of embarrassment. People were lined up behind us and starting to get restless, to wonder what was going on. They'd think we were poor. "Well, let's just take a few of these things back, then. We've really got too many things we don't need anyway." She reached into the cart and took whatever was on top—my white turtleneck, Adam's Windbreaker, the plastic-packaged socks. She tried to act like it was no big deal.

Finally, we paid and walked out of the store. My mother's neck looked stiff and stern, and she didn't even turn to look for cars as we walked through the parking lot. In the driver's seat, she sat for a long time, staring straight ahead without saying anything. Adam and I didn't dare, either. I wished things were like they used to be, back at our big tan-and-brown house—records playing, my own bedroom, my father bringing ice cream treats home. Everything seemed to have gotten ruined since Adam came, including my whole life.

BEFORE DRIVING BACK TO WISHBONE, we pulled up to a pay phone by an Amoco station on a very busy street. "Be back in a sec," my mother said, and I assumed she was calling Blake, who lived in Mankato. Maybe we'd go over and visit him. I couldn't imagine us in his house instead of the other way around. I couldn't even imagine him having a house of his own. Would there be flowered curtains and nice dishes? I didn't think so.

While she was on the phone, swinging her sunglasses around and around with her hand, Adam and I lounged back in the car with our bare feet up. The sun was hot, and the day was humid and still. I hated to think of school starting. With Sylvie leaving me for Carla and that group of girls I couldn't stand, who would I hang out with? Who would I even walk there with on the first day? Just then, Adam kicked my head from the backseat.

"Quit it!" I yelled, pulling my feet in out of the sunshine and sitting up straight.

"I didn't do it on purpose."

"Right."

"I didn't." He jiggled the back of my seat just to be obnoxious.

"Stop it!" I yelled, loud enough for my mother to hear. She gestured at us to pipe down, then I could tell she was wrapping up the phone call because she put her sunglasses on and turned her back to us. "You're such a brat," I said to Adam.

"You're such a brat," he said back, mocking me.

"I wish my parents would've never even adopted you," I said, crossing my arms and feeling the sticky vinyl seat stuck to my legs. "Everything was better before you came." I was hot and sick of waiting in cars for my mother all the time, and sick of Adam bugging me.

No reply, and even when I looked back in the rearview mirror, he didn't respond at all. He wouldn't even look at me . . . then I felt bad. I didn't want to be mean, but sometimes he just asked for it.

"Okay, we're going over to Blake's for awhile, and I want you to behave," my mother said, making no mention of the embarrassment in the store. She combed through her fine reddish hair, and tucked the sides back behind her ears. She was wearing it about shoulder length now, and it looked cute. She bared her teeth and ran her fingernail between them to get out pieces of something. For the first time I realized that she wasn't wearing her wedding ring. It was a thick gold band, absolutely plain, and I remembered asking her once why she didn't have a diamond like everybody else. "Iris, such questions," she had said, fingering the ring at the kitchen table. "It's really more elegant to have a plain band. It's more classy." She'd stuck out her hand and wiggled her fingers around, then sighed. "Besides, those big sharp diamonds get caught in your hair, they can tear your clothes, they can even hurt little babies. It's just not practical." But I always wondered if she hadn't secretly wanted one but was ashamed to say it.

"Where does Blake live?" I asked, hanging my arm out the window and privately watching how I looked in the side-view mirror, hair blowing, wearing a red T-shirt. I thought I looked pretty cute.

"You'll see," my mother said, and she turned on the radio to a pop station with lots of ads for chewing gum and shampoo. She took us down the hill, curving past the Viking Motel, and went all the way to First Street, then turned left. She drove slowly, looking at the house numbers; then she parallel parked in front of a plain white house that looked as if it might've belonged to a drug dealer. The red trim was falling off, and the screens were all rusty with holes in them. The yard had nothing but old bicycles lying around in various states of disrepair. Some were turned upside down, and some were jammed nose down into the dirt. There were four black mailboxes next to the front door. My mother rang a doorbell, and soon we could hear feet thumping down the stairs.

Blake opened the front door, which looked like someone had kicked it a few too many times. He held a can of beer in his hand. "Hey!" he said, all excited. He threw one arm around my mother and kissed her on the cheek, then put his hand out to shake with Adam—Adam went for that kind of thing. He just tousled my hair and laughed, then invited us all up.

We followed Blake back up the stairs and entered his living room, which had deep-blue flat carpet like a swimming pool, a tan-and-orange striped couch, a bookshelf full of small paperbacks all the same size, and an electric keyboard set up on a card table.

"I didn't know you played music!" Adam said, rushing up to touch the glossy black and white keys. "Cool."

"Adam," my mother warned, "don't even go near it or touch it. You'll break it."

"I will not," he said, "god." He stomped into the next room, which was sort of a dining room/lounge. In one corner, there was a small glass-topped table with three wicker-back chairs with metal legs. There was also a big flowered chair with a matching footstool, then a dresser painted black, with some folded clothes piled on top of it. Down a tiny hall to the right was the kitchen, which was a small square room with only one window that looked out into the backyard. All the cupboards were painted yellow, and the refrigerator, stove, sink were all green. Boxes of cereal were lined up on the counter—Wheaties, Raisin Bran, Corn Flakes—nothing sweetened or for kids.

It didn't feel like a lonely man's house; it wasn't great, but it was nicer than I'd expected. He and my mother sat at the kitchen table with cold cans of beer in front of them, talking. This left Adam and me to wander around the apartment, and we headed back to the living room, where the TV and the keyboard piano were. Adam turned on the TV, but there was nothing on except *Superstar Sports,* because it was Saturday afternoon. One team wore royal blue, and the other team wore red, and they did things like run through lines of tires and hang off ropes. This week it was the cast from *Dallas* versus the cast from *Eight Is Enough.*

I noticed pictures sitting on the TV table and got up to look. "Adam, look at this," I whispered. He looked over my shoulder at a big eight-by-ten photograph of Blake, a woman who must've been his ex-wife, and three kids. The oldest kid must've been about ten, and the youngest was a little girl who was maybe four or five.

"I didn't know he had kids," Adam said, grabbing the picture out of my hands. "I wonder if he told our mom that he does. You think?"

I settled back onto the striped couch, hands crossed over my stomach. "Yeah. He must have."

"Look at this one," Adam said, and he handed me a five-by-seven picture of Blake and his ex-wife. They were both dressed up, he in a white button-up shirt and tie, and she in a satiny peach dress with pearl buttons along one shoulder. She also wore a string of pearls around her neck. She wasn't pretty exactly, but something about her was good-looking. She had blond permed hair, a wide face, big smiling teeth, dark eyebrows, and a fun, lively look in her eyes.

But when my mother came in with a fresh beer, she took one glance at the picture and then looked again, long and hard, taking a big deep swallow of her beer. "Blake," she called to him, grabbing the picture and pressing it between her side and arm. "Blake."

He came in wearing his yellow pocket T-shirt and usual tight, dark jeans with a big belt. He saw right away what she had and looked first at us, then at her. "I just haven't put everything away yet. It doesn't mean anything, Marilyn." But my mother looked sad and far-off again. She didn't even answer, and I thought of my father back home, painting people's spiderwebby houses, missing my mother and wanting her back.

Naturally, we didn't stay long. The beers were drunk, the TV was snapped off, and we were off in the car again, the sun slanted down to the west a little, making it less hot, but not less humid.

When we got home from Mankato and climbed the back stairs to the apartment, I saw my father inside sitting at the kitchen table. I wondered how he got in, but then remembered it was Wishbone, and nobody locked their doors. The town was so small you didn't have to worry.

"Bill," my mother said. She adjusted the Kmart bags with her knee, opened the door to let me and Adam in, then let it slam behind her.

"Hi, sweetie," my father said, and stood up. I rushed over to him—it felt so good to have him there. He bent over to hug me. His long fingers patted me on the back, and I closed my eyes, then he kissed me on the cheek. "Adam," he said, "come here." Instead of a hug like I got, he hooked his arm around Adam's shoulder and pulled him close. Adam grabbed him around the waist, but it didn't last long, and they pulled apart.

"Marilyn," my father said. "I just had to talk to you. I hope it's okay."

"You could've phoned," she said, and slid out of her shoes like she always did first thing.

"I tried, but no one was home. I didn't want to miss you." He tried to meet my mother's gaze, but she was too busy unloading school clothes from the bags—all Adam's clothes, I realized with regret. "That's right, school starts on Monday, doesn't it?"

Me and Adam both nodded. "Unfortunately," I said.

"Gag," Adam said. He sat at the kitchen table with us, but my mother didn't sit.

My father motioned for me to sit on his lap, even though I was too big for that. I half sat with my legs trailing off the side. "I see you got some new clothes. Pretty nice."

"Well, mostly they're Adam's," I said, adjusting my weight so my butt bones didn't jut into my father's leg muscles. "I didn't get anything yet."

"Why not?" My father rocked me back and forth on his legs. It was good to be near him again, and then I noticed for the first time he didn't smell like butter, and didn't even wear his white creamery clothes either. He just looked regular, in tan shorts and an old green T-shirt.

My mother glared at us from the living room where she was removing price tags and labels from Adam's stuff. "Thanks to you, no, Iris doesn't have any school clothes. I'm practically broke, Bill! Did you know that? I have about five dollars to my name, and payday's not for another four or five days." She sat by herself in the living room on the dark green couch, legs and arms crossed, chewing on the inside of her mouth like she did when she was upset. "I can't do this anymore, Bill. You've got to contribute something."

"Can we talk about this in private?" my father said, giving my mother a mean look. His voice wavered, and he tapped me on the knee. "You kids don't have to worry about this. We'll figure it out." As if on cue, I jumped off his lap and followed Adam into our bedroom. I knew they were going to fight.

Adam and I acted like we closed our door, but we left it open just a bit and sat right behind it, listening. It felt like my fault again, but I didn't want any Kmart school clothes anyway. I was also starving to death since we hadn't eaten since breakfast, and with my knees bent up like this, I felt dizzy and shaky, like I might pass out.

"Well, then move back home!" my father yelled. He wasn't even trying to be quiet anymore, and I hoped the people down in Dana's salon couldn't hear him. "You complain you don't have enough money, but then here you are in a $275-a-month place, chasing all over hell with this guy I heard you've been seeing. What do you expect?"

"That's a lie," my mother said more quietly. Adam and I strained to hear every word, and looked at each other, puzzled. "You don't know."

"I *do* know. It's a pretty small town, Marilyn."

There was silence for awhile, and I held my breath in, felt my heart beat. My father spoke again. "I might as well tell you." He lowered his voice, and Adam and I strained further. "I don't want the kids to hear this, but the creamery is pretty much going under. I talked to Hanson at the bank about getting a second mortgage on our house, or getting some kind of extension for the payments on the creamery building, but he said they just can't do it with business as bad as it is." He cleared his throat. "Do you realize I was in there last, oh, what day was it? Wednesday? And no one came in. Not a single goddamned person! Even the high school and elementary have stopped ordering from us because they cut a deal with Pac 'n Save. That's our biggest order, remember?" I imagined my mother nodding sadly.

"It's just crazy. I don't know what to do but shut down—but hell, what then? What are we going to do, Marilyn?" His voice sounded on the verge of breaking. No wonder everything had been so hard. With her two miscarriages, nothing had been good in my mother's life, either. Even Blake with his big colored pictures of his kids and ex-wife—it was no good. I thought we should've all gotten back together. I missed my purple room and the backyard. Maybe then Sylvie would've hung out with me again.

For awhile, there was no sound, and it seemed like the argument was over, plus I had to pee. We swung the door open loudly enough so that they'd hear us, and stepped out into the hall. I couldn't help but peek around the corner when I was done in the bathroom. My mother and father were in each other's arms, holding tight, rocking gently back and forth. If only it would've lasted. If only I could've kept them together like that forever.

By evening time, when the heat bugs were screaming out their hot cry and it was unbearably hot and humid, my father was still at our apartment. For supper, he'd made us all fried-egg-and-onion sandwiches on white bread, one of my favorite things to eat in the whole world. Adam picked his onions off, and complained the greasy egg made his bread too soggy, but I figured he was probably just not used to eating good like that. My mother didn't turn on the TV for us as she usually did while she went off to write, but played Elvis records, just like the old days. They sat side by side on the couch, drinking iced tea with orange slices, talking about this and that, as old friends would've who hadn't seen each other for a long time.

I pretended that I was reading a book, but kept glancing up at them to make sure it was still real.

BY SUNDAY NIGHT HE WAS STILL THERE, and it all seemed the same as before except we now lived in a little apartment on Main Street. I was more worried about starting seventh grade than anything. Sylvie and I hadn't talked for days, so it looked like I'd be walking to school alone, which wasn't too bad since it was just around the corner. But I didn't know what to wear. It would probably be so hot I'd just wear shorts, but then if no one else had shorts on, I'd feel stupid. My homeroom teacher's name was Miss Rickhardt, who I heard was pretty nice and easy. She also taught English (my favorite subject), social studies, and maybe something else—that's how small Wishbone was.

THE FIRST DAY OF SCHOOL I DECIDED to wear blue jean cutoffs and a green-and-white striped T-shirt so it wouldn't look like I was trying to get really dressed up. I had pink Jelly sandals that I liked to wear, even though they made my feet sweaty in the heat. But I thought it seemed like a good outfit. Sylvie and Carla were going to stop in front of Dana's salon and walk with me, but Sylvie said they wouldn't come all the way up so I'd better be ready.

My mother's way of making us breakfast was to set the box of cheap-brand wheat cereal on the table and get out bowls. She leaned against the sink holding a cup of coffee in her hand while Adam and I shook out the dry flakes and dumped milk over them. Adam had stiff new jeans on and a long-sleeved shirt, even though it was a hot, humid day.

I sprinkled a sparkly circle of sugar over my cereal and watched it soak up the milk and turn gray. "Did our father leave again?" I asked, mouth full. I knew my mother would yell at me for talking that way, and she did. She was so easy to predict.

"Iris!" she said, setting her coffee cup down sharply on the counter. I could hear the rough ceramic bottom graze the tile, and it gave me shivers. "Not with your mouth full! Honestly, I thought I had taught you some manners." She was still in her pink-flowered nightgown, which was faded a soft white and had three little buttons at the neck with embroidery around them. Her hair looked wild and matted in back.

"Well, did he?" I asked.

"What?" She reached for the coffee percolator on the stove, the same white one with blue flowers we'd had all our lives. She poured another cup, and I watched it come out in a dark brown stream.

"Did he go to the creamery?" I asked, thinking that must've been it. I made a note in my head to go down there after school today, to maybe even invite Sylvie and Carla down for an ice-cream bar or a Drumstick. If my father was in a good mood, he might even give them all to us for free. I missed spending time at the creamery, especially since we'd moved to the apartment on Main Street. We never went down there anymore, and I hardly ever saw my father working.

"He just went to take care of some business," my mother answered coolly, not looking me in the eye. I kicked Adam under the table, wondering if he remembered what we'd heard my father say last night. Maybe with all the money my mother made as a teller in the bank, they could pay the creamery bills. I figured she must've made good money if she was working in a bank where there was nothing *but* money.

"At the creamery? Is that where he went?" Adam asked. He'd devoured his cereal, but left lots of soggy flakes at the bottom of the bowl that looked like wet pulled-off scabs.

"Yes, yes, of course," my mother said, and pulled out a chair to sit down by us. "You two with all your questions. What are you so worried about?"

I looked down. I didn't want to answer that, and from the way she asked it, I could tell she didn't really want an answer.

"Don't you think we can hear you guys talking?" Adam asked her. He got up, but didn't take his bowl to the sink.

"Forget it," she said stiffly. "Iris, get a comb. Let's braid your hair."

I didn't want a braid, but got a comb anyway. I could always pull it out later. I sat in front of my empty cereal bowl while my mother's long fingers made sections on my scalp and began pulling and twining the pieces together. My hair was thin and slippery, and the braid felt too tight. I could feel the white naked skin exposed on the back of my head where the sections were.

"Iris," my mother said softly.

I looked up, surprised. She put a hand on my shoulder. "Try not to move, honey." Then I heard her grip the end of the comb in her teeth, the dull sound of plastic on bone. It was a blue comb, thick and long and shiny, from Ben Franklin. "Iris, how would you like to go stay with your father for awhile? He misses you, you know."

"What do you mean?" She finished the braid and secured it with a covered rubber band. I turned around and looked up at her.

She went to the living room, pulled up the shade to let in the bright morning light, then set herself on the couch. "I mean just that. Go stay with your father." She drummed her fingers on the nubby fabric, not nervously, but lazily.

"What about Adam?" I asked. "Or you?"

"Well, we'll see. I was just thinking you might miss him, too. You know, with Adam it's a little different. They don't have the history yet."

I pushed in my chair and fingered the bumpiness of the braid down the back of my head.

"Iris!" Adam called from the bedroom. "Your stupid friends are across the street by the bank. Aren't you supposed to walk with them?"

"Quiet," I said, and rushed to look out the living room window without being noticeable. There were Sylvie and Carla and two other girls I knew in the cool group, Jennifer Barnes and Katie Schmidt, walking down the shady side of the street, already past our place and just turning the corner to the block toward school.

"Well go, Iris," my mother said. She got up to push the curtain back and look herself. "You can still catch them."

"No, I don't want to!" I bit my lip and knew that it was probably on purpose that they were avoiding me. Sylvie had confessed to me that Carla's mom said she wasn't supposed to play with me because of my mother and how she ran around with other men even though she was married and how she didn't take care of us kids.

I rushed to the bathroom and looked in the mirror. I couldn't go to school. My face was long with a pointy jaw, and my eyes looked too big for the rest of my head. They were a light washed-out brown, especially under bright bathroom lights, and my lips were faint and barely there. My nose was a little kid's nose with too-big nostrils. I could've easily stuck my whole pinky in one nostril. And my hair! I looked like a pinhead with the braid pulling every strand back tight and only a little chopped-off line of bangs over my forehead. I couldn't go! Why hadn't they stopped by like Sylvie said they would?

"Iris!"

I heard my mother calling for me, and quickly pulled out the braid she had worked so hard on. The hair fell out loose and a little kinky, as if relieved to be free.

To my surprise, my mother said nothing about the braid.

ADAM AND I ENDED UP WALKING together and got there barely in time. I rushed down the pebbly concrete hallway and entered Miss Rickhardt's classroom on the ground floor, right around the corner from the small gym, which was also used as our lunchroom.

The glass door was open, and everyone was milling around, trying to find their seats.

"Iris!" Sylvie came over from the other side of the room and set a hand on the desk in front of us. "Where were you this morning? We waited down by Dana's, and you didn't come, so I figured you just went with Adam or something." I caught her nervously glancing around the room, afraid someone in her new cool club might see her with me.

I looked her in the eye without saying anything, my secret way of telling her I knew she was lying. And then I noticed how pretty she looked. She was wearing a Lee denim mini-skirt and a flowered tucked-in shirt with a shiny clear belt around the waist. Of course they all probably had it planned to get dressed up the first day, otherwise nobody would've dared to do it. Everyone knew that even if you had new school clothes, you were supposed to wait at least a week or two before wearing them, just because.

"So, is Adam still causing all kinds of trouble at your house? I mean, in your new apartment?"

"No, not much." There was so much I could've told her, that I wanted to tell her: about Blake, about the creamery, about my mother, but it seemed as if she was only talking to me to be polite, not as a friend.

"Well, what else is new?" she asked, but then Miss Rickhardt was done digging through her files and told us all to get seated.

"I know you're lying," I whispered to Sylvie before she walked away. She looked back at me quickly, as if to defend herself, but simply shrugged her shoulders and shook her head as if she had no idea what I was talking about.

MISS RICKHARDT SAID THAT BOYS and girls were to be treated equally, and that in her class, no one would get special treatment. She seated us all boy-girl-boy-girl and said we were to treat each other as human beings instead of opposite sexes. I instantly loved her. She wore tons of jewelry—big raindrop-shaped silver earrings, bracelets in bangles up one arm, a long necklace with a large polished green stone on it, and even the barrette that held her long hair back at the nape of her neck was curly antique gold with flowers pressed into it. She was tall and long legged and had a kind of overbite with her front teeth that made her look young and fun. What an outfit for her first day, too—big flapping white pants, Jesus sandals, and a tight black-and-white polka-dot T-shirt. She dressed like a fashion model, only she wasn't pretty in a magazine way. Her skin was rough and reddish, a little oily, and her eyes were small and far back. But I loved something about the warmth she radiated. I started to think it would be my best year, despite Sylvie's ditching me.

First she handed out textbooks and told us to sign our names inside the front covers (of course everyone checked to see who'd had the book before them—one of mine had once been Sylvie's older brother's, way back when) and write what condition they were in. Then she gave us a list of all the supplies we were going to need, which weren't that many. I would have to buy some colored pencils and a protractor. I just hoped my mother and father could afford it.

Next, after everything had been handed out and everyone was settled, Miss Rickhardt told us to get out a sheet of paper. "Now I want you to write down what your expectations are for this school year," she said in her slight lisping voice that sounded smooth like music. She leaned up against the radiator and crossed her arms. "Think about the kinds of things you hope to learn, what you've had trouble with in the past, what you're interested in. Just write about those kinds of things, about you and school, for the next ten minutes or so." She turned her back to us and looked out the window. The T-shirt clung to her bony back, and her shoulder blades stuck out like angel wings.

I turned to my sheet of paper. Me and school? Nobody had ever had us write about things like that before. I didn't quite get the point, but started to write anyway. Miss Rickhardt was still turned to face the window and wasn't even watching to make sure that we were doing it, like my old teacher, Mrs. Scholhauser, would have. I wrote:

> This year I want to know more about other states in our country, especially Hawaii and Alaska because no one ever talks about them and they're part of the same country. I hope you might read us good books out loud like I heard another teacher does.
>
> I actually love school. The only problem I have is with math, even though my mother said she's not good at it, either. I expect I will be smarter after this year. Is this what you mean? I hope we might get to write short stories and make a little magazine of our whole class's stories. Maybe we could sell them up at the bank or the grocery store, and people would think they were neat.
>
> My mom is a writer, by the way. Or supposedly.
>
> Cool earrings. Hope you don't mind my saying that.

After awhile, Miss Rickhardt went around and collected them, and I started to feel nervous that I'd put the complete wrong thing. But she smiled when she took mine, and I noticed her two eyeteeth sort of winged out onto her lips. She was not perfect, and I liked that.

Next was the dreaded lunch hour. We all stood in line with our lunch tickets and waited for the woman with the paper punch to make a hole for Monday. Little green dots littered the floor all around her like confetti, and it took her a long time for each punch. I couldn't seem to find Sylvie. There was a girl behind me, Jenine Buck, who was from a farm and kind of shy, but I talked to her and asked her how she liked Miss Rickhardt.

"She's kind of weird," Jenine said. "She dresses like a total hippie." Jenine herself was dressed kind of strangely. She wore light-blue corduroy gauchos and a really stiff Western shirt with pearly snaps, like a cowgirl. She also wore red tennis shoes and no socks, and her hair was up in a shaggy ponytail that sprouted out the top of her head like a flower. Pieces fell out and hung around her ears and down her neck. Everyone always joked that she smelled like manure from her farm, but I honestly didn't smell anything. "Don't you think she's weird?" Jenine asked.

"Oh, I don't know." I shrugged my shoulders and didn't pay much attention, looking instead for Sylvie, but she was either not in line yet or already eating, because I couldn't see her.

As we slowly moved up the little ramp to the lunch line, there was a warm, wet smell of beef and noodles and the sight of silver—silver counters, silver pots, silver ladles and big spoons, even silver walls back behind the stoves, which you could see from the lunch line. The cooks were all ladies from town, and the one who filled my pale blue tray was Esther, a tall strong-looking woman who said, "Dere you go," instead of "There." She wore clear soft plastic gloves, and as she dished me up a sticky portion of hamburger hotdish, I imagined how by the day's end, her hands would be all steamy and warm inside them, how the air would feel so cool and fresh on her fingers when she took them off, wiggled the tips, and said, "Ah." She then handed my tray to a lady named Judy, who spooned a syrupy pool of fruit cocktail into one of the smaller sections of my tray, and I noticed for the first time how much the cubes of peach and pear looked like colorful dice without the dots. Every now and then there was a flash of red—a tiny maraschino cherry.

"Want some bread?" Judy asked, and wiped at her forehead with the back of her arm. Most of her hair was packed away in a hairnet, but some slipped out. I could tell it was dyed because it was a hard jet black, the same tone all over. Plus, she was old. She often came into the creamery for milk and cream, and I'd noticed her wobbling on her legs. "Bread?" she asked again, because I was taking too much time.

I nodded, and she dug inside a white plastic bag, then slapped a piece onto my hill of hotdish. I could see it getting soaked already with orange grease and meat chunks, turning gummy like glue. Sylvie and I used to make dough balls out of the bread by tearing off the soft crust and rolling the bread, hard, between our palms, then biting right into them. It would always stick in a gagging way to the back of your teeth and top of your mouth. I wondered if she did that with Carla. Probably not. Carla seemed more proper and prissy, especially since her parents were both high school teachers, and they lived out in the new part of town, which I'd heard my parents call Teacherville. All the houses there were low and wide, painted in dark browns or dusty greens, with shrubs and curved driveways and attached garages. It was across the highway and almost in the country and seemed like a whole different town. I used to want to live there so bad, but Sylvie always convinced me that our old two-story houses were better because they had more flavor. She got that kind of talk from her mom.

After I got my plate, with Jenine following close behind me, I stood at the milk machine, stuck a pointed paper cup in a plastic holder, and squirted myself a stream of bright, white 2 percent. I hated skim. My father had said to never drink skim. It'd give you rickets, he always said, whatever that was. He said it was like blue water for fish to swim in. "It's for the fish," he'd said, and laughed, his eyes sparkling. I really missed him.

Holding my tray out in front of me like a hot dog vendor, I scouted out who was sitting with who, and tried to find Sylvie without being too obvious. The gym was made of shiny pale bricks and had an enormously high ceiling, so that the chatter of people's voices reached up and echoed. Huge windows with metal cages over them like a prison let in dusty lengths of sunshine. I walked to the end of the gym and finally spotted Sylvie with Carla across from her, plus three other girls, one who also lived in Teacherville.

Holding steady so I wouldn't spill anything, I walked toward them, not making eye contact, to see if there was enough room for me to sit down. It seemed like there probably was, but when I got near them, Carla put her hand over her eyes, whispered something to all of them, and they all clustered together over the long fold-out table. Whatever she'd said made one of the girls, Denise, almost spew out the milk in her mouth. They eyed me quickly and tried to stop laughing, but couldn't. Even Sylvie. Sylvie was laughing just as hard as any of them.

I almost cried—almost—but thankfully I turned around and acted like I was looking for someone else. But when I turned to go the other direction, I accidentally slammed into Jenine, who I had no idea was still following right behind me. Our trays crashed together, and milk sprayed up and splashed down onto our food. "Whoops!" Jenine said laughing, because no other harm had been done, just milk in our food, milk on my hand. All of this right in front of Sylvie's new group, and to top it all off, Jenine asked, or assumed, that I was sitting with her.

"Should we sit here, or over there?" she asked, pointing with her head to an empty spot two tables over. "Let's sit here." And so I sat with her, because there was no one else. I tried to listen to her talk on and on about her zillions of brothers and sisters and how mad she was that she had to walk all the way down the driveway to catch the school bus instead of getting a ride with her mom. I looked down at the little white lakes in my hamburger hotdish, at the cloudy puddle of fruit cocktail. It wasn't right. Nothing was right, and just when I thought I'd had everything under control, tiny drops of tears crept out, and with my head hung, I could feel them rolling down my cheeks, onto the cold food.

"What is it?" Jenine asked, shaking my arm. "What? You can tell me. What?"

NOT ONLY DID I DECIDE TO GO stay with my father again, but I decided to leave my mother behind for awhile. I didn't want to talk to her, or see her, or be nice to her, or do anything with her. I'd decided that everything that'd happened was her fault; it had to be. She didn't have to leave my father or get a boyfriend when she was already married or drag me and Adam to live in a tiny apartment above a hair salon. There was no reason for any of it, and to punish her, after school, when no one was home, not even Adam, I started to pack my things in brown grocery bags. We didn't have any luggage like my Grandma Laura did. We never really went anywhere, or when we did, it was just some lame day trip to Mankato or somewhere close.

I carefully emptied out my dresser drawers and placed the folded stacks of shirts, shorts, and pants in the two empty bags. That was all I could take at the time, but I planned to sneak back again the next day when my mother was working at the bank. Just as I was about to leave down the back stairs, I remembered my toothbrush, nightgown (which hung on a hook on the bathroom door), and my diary, given to me by my cousin DeeDee for my last birthday. I only wrote in it every now and then, especially since it had only a tiny space for each day. It was kelly-green plaid with a brass clasp and baby padlock.

My arms were full of the two stuffed bags, and as I was adjusting them with my knees to open the door, Adam sauntered in. He had clear dots of sweat above his lip, and his dark hair was all whipped back like he'd just come out of a windstorm. "God, it's hot," he said, and walked right past me.

"Of course it's hot if you wear long sleeves and long pants in summer," I said, resting the bags on the counter for a second. "Duh."

"Duh," he repeated, but unbuttoned the stiff dark flannel. He threw the shirt over a kitchen chair, and I noticed the waves of ribs running down his chest, so skinny. The center caved in with an odd dip that looked too deep to be healthy. It looked like someone had smashed it in with a fist.

He rubbed his hands up and down over his nipples. "What're you looking at? Geek." Then he noticed the big brown grocery bags with all my stuff. "What's in there? Are you running away or something?" But he didn't say it like a question, he said it like an accusation. He poured himself a glass of green Kool-Aid, and the glass beaded water down the sides.

"Yes," I said. "Yes!" I pulled the door open and stepped out into the heat. Everything was hot to the touch: the wooden railing that went downstairs, the door handle, the air, the dry gravel below. With the sun in my eyes, I rushed down the stairs, into the alley, and back toward the railroad tracks. This was my old way home.

After the tracks, it was all houses instead of stores. I walked under the cool shade of maples, constantly stopping to adjust the bags in my arms. I knew all the cracks of the sidewalk, where the concrete squares spun at a slant from big tree roots, where the wide sidewalk pieces became smaller ones with grass growing in between, where there was a cement ledge in front of a house that I walked on like a balance beam and dismounted like a gymnast when it stopped.

Cars rolled by full of high schoolers who tipped cans of pop up to their lips and cruised around with nothing better to do. When a station wagon full of them stopped at an intersection to let me cross, I could feel its deep drumming radio like a heartbeat. Even after they were past, I could still feel the beat, like a pulse, heavy and slow, in my chest. But I was almost there.

THE HOUSE WAS COOL and dark inside, no car in the driveway. Nothing but the hum of the refrigerator, the grinding of the kitchen clock, the occasional flutter of maple leaves against the windows. I set the bags down on the dining room table and rushed around the house, looking for changes, clues to how my father had been living these months. But it was quiet; there was nothing.

In the living room, I flopped down on the plaid couch, which was so much softer and more welcoming than the scratchy green one in the apartment. I remembered how we'd all sat there the day Adam arrived, even Sylvie, Grandma Laura, everyone. I closed my eyes and let myself miss it, wished again for what was, for how safe and whole it had been without a brother to share it. I thought of my mother's two dead babies, and turned inside to face the couch. I hugged myself up to it, throwing an arm over the top like it was a person, someone to hang on to.

Later, when the darkness started to creep around the edges of the afternoon, I heard my father's car pull up in the driveway. I jumped up and ran for my bags of clothes, set them in front of the entryway so he would know I was there, and took the stairs by twos to my room. It smelled like wood floor polish when I pushed open the door, and was exactly the same as I'd left it. The purple walls were so familiar, and one of my cardigans was still draped over my rocker. I heard my father open the front door and felt my heart pound with excitement.

"Marilyn?" my father called. It was so quiet I could actually hear the crunch of the paper bags when he picked them up downstairs. "Iris? Iris, are you here?" I heard him climb the stairs slowly.

I didn't answer. Instead of going under the bed like I usually did when I played dead, I lay sprawled out right on the floor just below the window. I turned my head to the wall and flung my arms out to the sides like an accident victim. As he stepped into my room, I didn't breathe. That was how dead I could get.

He stood above me, and I squinted up, barely. There was light behind him from the hallway window, plus he was wearing white and he looked like an angel. I noticed he had the soft oily smell of butter on him. I closed my eyes again, tried not to react. "Iris, you're doing this again, playing dead?"

His bones popped a little as he crouched down to my level. I saw his hands hang suspended between his bent knees, so helpless they seemed, and red and rough. He reached out and touched my cheek. "Why?"

Chapter Seven

Memory: My father and I sit in the back of the creamery. It's after hours. He hands me samples of butter to taste. Pale little smears on wooden Popsicle sticks. "What do you think of this one?" he asks. "It's a Wisconsin unsalted. From a Guernsey." He perches on a stainless steel stool, one leg stretched forward expectantly. We both wear paper hats and sanitary gloves.

I lick it. Feel the creamy slickness melt across my tongue. "Good," I say. "Mmm."

"How about this?" He hands me another. I can hear the clock grind in the store out front. Cars drive by, splashing through the rainy dark. "It's a Melrose salted. Double cream." He looks at the container from which it came. "Actually, doubled churned, too."

I taste. A smooth salty warmth in my mouth. I am reminded of popcorn. "Wow," I say. "This one is really good." The flavor trickles down my throat like syrup. "I think this one's the best. A plus."

My father stands up, and I think he will applaud. He does. "That's it!" he cries. "We're going to win with this one!"

I don't know what he means, but concur. "First place," I say. "Guaranteed."

Living with my father again was good, but felt strange because the house was so big and quiet with only the two of us. Plus, it didn't have that cozy feel like when my mother was around, singing, watering plants, typing away in her office. I thought it felt even lonelier than it had before, but at least my mother would be punished for what she'd done. I hoped she missed me, and was sorry.

The first night I stayed at the house, my father was excited and ordered a large sausage-and-pepperoni pizza for us from The Food Haus, the one and only restaurant in Wishbone. It was actually right by my mother's apartment over Dana's salon on Main and was run by an old German couple, the Steingartens, who lived in the back. The restaurant was dimly lit, paneled in dark brown, and had bubbling beer signs and pictures of shaggy Schmidt beer horses for decorations on the walls. They used to serve only beer and food that could be cooked in the small toaster oven behind the bar, but they had a whole menu now with pizza, shrimp, steaks, bacon cheeseburgers, and even malts. On Friday and Saturday nights, all the people who lived in Teacherville went out to eat there and spent lots of money. Once I went in there with my mother to pick up a pizza, and they were all sitting around a big table in back, empty glasses and plates all around, cigarette smoke billowing up in a cloud. My mother always said they acted as if they owned the place, but I thought she was probably just jealous.

But my father gladly went driving off in his old beat-up sedan to pick up the pizza for us while I waited at home, watching TV in the family room. I sat in the big flowered chair with my feet up on the wooden footstool, which was my mother's usual spot. There was nothing on at this time but news and game shows, so I watched one show where the person had to go into a glass booth where hundred dollar bills were flying around everywhere and try to grab as many as she could and stick them in a pouch. The woman was going wild, and her large breasts, which strained against her tight white blouse, were bouncing as she grabbed and jumped. When her time was up, the money that wasn't caught fell softly down to the floor like autumn leaves, and she looked sad, like she hadn't gotten enough. The game show host patted her shoulder and ushered her away.

It was stupid. I knelt in front of the TV to switch channels, but the phone rang, so I ran to catch it in the kitchen. "Hello?" I never even stopped to think of who it might've been.

"Iris?" It was my mother, sounding mad and put out. "Is that you?"

I pulled up a stool and sat twirling the mustard-colored phone cord. It was a long cord. "Yeah, it's me."

"Well—" She made a sound I hated and couldn't ever duplicate. It was the sound of tsk-tsking with her mouth barely open with a little spit behind her teeth. It was hard to explain, but it drove me crazy and always made me feel ashamed. "What are you doing there?"

I started to think I was in trouble, but then realized that she was the one who'd asked me if I wanted to go and stay with my father in the first place. "I'm staying here now," I said. "Like you asked me if I wanted to."

She sighed and tsk-tsked again, and I could hear Adam hollering something in the background. "Well, Iris, did you ever think about *telling* me? You think it's okay to just pack your bags and take off without letting your own mother know?"

I didn't answer since I was pretty sure it was one of those trick questions that didn't really require an answer.

"Well?" she asked again, and I was even more confused.

"I don't know. I'm sorry, I guess."

"You guess." My mother laughed, but it was a cold laugh, like a cackle. "Iris, only you. You *guess* you're sorry." She waited, but I offered nothing. Then she got sweeter right away; I knew her tactics. "Honey, you know I love you. I just worry about you. It's just—this is a hard time right now for all of us. You have to hang in there."

"I know."

She jumped right back at me. "Do you? I mean, do you really understand what's happening right now in our family? It's in a transition, but you don't need to worry about it, honey. All right?

Don't worry about it. Just enjoy your time there with your father. He loves you, too."

"Okay." I saw the headlights of his car pull up to the house and got excited because I was starving.

"Okay, Iris. Put your father on now, would you, please?"

"Just a second." I heard the car door slam and went to the back door to let him in. "He's just coming in the door. He got us a pizza from Food Haus, pepperoni-and-sausage."

"Really," my mother said.

"Here he is," I said, and waved the phone out to my father. He slid the big cardboard box onto the counter and threw his keys alongside it.

"Who is it?" He fished his wallet out from his back pocket, took off his watch, and threw them both on the counter. He always had to empty his pockets the instant he got home. My mother said men tended to do that since they didn't have purses.

"It's your wife," I said, something I had never said before and which sounded strange coming from my mouth. "She wants to talk to you."

He finally took the phone, and I was released, able at last to open the pizza box and inhale the sweet, warm tomatoey smell. The Steingartens had a way of frying their pizza crust first, so when I picked up a piece, the bottom was greasy yet crispy and doughy, so perfect. I should've waited for my father before eating, but he signaled that I should go ahead, and I couldn't help it—I did.

I didn't even eavesdrop on their conversation when it would've been so easy to do. I was too hungry to care.

LATER THAT NIGHT, after I'd brushed my teeth and put pajamas on, my father and I sat in the family room. It was still warm enough for the windows to be open, but I wore full pajamas and slippers because there was a breeze. My father always liked it cool in the house. In fact, my mother used to complain in the winter because he insisted on turning down the heat and sleeping with the windows open, even with snow on the ground outside. He said it made for better sleep, better breathing, and clearer thought in the morning, but my mother would come stomping out of the room some nights wrapped in quilts and a robe and crawl in bed with me. "It's so cold I can see my breath!" she said once, then curled up beside me, falling instantly asleep. I remembered lying there stiff and tense with her filling up my bed. She clutched one of my pillows to her chest and bent one knee up over the edge of the bed, as if climbing toward something steep and high.

"Your mother and I were talking," my father said, startling me for a second because it was so quiet. We both had books open on our laps, mine a social studies text, faded with frayed corners, and his a spy novel, a shiny black paperback with raised red letters. I slapped my book shut and stretched loudly.

"It's your birthday pretty soon," he said as he grabbed his cigarettes and lighter off the end table. He set the open book over his knee and lit up. "Maybe you'd like to have some of your friends over for a party."

I hadn't thought of my birthday, September 13. "Maybe."

"Your mother thought it might be fun," he said, and he blew smoke rings like he used to do to entertain me. "But it's up to you." He shrugged.

I twisted the ends of my hair, which were split and bleached from the sun, and noticed that my father looked old. His hairline was starting to reach farther back, and his face looked grainy and tired with dark pouches under his shiny blue eyes. He seemed tired, and I knew he must've been lonesome, having been on his own like this for weeks. Or had it been months? A month? I couldn't remember anymore.

I thought about who I would invite if I had a party, but Sylvie wasn't even an option anymore, nor was anyone at school for that matter. But then I got a great idea. DeeDee! I hadn't seen her for so long and thought maybe she could come and stay for the weekend. Of course then I'd probably have to ask Melanie, too, and maybe even Noel, Carter, and David, but that would be okay. It would be like old times with all the family. Maybe Grandma Laura could come, too. And Adam, of course, would have to be asked.

When I told all of this to my father, he made it sound like it was the greatest idea ever. I could tell he was relieved that it would be only relatives.

AT SCHOOL THE NEXT WEEK, Miss Rickhardt put us into groups, had us "adopt" a state and a president, and assigned us to report on them to the class. Of all the luck, I wound up with Sylvie in my group, as well as Jenine, who thought I was her best friend since we'd eaten lunch together that one day. When we pulled slips of paper out of a big crumpled paper bag that Miss Rickhardt walked around shaking, for the state, I got Hawaii, and for the president, Jenine pulled out William McKinley. Hawaii was good, but I'd never even heard of McKinley. Sylvie sat with her legs crossed and her foot jiggling up and down, looking completely uninterested. I could tell she felt awkward because she kept glancing down at her desk, then glancing sideways around the room, but never looked at us. There were also two boys in our group, Joel Heider and Lance Neisenbaum, but somehow Jenine took over as the leader since no one else was talking. The two boys were kind of shy and dense.

"Well, let's get to work," Miss Rickhardt said, and she clapped her hands twice. She had given us the afternoon to go to the library, look up books, and read articles in the encyclopedia. She said this was "hands-on" learning, the best kind, with a gleam in her eye. The whole class followed her down the dark hallway, past the band room, around the corner, and past classrooms. I hung back by myself, and watched Sylvie's group magically form again.

As they walked, they clustered up together and whispered, putting arms around each other's shoulders. It seemed they'd all agreed to wear jeans today with sandals and tank tops since that's what they were all wearing, every one of them.

The school library was tiny—smaller even than a regular classroom—but I loved it. The heavy papery smell of old books made my nose itch the minute I walked in. To the right was a small alcove for children's books with little pink chairs to sit on, and straight in back was Miss Nevin's desk, a plain oak table with junk piled high all over it. When we walked in, I could smell her right away. It was the nicest blend of chocolate combined with the waxy almondy scent of face powder and lilac perfume. It was a smell I could've recognized anywhere. To the left was the main part of the library, with wooden shelves full of books, and a square carpeted space in the middle full of big pillows.

"Okay, hit the books!" Miss Rickhardt said, and looked so excited you'd have thought she was going to a carnival or something. She stood in the middle of the library, hands on her hips, smiling. Today her outfit was a green corduroy skirt with a plaid shirt, a crocheted cream-colored vest, and tall brown boots. Every day it was exciting to find out how she'd be dressed. She'd actually worn cowboy boots last week, which was pretty unusual for a woman in Wishbone.

Sylvie, Jenine, Lance, Joel, and I found an unoccupied corner, and just sat there, barely talking. We weren't used to this kind of thing and didn't really know how to go about it. Luckily, Jenine had the idea that we should each go on a search for books. Joel, with his sleepy eyes and big red lips, said he'd go look up Hawaii in the encyclopedia, and trudged away like he was about to fall over. Jenine and Lance went off to look in the card catalog, which our whole class was cluttered around, so Sylvie and I just sat back and waited. In a way, I'd been hoping to talk to her, but now that I had her alone, I didn't know what exactly to say. I just wanted it to be like the old times.

"So how are you?" Sylvie asked finally. She sat with her legs stretched out in front of her, her ankles crossed. For the first time I noticed that she seemed to be wearing a bra under her tank top. So many times in the past we'd talked about when we would get one, and how, and where, and what kind, and to see the bumps of straps under her shirt now made me sad in an odd way. I supposed they all had them now, made as a group decision.

"I'm pretty good," I said, unsure of how much to offer. But Sylvie's eyes had that old familiar sparkle, and I couldn't help telling her more. "I moved back in with my dad."

She seemed surprised. "Really? Wow. What did your mom say?"

"Mmm, she didn't care. She's too wrapped up in her life, you know."

Sylvie nodded, and bloused out her tank top a little, as if she didn't want the bra to show. "What about Adam? Is he still being a turd?"

"Yeah, as usual. He's still with my mom in the apartment." Suddenly it sounded so strange, to hear myself explaining my divided-up family. "He likes it there, I guess."

Sylvie twirled one of her fake diamond stud earrings around in her ear. "Gol, that's so weird how your mom and dad just split up. Do you think they'll get back together or what?"

I had to think about that for awhile. It had never occurred to me that they wouldn't, but now that Sylvie mentioned it, maybe they wouldn't, ever, be together again. "I don't know. Maybe not." The thought made me panic, and apparently I couldn't hide it, because Sylvie put a hand on my knee.

"Maybe they will, Iris. You never know, but . . ." Sylvie looked as if she was going to tell me something, but stopped herself.

"But what?" I said. "You can tell me. *Tell me*," I whispered.

She put her head closer to mine, a hand over her mouth. "Carla's mom told her your mom has a new boyfriend."

I sighed, relieved, and waved a hand as if to dismiss it. "Oh, that was Blake. They were just like that for awhile, but they don't see each other anymore. He lives in Mankato. That's completely over." I was almost glad for a chance to explain the whole thing and to clear my name again with Sylvie's new group.

But Sylvie looked at me strangely.

"What?" I asked, worried there was something else.

"Well," she said, wrinkling up her face apologetically. "I guess there's a new one even after that guy. That's just what Carla's mom said, anyway. Someone from Wishbone." She shrugged her shoulders and shook her head. "I have no idea."

It couldn't have been. Just when I'd thought things were getting better, my mother seemed to sink deeper and deeper. No wonder she didn't want me around the apartment anymore. With Adam always out running around, she could have the whole place to herself and all her boyfriends over. The whole idea made me sick to my stomach.

"How are we doing?" Miss Nevin said, pulling up a library chair. Her almondy lilac scent came washing over us, and I nudged Sylvie, since we used to joke about it. "Are we finding some good information about our topic," she asked, "or are we just visiting?" She was a large, chubby woman, and breathed heavily. Her calves were thick and solid, and her face was puffy and red with the faintest sprinkle of tiny freckles. In fact, it always reminded me of when a frog blew its chest up—that texture. But her mouth was petite and painted in frosty coral, her small eyes flashy and dark behind slightly tinted glasses. There was something beautiful and comforting about her, almost elegant in the way she carried herself.

"We were just waiting to use the card catalog," Sylvie said quietly. Both of us always had a hard time speaking up to teachers and adults, and ended up kind of cowering in fear.

"Mm-hmm. Mm-hmm. Well, it's free now," Miss Nevin said, and she held out a palm, directing us to it. With a couple of loud grunts, she rose from the tiny chair and walked daintily back to her desk.

"Mm-hmm. Mm-hmm," Sylvie said to me quietly, making fun of her. "Mm-hmm. Mm-hmm. Mm-hmm."

I answered back the same, but couldn't help bursting out laughing when Sylvie kept doing it. She'd always been so good at imitating people, but when Miss Nevin looked over at us and put a finger to her lips, I tried to hold back. It felt so good to laugh with Sylvie again, and I told her outright before the last bell.

"I miss you."

Before running off with Carla and Jennifer, she loaded up her backpack and smiled. "Me, too."

But things didn't change. We still didn't hang around together, but were only friends from a distance. It almost made me wish I could've moved to a different town.

AT LEAST I HAD MY BIRTHDAY PARTY to look forward to. Sometimes it was just easier to be with your family; they'd always take you in no matter what and wouldn't drop you for any reason, like friends did. My father talked to both Aunt Patty and Aunt Deb, but the two older boys had something going on, so only Noel could come—if Aunt Deb could drive him down, if she didn't have to work. But DeeDee and Melanie were both coming for sure, and Aunt Patty said she might even come and stay with my mother.

On Saturday, I called to invite Grandma Laura, who always sounded so happy and thrilled to hear my voice. "Iris! It's you! Hi, honey! How are you?" How could I not have felt loved with that greeting? She said she wouldn't miss my birthday party for the world and asked what I wanted for a present.

"Umm, I don't know. I can't think what right now. Maybe clothes." I thought of the jeans and tank tops and denim skirts

Sylvie and her friends wore. "Maybe a Lee jean skirt?"

"All right. Well, you let me know, or maybe I'll just give you money and you can pick them out yourself." Her voice wavered off, and I could hear her breathing.

"It's up to you," I said. "Anything's good."

"Is everything okay, Iris? Are you doing all right?"

I twirled the phone cord and paused, wishing I could go live with her again, like last July. We could eat frozen pizzas or more of her fancy Italian recipes, and she could wash my hair in the sink. "I'm fine," I said. "Really."

We said "Good-bye" and "Love-you," and I thought about calling Adam next because, of course, he had to be invited, but I didn't. I didn't want to have to talk to my mother just then.

THE NEXT SATURDAY—the day of my birthday party—I decided to go up to the creamery with my father in the morning for old time's sake. Melanie and DeeDee weren't due to arrive until after lunch, and I still wasn't sure whether or not Aunt Deb was bringing Noel. Other boys might've felt funny being with so many girls, but knowing Noel, he wouldn't care at all.

By the time I came downstairs, my father was already awake, showered, and dressed, and sitting at the kitchen table with a cup of coffee and a cigarette. "Happy birthday," he said, and blew three perfect smoke rings up into the light. I had almost forgotten that today was actually the day. Usually birthday parties never happened on the real birthday, but this time I got lucky. When I pulled out a chair to sit down next to him, I found a big present, wrapped in pink bubblegum giftwrap.

"Wow," I said, reaching for it. "What's this?" It was bigger than a toaster, but not bigger than a suitcase. When I picked it up and set it on my lap, it was heavy.

My father just sat back, enjoying, which was how he always was on Christmas and birthdays. He loved giving presents more than getting them. "Open it. I want to see what's in there." He dabbed out his cigarette in the ashtray I'd made back in art class one year, still the same green with a painted orange inside and my crusty thumb-pinched edges.

"Like you don't know," I said, smiling, and I tore at the pink paper. If the box showed what was really inside, I had a radio/cassette player. It was! Inside the molded Styrofoam pieces was a shiny silver-and-black radio with a cassette player on one side. I couldn't believe it. "Oh my god! This was probably too expensive."

"It's from your mother and me. From both of us." He got up and put his coffee cup in the sink. "Oh, and also from Adam."

"Thanks. I love it." I pushed the buttons, opened up the cassette holder, checked to see if everything worked. "Now I can get some tapes instead of the 45s Sylvie and I always get. Or used to."

He looked at his watch. "Well, I have to run. Are you going to come up later? Why don't you."

I looked at the clock—only 7:30. "I'll come up later." Instead of his usual white creamery work outfit, I noticed he wore dark brown pants, a white shirt, and a short red apron around his hips. "Why are you wearing that?" He looked funny, younger, like a stock boy.

"Long story, but there's a new guy up there working with me. Actually, he's kind of taking the place over, making it into more than just a creamery. Anyway, I'm going to stick with it, making the butter and cheese, but we'll see how it goes. I guess he wants to make it into a sort of convenience store." His face winced a little before he said good-bye, shrugged his shoulders, and rushed off, and I knew only too well how he loved his creamery. He must've really run out of money, and I wished he hadn't spent so much on a birthday present for me. Still, I instantly ran to the family room, where there were some Johnny Cash and Waylon Jennings tapes, and slid one into my new cassette player. It was corny music, a burning ring of fire, but I knew it was going to be great to have my own music up in my room. If only I could've shared it with Sylvie.

AFTER CHEERIOS AND SOME CARTOONS, I showered, dressed in cutoffs and a striped tank top, and walked up to the creamery. It was exactly two blocks to the railroad tracks, but after one block I had to cross the street to avoid the old men sitting on the porch of the men's boarding home. There was Vick, Eugene, and then Waldo, who was especially crazy and always beckoned for me to come and sit on his lap, even though he had a huge wet pee stain on his overalls. He had a bright pink face and white fuzzy whiskers, wore black-frame glasses, and always had a striped railroad hat on. Ever since his wife had died, he'd lived at the boarding home, and it seemed all he and the old men did was sit there all day on the porch, watching Main Street go by, even though there was nothing much to watch.

After the tracks, which people didn't even stop for in town because trains were so seldom, there was the feed mill, by far the tallest building in Wishbone. It stood silver and slightly rusted, with Christmas lights on it year-round because no one wanted to go through the hassle of taking them up and down season after season. In the fall, trucks full of feed corn and soybeans had to wait in line—like it was a McDonald's drive-thru—and ended up spilling lots of their crop onto the sidewalks, where pigeons nibbled at it. There was even a feed mill store, which I had never been in since I couldn't imagine what they would sell that would be that interesting. Through the big glass window, the place looked practically empty except for a couple rows of fertilizer and some green or blue Purina caps with the red-and-white checkerboard logo. Just about every farmer in Wishbone wore one of those, covered with feed dust and greasy black fingerprints from working on their machinery. I liked the smell as I walked by—a sort of sweet, nutty odor that reminded me of oatmeal. There were also wooden boards instead of cement on part of the sidewalk there, and whenever Sylvie and I used to walk down the street, we would avoid the empty hollow-sounding planks since it seemed easy to break through and fall in.

After the feed mill, it got more interesting. There was the Wishbone lumber company, with big trucks roaring in and out of its garage, then a Laundromat, a cabinet shop, and The Food Haus, which had those cloudy cubelike cafe windows that you couldn't see through. It always smelled like fried onions and hamburgers, or at night, pizza. The next block was really the heart of Wishbone: there was the bank, made of black brick and containing the only public clock in town right above its doors; the post office, where absolutely every old person in town went at 10 a.m. to get their mail because Wishbone wasn't big enough to have home delivery; Rexall Drugs, which was always the first place to decorate for Valentine's Day, Easter, Halloween, and Christmas, and was the best place to buy candy; Jay's hardware store, where Sylvie and I used to get 45 records; Ben Franklin, my absolute favorite store; and Dana's hair salon. As I walked past, I almost forgot that my mother and Adam were right above it, in the tiny apartment with the tar-papered back balcony. I hoped they couldn't see me. I hoped they weren't looking out the window or anything, like I always did when I lived there. I walked quickly, with my head down, and kept going, fast—past the liquor store, the bakery, the shoe store— until I reached the single stoplight in all of Wishbone and turned right. If I kept going, after less than a block, I'd walk right into the cornfields. Uncle Robert always made jokes about it, saying you had to pay attention where you were going in Wishbone or you'd find yourself smack dab in the middle of a cornfield. He thought he was a big city slicker because he lived in Mankato, which wasn't even like a real city, not like Minneapolis.

And then there was the creamery—a small red brick building with a glass front door and two small windows in front. When I walked in, I noticed right away that the usual bell didn't ring, but a kind of electronic beep went off. I couldn't believe how different things looked. Some of the coolers that used to hold milk and cheese and little plastic tubs of cheese curds were gone and had been replaced by racks of Hostess stuff—Twinkies, chocolate cupcakes, apple pies—and also racks of Doritos, Funyuns, Old Dutch potato chips in foil bags. Everything seemed so colorful and bright, unlike before where there was the dark gray metal of milk crates, the whites and pale yellows of cheeses and butter, the bland whiteness of milk and cream. Now, behind the counter, you could buy little yellow tins of Anacin and blue strips of Di-Gel, small orange horoscope books, cigarettes sealed in plastic, and stacks of the local paper, the *Wishbone Weekly Register*, which was usually full of the same people week after week and all the popular kids who won awards and played on all the sports teams. I only made it in there once, when I got second place in the spelling contest last year and made it to regionals. The clipping, all yellow and feathery now, was still hanging on the refrigerator at home. I'd always been good at spelling; it just came naturally, like knowing when to turn when you were in a new town and didn't know your way around.

No one was in the front part of the creamery, even though the beeper buzzed on me when I came in. I walked toward the door that led to the back, but almost bumped into a man who wore the same thing as my father had been wearing: a white shirt, brown pants, and a red half apron, only this man wore a tie with diagonal blue-and-silver stripes. "Hello!" he said, reaching out his hands so we didn't smack into each other. "Can I help you?" He was much shorter than my father, a little chubby with a belly hanging over his belt, and wide-set dark brown eyes. He had a mustache that was just starting to turn gray.

"Yeah, I'm looking for my father," I said quietly. "This is his creamery."

The man straightened up, clasped his hands behind his back, and looked at me, his eyes twinkling. "Of course. You're Bill's girl. It's Iris, right? Like the flower?"

I nodded, and twisted my foot around nervously.

"I should have known. You look just like him. Spitting image. That's really something else."

If only he knew I was adopted, I thought, then he wouldn't be saying anything about my looks. I didn't look like anyone but myself. I was beginning to think he wouldn't let me in back to see my father, when suddenly my father came in through the front door, carrying some paint cans. His face looked grim and serious, but when he saw me, he brightened up. "There's the birthday girl," he said, and nudged me with his elbow. "Oh, this is Verne Ott. He's redoing the place. Verne, it's someone's birthday today." My father set the paint cans down behind the counter.

"Oh, really?" Mr. Ott said. "How old?"

"Twelve."

"Well, I'd say that demands a treat! Pick anything in the store you want, Iris. Anything at all." He folded his arms across his chest and laughed a little. "You know, my parents used to have a general store when I grew up, and every year for my birthday they'd let me pick anything I wanted. It was the darndest thing. Hard, too. They called it Pick of the Crop, and I would stand around for hours, seriously *hours*, trying to pick the best thing." He gestured with his hand around the store. "Go ahead." He seemed so pleased, as if he was the one getting to choose. "Pick of the Crop."

I hated it. I didn't like things forced on me like that, even though he was trying to be nice. I couldn't figure out if he was my father's new boss or coworker or what, but things between them seemed stiff in a fake trying-to-be-comfortable way. Mr. Ott seemed to be in control, and my father seemed lost in what was once his prized creamery.

As I walked around the newly arranged aisles in the cramped little store, scanning rows of squeeze-out-of-the-tube cheeses and Triscuits and Chicken in a Biskit crackers, I couldn't believe that to the left in the big glass cooler there were tubs of Parkay margarine for sale. To my father, margarine was like a sin—an evil, unnatural thing that looked and tasted like plastic and was full of food coloring to make it look not as much like lard, which it really was. There were several different types of margarine for sale— white-and-yellow plastic tubs of it with little flowers ringing the bottoms, big blocks of it, and foil-wrapped silvery sticks of it. Next to all the margarine, my father's butter, in its familiar white waxed paper with plain black lettering, looked so old-fashioned, so out of date, and seeing it there made me feel tender toward my father and his beautiful butter. I reached out quickly and picked up a brick.

Mr. Ott seemed totally confused by my choice. "Butter? That's what you're going to pick?" He shook his head, laughing. "I would've thought a kid your age would take something like Doritos or maybe a bag of Snickers, but you've got the butter. Isn't that something else—a pound of butter." He crossed his arms, grabbed his elbows, and scratched them. Then, turning to my father, he winked. "You must've really trained her good!" He exploded with laughter after he said it, even though I didn't see the joke at all. Somehow I got the feeling my father was being made fun of, and I had to stand up for him.

"Homemade butter is the best," I said, and could feel it melting slowly where my fingers gripped around it. "I think we're out at home and I need some for something."

But my father frowned, and soon some kids came into the store to stand and decide in front of the new, bigger candy rack. There was everything from Stark Candy Wafers to Reese's Peanut Butter

Cups to Nut Goodies to Tangy Taffy to Blow Pops to *every*thing. Mr. Ott really knew how to reel people in.

I stood by the door, watching cars pass under the slanting autumn sun, then followed my father outside. He gripped two paint cans in his hands, which made his arm muscles bulge tightly. "What's the paint for?" I asked, sitting on the front cement steps. I watched as he pried the lids open with a screwdriver, and saw one was a thick creamy white and the other a cheerful marine blue.

He didn't answer at first, but looked up. I looked up, too, at the sky, shielding my eyes from the glare, but saw nothing. "What?" I asked.

"The sign," he said, stirring the white paint. "We have to change it."

I looked at him, concerned. "You mean it's not your creamery anymore?"

"That's right," he said. "I'm just a worker." He stirred the oil down into the white paint, and it swirled in yellowish, then disappeared.

"But why?" I knew it was risky asking so many questions, but he didn't get upset like my mother would've. He didn't say, "Iris, so many questions!" and storm around. He just sighed, and rested an elbow on his knee.

"I don't even know anymore what happened," he said. "I really don't."

I wanted to reach out and hug him, but the sign needed to be stenciled and painted, and I supposed it would say Ott's Convenience Store or something like that. What a stupid-sounding name: Ott. Maybe the store wouldn't be popular and would turn back into a creamery soon. Maybe Mr. Ott just didn't have the charm that my father did.

WHEN I RETURNED HOME from the creamery, my pound of butter a soft greasy brick in my hand, everyone jumped out from hiding places all over the house. Noel was there, even though Aunt Deb had had to leave to take Carter and David to some soccer thing, and Grandma Laura was there, and my mother and Adam, and the last ones to jump out were Melanie, DeeDee, and Aunt Patty. They all wore pointed Flintstones birthday hats that said "Yabba-Dabba-Doo" with stretchy strings under the chins, which had to have been Grandma Laura's idea. On the dining room table, there was a chocolate cake with pink frosting and a ballerina in the center, and twelve candles punched into the frosting. I couldn't believe this was all for me, and had a hard time holding back tears.

"What's wrong, Iris?" DeeDee said, and she came over to put her arm around me. "It's your birthday. Don't cry."

But I couldn't help it. I cried and cried, and soon everyone started bringing around presents, not knowing how to act. It took me about five minutes to recover, even though I couldn't exactly explain what had happened, what had come loose inside me. Suddenly I had a new Lee jean skirt from Grandma Laura with a ten dollar bill stuck in the pocket; two print turtlenecks—one with little red hearts and one with blue Scottie dogs on it—from Melanie and DeeDee; a heart-shaped jewelry box from my mother with lilacs painted on the lid; an Olivia Newton-John cassette tape from Adam; and a big, purple pottery bowl from Noel, who always picked out weird birthday presents. "It's for collecting things in," he said, explaining it when everyone laughed. "Or for baking."

In the afternoon, Grandma Laura, Aunt Patty, and my mother all sat around the kitchen table, drinking coffee and talking about Aunt Deb, who wasn't there. A couple times I caught them saying she had too many boyfriends or that she'd gotten too wild without her husband, Wayne, and wasn't taking care of her boys very well. Every time I ran in there for something, my mother was rearranging dishes or the way the mail was stacked on the counter, since she hadn't lived in the house for months. It was as if she had to go through everything again and leave her mark, though I was wondering if this meant she planned to stay, to move back in. I wished, and yet, I sometimes wished not.

The five of us kids kind of lazed around the family room all afternoon, the TV on but no one really watching it, occasionally playing a cassette tape on my new tape player, but mostly just talking. Melanie, who'd just turned fifteen, sat in my father's big chair with her legs slung over the arm of it. She wore brand-new overalls with a tan-and-green striped turtleneck and brand-new white Nikes with red swooshes. As always, everything she and DeeDee got was the most expensive and the best brand. Her hair was cut in a new way, kind of feathered around her face and long, like Farrah Fawcett, but because it was so thin and mousy, it looked bad and hung there limp and greasy, especially the bangs. She still had the same pink glasses, and her dark piercing eyes peered out the tiny frames. She was always blinking.

"So, like, where's your best friend, Sylvie?" she asked, twirling pieces of her new hairdo in her fingers. "I thought you guys were inseparable. At least last time I was here you were."

Adam turned the TV to a college basketball game, and the announcers' voices blared loudly, mixing with Captain and Tennille on the tape player in a bad way. "Adam," I shouted, "would you turn that stupid game down? I can't even hear Melanie."

I sat on the floor next to DeeDee, who seemed to have gained more weight since I'd last seen her. Her face and neck were thick and full and covered with freckles, and I noticed that even her hands, as they picked at the green shag carpet, were a little pudgy, her fingers like short plump sausages. "Umm," I said, grabbing my feet. "She's just kind of busy with other stuff."

Melanie snorted, and jiggled her foot up and down, glancing at the TV, then out the window. "Did you guys have a fight? I bet you did, right?" She glanced at the TV again, and it was funny how she was asking all these questions, but I could tell she wasn't really interested.

"Not really a fight," I said. "I don't know. She's got a bunch of new snotty friends."

Adam and Noel lay on the floor in front of the TV, their chins propped up in their hands. Suddenly Adam rolled over to face us. "It's because no one likes Iris anymore in school since she's so weird, and because she plays dead and stuff, and is a big teacher's pet."

"I am not! How would you know anyway?"

"Because everyone says so," Adam said, and sat up, reaching around his knees. "And everyone says our mom is a runaround. That's the part that I agree with, and I say, 'No shit.'"

"Adam," I said, but I didn't know what to say next.

"Adam, you shouldn't say that," DeeDee said. "Especially when your mom might hear you." DeeDee was always sticking up for whoever was being talked about. She leaned back on her hands, ankles crossed, and the way she sat accented her big belly pressing against her belt. "And Iris isn't weird."

Adam got up, flopped down on the couch, and clasped his hands behind his head. "Oh, okay, Fatso," he said sarcastically. "Whatever you say, Fats."

I froze up like an icicle, straight and narrow and stiff. That was going too far, and especially with DeeDee, who was so nice to everyone. Even Melanie and Noel seemed shocked and frozen, too, and before I knew what was happening, Melanie walked over to Adam, slapped him hard on the arm, and said, "You little snot." Then she walked out of the room, toward the kitchen, and I assumed she was going to tell on him.

So did Adam, apparently, since he ran out the back sliding door, even though it was cold out, and left it open, letting in the wind. DeeDee stayed where she was, head down, fingering through the tangle of shag carpet.

"He didn't mean it," Noel said. "He just has problems. Remember?"

I knelt beside her and put a hand on her shoulder. "It's okay, DeeDee. Adam's just a total brat. You know that." But I could see the tears running down her cheeks, and I understood exactly how it was with Adam, how bad he could make you feel.

THAT NIGHT FOR DINNER Grandma Laura set up the grill in the front yard and fired it up for burgers, even though it was chilly outside. Everyone hung out, drinking pop, bundled up in jeans and sweatshirts and jackets, my mother constantly running into the house for a spatula or salt and pepper or a platter. Adam was still nowhere to be seen, and we had all decided not to tell on him, even though he deserved getting yelled at. Still, there was a sad, ruined tone to my birthday party, and I felt bad when I watched DeeDee standing with her arms wrapped around herself, as if to hide her weight problem. She really wasn't that fat, but because she was so short and wide, any weight on her seemed exaggerated. I had always been skinny, and hoped that she didn't compare herself to me, since, if anything, I was underweight, but I knew she probably did. I was the same way with all of her and Melanie's nice expensive clothes.

The night was dark and clear, and there was almost no traffic except for some people still coming home from work. They parked their cars, flicked off the headlights, and trudged up the sidewalk. I could see bats swooping down above our heads, but as it got cooler, they usually started hibernating. I'd learned about this in school when we'd studied mammal behavior in biology. My mother was terrified of bats, and when she came out with a plate of sliced onions and a bat swooped near her head, she almost threw the plate in the grass. "God, I hate those things! Here," she said, pushing the plate into my hands. "Here, take this. I have to go in. I can't stand it." She covered her head with her hands, ducked, and ran at a slant toward the side door, which led into the kitchen. "Where did Adam go off to?" she shouted from behind the safety of the screen door.

I just shrugged and said, "Who knows?" then mumbled to myself, "Who cares?"

Just as the burgers got done and were being slid onto the plate, my father pulled up, cut the lights, and got out of the car. I realized suddenly that this would be the first time we were all together in the house again as a family. "Hi, sweetie," he said to me, then he stared at my mother behind the screen door. "What's with her?" he asked.

"You know," I said. "Bats." We all went inside, where the table was set with lettuce, sliced tomatoes, pickles, mayo, mustard, and ketchup.

"Everyone ready for a Blue Moon burger?" Grandma Laura asked, wiping her hands on her pant legs. These were her famous burgers, grilled to a very well-done that was almost crispy, then served on a toasted bun with blue cheese melted on top and grilled onions sprinkled over that. It was my absolute favorite way to eat a hamburger, especially when the bun crunched, although I saw that Melanie had ordered hers plain, and DeeDee had hers with cheddar instead and no onions. But everyone else loved them just as they were and ate quickly. Still, Adam didn't come home. He would've loved a Blue Moon burger, I knew. Grandma Laura pulled open a big bag of potato chips and sprinkled them out into a Tupperware bowl. We all grabbed some and ate, and watched fireflies dart around the backyard.

LATER, AFTER ICE CREAM AND CAKE on pink Flintstones paper plates—which my Grandma Laura had bought and again made me think she didn't really realize how old I was—everyone relaxed in the family room. Adam had snuck back in without our knowing when, but sat as if mesmerized in front of the news. My mother and father seemed to get along okay, although I noticed they sat on opposite sides of the room, which may've only been because there were so many people—nine people, counting me. I was scrunched between Grandma Laura and my father on the couch, and my mother was in the recliner with her feet up. Maybe she felt glad to finally be home, to be out of the cramped apartment, and to relax with us again. But if she did, she didn't say.

THAT NIGHT, MY MOTHER and Aunt Patty headed back to the apartment and left my father and Grandma Laura as the only adults to stay with us kids. Adam stayed, too. Before leaving, my mother kissed my father quickly on the lips, then gripped her purse close to her body, as if hiding something. She left with Aunt Patty, promising to be back tomorrow to see everybody before they took off.

"Now be good, you two," Aunt Patty said to the girls, even though everyone knew they were always good, that it was Adam who was usually the one to watch out for, but DeeDee agreed that she would be and Melanie just rolled her eyes, which was the way she reacted to most everything these days, as if it was all so silly and ridiculous.

All of the kids decided to sleep in the family room, except for Melanie who said she needed more privacy and took the couch in the living room, just a room away. It was something we'd all always loved doing as cousins, these slumber parties, and even though it wasn't even nine o'clock yet, everyone was mostly sacked out on the floor. We all tried to watch TV, which of course hadn't been turned off all day, but my eyelids were heavy and I had a hard time staying awake. Noel was up on the couch, since he'd won the coin toss, and Adam, DeeDee, and I were on the floor in front of the TV, facing the sliding doors. Adam had been acting very nice, almost polite to everyone since he'd come back, especially to DeeDee, even though she wouldn't say anything to him. She lay next to me in a plaid flannel sleeping bag with Adam on my other side. We talked quietly about what we should do tomorrow, then slowly faded out until I could hear everyone's heavy breathing. Finally, I dragged myself out of grogginess and managed to snap off the TV, which had been casting a bright blue light across the room. It felt like a great relief to have it off.

I flopped back down and burrowed into my sleeping bag, enjoying the quiet darkness, and remembered before dropping off that it was the end of my twelfth birthday, and that I was adopted, and that I still didn't know who'd given birth to me in the first place. Maybe I'd dream about her.

Later—it could've been close to morning or just the middle of the night—I woke up from a sound of movement. I thought it was just our cat, which I always used as an excuse when I got scared, but as I lay still and opened my eyes, I saw that Adam wasn't in his sleeping bag, but was over by DeeDee. I turned over and pretended to be asleep, but really my eyes were open wide, trying to see what was going on. As my eyes adjusted to the dark, I could see the pale white skin of DeeDee's bare stomach. Adam said to her quietly, "Sssh!" when she made a sound. I didn't know what to do or think, but it didn't matter because I couldn't seem to move or speak. I was absolutely frozen with fear and kept thinking, What can I do? What can I do? Why can't I yell or say something? But I couldn't. I watched Adam kneel beside her, being very careful to be quiet and not make rustling sounds. He kept looking over at me, and up at Noel on the couch, so I scrunched my eyes up so they wouldn't look open. I didn't want to get involved. I didn't know what to do. I watched Adam slide in next to DeeDee in her sleeping bag. DeeDee let out a small little sound, but Adam grabbed at her mouth and froze when Noel rearranged himself on the couch, then dozed off snoring again. I was terrified that Adam was going to come over to me next, and I lay there, eyes open, breathing heavily, waiting to fight back if he did.

I don't know how I ever managed to fall asleep, but when I opened my eyes again, it was morning. I found everyone in the kitchen, eating bowls of Froot Loops or Apple Jacks, which someone must've brought over special because we never had that kind of cereal around. Melanie was sitting up at the counter, drinking coffee—even though she probably didn't even like it—trying so hard to be like an adult. Grandma Laura sat at the kitchen table with DeeDee and Adam, who were both acting totally normal, and I was beginning to wonder if maybe I'd been dreaming or seeing things last night, but I couldn't get rid of the image of DeeDee's pale skin that looked so white in the dark. It made me shiver to think of it.

"Good morning, birthday girl," Grandma Laura said, and pulled out a chair for me to sit beside her. "Are you hungry? I was going to fix eggs and bacon, but nobody wanted that. How about you?"

"Mmm, I'm not really hungry yet." I glanced over at DeeDee to see if I might've been able to get a secret look from her, but she looked down into her bowl of peach-colored milk, a few soggy *O*s left floating in it. Adam refilled his bowl with more Froot Loops, his foot jiggling up and down, wobbling the table.

"Well, your mother and Aunt Patty are coming over any minute. You're sure? Because I might make a big breakfast for them." She sat back and crossed her arms over her pink fuzzy robe.

I must've looked kind of strange because she reached out and put a hand on my forehead. "Are you okay, Iris? You seem a little under the weather." She took her hand off my forehead and cupped her hands around the back of my neck. "Hmm. You don't seem to have a fever. What is it? Is something wrong?"

I wriggled away and sat down. "No, I'm okay. I'm just . . . I don't know. Tired." When I said that I looked Adam right in the eye, hoping he'd know that I *knew*, but he just smiled and shrugged his shoulders. "Iris is always a zombie in the morning," he said, then picked up his bowl and drank every last bit of milk down. DeeDee looked up at me quickly, and I could sense something not quite right in her light blue eyes, but unfortunately, I didn't get a chance to talk to her about it.

LATER, MY MOTHER AND AUNT PATTY arrived with a box of powdered doughnuts and a gallon of orange juice. My father was the last one up, since Sundays had always been his only day to sleep in, even though the latest he could manage to stay in bed was eight o'clock. He sat at the kitchen counter now in his robe and pajamas, and with my mother rooting around in the cupboards right next to him, it felt like home again. When I had the chance, I nudged DeeDee and motioned for her to follow me upstairs to my room. Usually we hung out there when she came over, but with everyone here, we'd had no privacy.

"You don't want a nice big breakfast?" Grandma Laura asked, turning around in her chair to look back at us. "I could make blueberry pancakes." She smiled, and I noticed for the first time her teeth were yellow, almost brown, and cracked in places like an old teacup. Her short gray hair was so thin that you could see right through to the scalp, and suddenly I got the feeling she might die soon. I had never before thought of her dying, and seeing her smile at me so openly set off a crack in my heart.

"No, maybe later," I said. "I'm just not hungry. And DeeDee already had breakfast, right, DeeDee?" I turned to her, and she nodded, but didn't say a word. This made me even surer that something had happened last night that shouldn't have.

"Hey, wait up," Adam said, following after us. He hung on to the railing of the stairs, pulling on it like he was going to pull it out of the wall. He was always so destructive and dangerous like that. His dark hair had a cowlick right at the center, and in the mornings his bangs stood straight up and flipped open in the middle. "You guys always just sit up there all the time. Stay down here, and let's all do something together. We should go outside or something."

I didn't even answer him. "Come on, DeeDee. Let's go up to my room." We both stomped up the stairs and left Adam at the bottom, looking up after us.

Once we were in my room, I carefully shut the door, turning the old-fashioned glass doorknob. DeeDee always said how wonderful our house was to have old things like that—the clear doorknobs like little chunks of ice, windows with real painted sills you could set things on, wooden floors you could slide around on in your slippers, old hissing radiators that were the best to sit against when you came in from ice-skating or the cold walk home from school. She didn't have things like that in their house, which was new and modern with thin metal frames around the slide-open windows, tan carpeting, metal doorknobs, and a heavy Lysol smell hanging over everything. I loved my room, which was dark and cool from the big shade tree outside, and I breathed in the smell of my clean, light blue bedsheets and the lemony wood floor polish.

"DeeDee?" When I turned around, she was already flopped on my bed, clutching the white eyelet comforter up to her chest, looking sick. In fact, when I sat down beside her and set a hand on her back, her eyes snapped shut and her mouth opened, but she didn't say anything. Her whole body shook. I didn't know what to do, so I simply lay down beside her, facing her, and tried to hold her.

"Ssh," I said quietly. "Ssh. It's okay." I patted her back like a little doll.

She tried to sit up, then decided against it. She tried to talk calmly

but ended up blurting out words. "I—hate him. He's just . . . mean."
I nodded, rubbed her back in circles. After awhile, I managed to sit
up and rock her back and forth in my arms; I hummed quietly to
soothe her.

Her wide solid body felt good in my arms, warm, and I could
imagine how amazing it must've felt to be a mother and hold a
little child in your arms every day. I dipped my nose into her damp,
mussed-up hair, and could smell her almond-scented shampoo.
Vidal Sassoon.

"Just don't say anything to anyone," she said.

I went to sit in the small rocking chair in the corner, my butt
barely wedged in. I still didn't really get what had happened. Not
exactly. DeeDee rested her forehead on her knees and sighed.
Maybe I should've run and got my mother. Maybe I should've
told on him before it was too late, but then I thought he'd probably
get sent away, or maybe we both would, or maybe he and DeeDee
would both get in trouble. I didn't know.

DeeDee was lying on her back now, hands crossed over her
chest, fingers laced together. "I wish he never would've come here.
To your family, I mean." She looked like she might start crying, and
put her hands up to her face.

I stood beside the bed and looked down at her like a concerned
parent, but just as I was trying to figure out what to say, we were
called downstairs to start saying good-bye to everyone, and that
was how my twelfth birthday ended—with DeeDee and her
secrets and puffy red eyes, and Adam the same terrible person he
was when we'd got him.

AFTER EVERYONE LEFT, I spent the rest of the day hidden in my
room, listening to Fleetwood Mac, trying to understand the people who were supposed to be my family.

Chapter Eight

Memory: My mother hands me a small white paper bag. I think candy is inside, but I'm wrong. It's bright white sanitary napkins, folded in threes like little baby diapers. We stand in the tiny apartment bathroom while the lights buzz. It's a Saturday morning.

"The thing is," she says, "you always want to be prepared for the worst." I must look at her puzzled, because she revises. "I mean, be prepared for anything. Any-thing." She looks in the mirror and smooths her eyebrows. "Did you know I was voted Most Unpredictable in my high school class?" She smiles, studies her teeth up close. "But then I was also voted Best Looking and Most Talented, and look where that got me."

She snaps off the light, and I feel her fingertips on my back in the dark.

I think of all the bleeding ahead.

It was true: my mother had a new boyfriend. I saw them driving down Main Street in a red car, my mother's auburn hair blowing out the open window. I thought she might have even seen me, and I couldn't believe how obvious she was. How could she have been so obvious? It wasn't as if Wishbone was a big city you could disappear in. Everyone knew everything, saw everything, and eventually heard everything, so if my mother thought she was pulling off a secret, she certainly wasn't. Everyone would know, especially my father. She must've been breaking his heart.

It was the beginning of October, and she and Adam still lived in the apartment above Dana's salon. I stayed with my father, which at first seemed kind of lonely, but eventually I preferred it. When I came home from school, the house was dark and quiet, the clocks ticking, refrigerator humming, everything locked and in place. I often sat at the dining room table and had a glass of milk and some graham crackers, felt the smooth polished wood under my hands, scuffed my stocking feet on the braided carpet underneath. It was utterly quiet and still, except for the cat, who stretched and yawned from a nap under the piano, came padding over to me, and rubbed herself against the leg of my chair. That was my only greeting.

Ever since the incident with DeeDee and Adam, I hadn't said anything to anyone, but had felt myself turning inward, confused. It didn't seem right for Adam to just get away with it, but the truth was I was scared to tell and didn't really even know *what* to tell. Plus, my own body was starting to change, and it made me feel gross when I thought about Adam—ashamed. I was starting to get long wiry hairs on my crotch and under my arms, and my nipples were just starting to bloat and puff a little, leaving small nuggets underneath, the size and shape of walnuts. I didn't have a period yet, but knew about it from a movie we'd seen in school. It had been very strange and formal when all the boys were herded out without explanation to go play dodgeball with Mr. Baxter, the P.E. teacher. We girls were left to cluster up in the desks at the front of the classroom, and were given small white booklets covered with bright blue, red, and yellow flowers. The cover said: *What Every Young Woman Should Know About Her Body.* The companion movie showed a completely naked girl with boobs and pubic hair, then switched to pink-and-blue diagrams that showed how to insert a tampon and how you could become pregnant. It shocked me, really, at the time, and now I started to wonder how much had really happened with Adam and DeeDee. Now she'd never come over anymore, and I had no one to really hang around with. Certainly not Adam. And although I sometimes talked to Sylvie since she was in my class, it wasn't the same.

ON FRIDAY I WENT TO SCHOOL, dreading it. It was like I had no group to belong to. There was the cool group, which Sylvie belonged to, then the group of shy, dorky girls from farms, then there was the sort of medium normal group who were super good in school but not really social or fun. I was somewhere on the fringes, and when it was free period, I took a book and sat with my back against the industrial arts building, where there was shade and where no one would bother me. I was reading this great book by Norma Klein about a young mom who was dying of cancer and trying to say good-bye to her family. I was toward the end now, and it was really starting to make me cry. Sometimes I held the book in front of me and acted like I was reading, but really I watched everyone. Sylvie's group of girls was starting to talk to the boys in our class, and I watched as one guy, Steve Rogers, walked over to them, hands in his jeans pockets, hair blowing in his eyes. He was probably the cutest boy in our class—blond hair, big brown eyes, thin but not skinny. He didn't sit down with the group, but stood there while they all looked up at him like he was a god.

I continued reading. It was like books were my only safety and joy; I happily forgot about my own stupid problems and worried instead about this woman who was dying and leaving her baby and husband behind. I tucked my hair behind my ears and held the pages open with my hand so the wind wouldn't blow them, when suddenly Sylvie came running up to me, breathless. "Hi," she said. She didn't wear a jacket, even though it was getting close to freezing at night now. She wore brown corduroy overalls and a cream turtleneck. The strong wind whipped her bobbed hair up in a frenzy. "Hey, what are you doing tomorrow night?" She glanced back at her group, and I began to wonder if she was ready to pull some prank.

I pretended to run through some sort of schedule in my head, even though I knew I had absolutely nothing going on except some homework and a visit to my mother's. "Umm, not much," I said, squinting up at her. "I had a birthday party awhile ago. But nothing much is going on this weekend."

"Why didn't you invite me to your party?" she said, as if shocked, but we both knew why.

"It was just family, DeeDee and Melanie and stuff. It was no big deal." I slipped my finger into the book to save my place and wondered what this was leading to.

"Well, Carla and Jennifer and I kind of decided that we want you to come to a slumber party Carla's having on Saturday." She glanced back at them again, as if to see if she was doing the right thing. The wind continued to roar through the tall elm trees across the street, and the sky darkened.

I thought it over for a second, a million questions running through my head. Why now? How did you suddenly just decide to let someone into your group like that? I almost said right out, In Teacherville? Because that had always been a sort of off-limits place unless you were from a certain rich class of people. Really I was dying for this, but I didn't want to seem too easy, too desperate. "Saturday night, you said?"

Sylvie nodded, and when she pressed her lips together, deep dimples emerged from her cheeks. She looked so cute.

"I guess I could come. Is it someone's birthday? Like, should I bring a present or something?"

"No, it's just a slumber party." Carla waved a hand at us and shouted something I couldn't hear over the wind. "Come on over with us," Sylvie said. "We can chat about it."

I did go with her, but felt suspicious, especially when I remembered what Carla's mom had said about my mother, that she was a runaround. I felt obedient and small as I followed Sylvie and was granted entrance into the cool group for some reason unknown to me. Be careful, I kept thinking to myself, there's got to be a trick somehow.

When I sat down, I found out I was right: one of them had a crush on Adam. Of all the most unbelievable things. On Adam. "So what's he like at home?" she asked. It was Jennifer Barnes, who I barely even knew since she had Mr. Jowolski for homeroom. She had wavy blond hair with bangs, naturally dark red lips, and this sweet wholesome look, like she could've been in commercials advertising soft toilet paper or soap. In fact, Sylvie had told me once that her mother had entered Jennifer's photographs in contests, hoping to get her started on a modeling career. It would've been her luck to get famous, too, since she seemed to have everything else she wanted. Nice house in Teacherville, a new girl's lavender ten-speed bike, her own room with her own bathroom in the basement, a real stereo. All this I knew from Sylvie.

I sat with my elbows on my knees, hands crossed in front of me. If they only knew Adam; if I could've only told them the truth, then no one would've had any "cute" crushes on him. But I couldn't now. "Well, he's actually kind of a brat. I mean, we don't get along that well." They laughed, and I shrugged my shoulders. It was the six of us—Sylvie, Carla, Jennifer, Katie, Denise, and me—and we sat in a circle by the baseball diamond, shivering in the cold wind. I was the only one who wore a coat.

"Well, does he like anybody right now?" Jennifer kept digging for clues about Adam, although given what had happened, or maybe happened, with DeeDee, it was hard for me to even hear the mention of his name. Still, I knew what these girls expected. It was cool for them to have a crush right now, even if nothing ever came of it—it was cool to be the one longing for a boy. Jennifer looked around at everyone, and raised her eyebrows.

"Umm, I don't think so. He hasn't mentioned anybody," I said. It was the best I could do.

Denise Kramer, a very snotty girl with gray uneven teeth, ratty dishwater-blond permed hair, and a square, boyish body, piped in, "Well, you guys aren't actually brother and sister, are you? Because I know he was just adopted, obviously, and weren't you, too? That's what Sylvie said." She crossed her arms over her pilled white sweatshirt with a big Minnesota Vikings logo on it.

I couldn't believe Sylvie had betrayed me like that. I couldn't believe it. "Well, it's not really anyone's business—" I tried to beg off, felt my face flame deep red with shame and embarrassment. I swallowed hard, but Sylvie jumped in and tried to save me.

"I'm sure, Denise! Just ask a question like that, why don't you!" Sylvie did a good job of scolding her, and pointed across the grounds for distraction. "Isn't that him right there? In the jean jacket and red turtleneck?"

"That's him," I said, and felt, heavily, as if he would always be a stone around my neck.

"God, he's cute," Jennifer said, and I had to believe from the sound of her voice that she said it more for show than from honesty. "I especially love his eyes. They're so flashy."

I just about gagged. "Yeah, right," I said under my breath. Luckily, the bell jangled us all to our feet, and it was time for English with Miss Rickhardt, who had recently told us and written on the board that we were to address her as *Ms.* Rickhardt, not Miss. I didn't really see what the big difference was, but she'd lectured on it passionately the other day—"Be your own *woman*," she'd said—so I did my best to remember.

"So come to the slumber party on Saturday night, okay? Can you?" Carla asked me as we walked up the tiny hill, back toward the drab brick school building. "I would really love to have you." Fake, fake, fake.

"I guess I can come," I said, but I hovered back away from her a bit. It was all too much, too fast. I already knew things like this never lasted.

IT WAS A DARK GRAY BLUSTERY AFTERNOON, and Ms. Rickhardt said instead of our usual hour of grammar and English language, she wanted to try something new. She had on a cream-colored calico Gunne Sax dress with a lace-up top and flounced skirt, zip-up tall brown boots, and a big brown ribbed cardigan sweater. Her long hair was held back with a plain metal barrette, but curly pieces by her ears fell out and framed her face. She spoke with a slight lisp, while walking across the room, pulling down the cracked yellow shades. "Now I just want to try something here. Instead of language as we read it in books and hear it on the radio and TV, I'm going to play some music on the record player, and we're all going to move to the music in the dark." She walked toward the door and flicked off the lights. The fluorescent bulbs overhead sizzled and died with a pop. "Can everyone help me push the desks off to the sides?"

We were all confused about what was happening, but pulled on the wooden seats of our heavy desks and swung them off toward the walls. "Great, super," Ms. Rickhardt said, standing at the front of the room, tall and still. It wasn't completely dark in the room, but felt shadowy and brown, like my bedroom at dusk. Shafts of light entered through the gaps of the shades, but it was a dull flat light, all shadows. Ms. Rickhardt went over to start the record player, and the grainy loping sounds of piano and saxophone music could be heard. "Now move like animals, or like music, or like water, whatever. Just move. Don't pay any attention to anyone else."

The music dipped up and down, curled and looped through the room. At first no one did anything except walk around awkwardly, but then Ms. Rickhardt stopped the record for a second, and pushed us to do better. "Really, this is just an experiment. You don't have to feel stupid, because there's no right or wrong way to do this. You can just relax and try to see into the music. You can dance or glide or rock or roll on the floor. It doesn't matter." She stopped, peered at us in the darkness, making eye contact with everyone. "Now come on. Show me that you're creative. That you're not afraid."

The music began again, and I closed my eyes, rocked my knees slowly up and down, then pretended that I was a snake. I pointed my hands together flat at the palms, crouched down, and slithered around the room. The music grew mysterious, complicated and low, then boomed to surprises. I imagined myself in the water, under a hazy liquid pale green, the sun barely finding me. I didn't even notice what other people were doing, except once when Ms. Rickhardt accidentally bumped into me, I saw she was hopping around like a rabbit, her head shaking back and forth strangely.

When the music stopped, I came out of it, like a trance, and collapsed my shoulders. Ms. Rickhardt turned off the record player, flapped open the shades, and fumbled with the light switch. Her face was sweaty and excited. "Okay, okay, great! That's great! Super. Now everyone get the desks back in order, okay—" She waited at the front of the room, hands clasped, as if barely able to hold back some discovery she'd made. "All right, now I want you to write about it. I want you to take out a clean sheet of paper, and write down whatever it is the music made you think of or become or remember." She flew up to her desk in the corner by the window, and tore out a sheet of paper from a beat-up notebook. "I'm going to do it, too. This is fantastic. What happened with the music? Just write about it. Write, write, write."

I sat with my head down, my long hair hiding my face on either side. At first the page with the watery blue lines was blank, but as soon as I began writing, I quickly had a full page and more. The writing came easily for me, and I elaborated on Adam, my mother and father, the creamery, my Grandma Laura, DeeDee. When the time was up, I handed in the longest of anybody. "Wow," Ms. Rickhardt whispered when she collected my pages. "You're quite a writer, Iris. Fantastic." Her praise sent me floating away, happy as my snake had been, weaving and diving through the imaginary musical waters.

ON SATURDAY MORNING, I woke up with a sick feeling in my stomach that I knew was just nerves. Instead of jumping right out of bed, I shoved my pillows up against the wall and reached down for the book I was reading. There was something queenlike and royal to propping myself up in a dark room, book spread out cleanly on my bent knees, shades raised just an inch or two to let in the light. I was almost to the end of *Sunshine* by Norma Klein, and it was breaking my heart. In fact, I could've finished it the night before, but I'd saved the last twenty or so pages as a treat for today on purpose.

I could hear my father downstairs in the kitchen, could smell the coffee and hear the crunch of newspaper pages being turned and straightened. He didn't work on weekends anymore since Verne Ott's wife and teenage son, Kevin, worked there now to help out. I thought my father felt squeezed out, unneeded, and worthless. He only did actual creamery work on Mondays and Thursdays, and as a result, a lot of business had slacked off—farm families who used to come in for all their butter, cream, milk, and ice cream didn't really do it anymore because it wasn't all that fresh and the whole atmosphere of the store had changed. It was more like a quick-stop place instead of a creamery. I thought soon my father might even be fired, or maybe not fired, but forced to quit because there just wouldn't be any work for him. Although I'd heard him telling someone on the phone last night that Mr. Ott was thinking of installing two gasoline pumps, which might really turn the place around. I doubted my father would keep working there then. He had too much pride for that, but it made me sad to see all the butter-making prize trophies downstairs, the raised gold cows a salute to a past that no longer had a place.

After finishing the book, and crying so hard I had two perfect clear streams of snot running under my nose, I got up and headed for the shower. There was a chill in the house, the sun still blocked by trees in the east, and I nosed my feet into the slippers my mother had knit for me. I skated off across the slick hardwood floors, swinging my arms fiercely like an Olympic speed skater, until I reached the brown braided rug in front of the bathroom door and stopped, arms raised in the air. I could hear the crowd roar.

AT ABOUT SIX THAT EVENING, Sylvie called me. "How's it hanging?" she said, not so much a question as a greeting. She never used to say that until she'd started hanging around with Carla. "You ready to go? Denise's mom is going to pick me up, and we can stop by your place in about ten minutes, okay?" Why did she sound so much older suddenly? So powerful and in charge.

"Okay." I felt my stomach tense up again, afraid—I didn't know of what.

"See ya soon," she said. "Ciao." My mouth hung open in disbelief at her "ciao." It seemed unbelievable that she would say such a thing seriously, and to me, of all people.

I packed a small duffel bag with my nightgown, slippers, and an outfit for tomorrow—jeans and a University of Minnesota sweatshirt my father had bought me once when he went to a game up there. Then I sat out on the front stoop, twirling dried-up autumn leaves between my palms by their long brown stems. Our big maple in front sent down a sprinkling of intensely bright golden leaves, and the tree toward the back sent down layers of dark red smaller, smoother ones. I liked the old dusty smell and thought that I could've probably told Ms. Rickhardt about it and she'd want me to write a poem highlighting all the details. Maybe I'd write a poem and just give it to her, as a surprise. I could imagine so clearly the look on her face if I did that—her forehead and long chin would shine, she'd tilt her neck to the side, she'd smile and show the overbite of her teeth.

Denise's mom leaned on the horn before she'd even pulled up to the curb, which I found funny for some reason. She drove a big green station wagon—the kind with an actual door you could open sideways in the back. She worked in a factory three towns away where they made plastic ice cream buckets. The only reason I knew that was because I always seemed to be at the creamery when my father got his big shipments of buckets. They'd come in big rectangular boxes and smelled in a weird, plastic fruity way like melons. My Grandma Laura thought they were valuable things to have, and asked that we never, never throw one away without saving it for her.

I waved to Denise and Sylvie in the car, and slung the duffel over my shoulder, sprinting across the lawn, as if there was some mad hurry. No one was in the front seat next to Denise's mom, so I naturally popped open the back door and squeezed in next to Sylvie. "Hi," I said. "Thanks for picking me up."

"No problem," Denise's mom said, winking at me in the rearview mirror. She wore a black hooded sweatshirt, and her short curly hair was matted up in the back and tired-looking. "I didn't work today, so I'm just on my way to the grocery store." She smashed out her cigarette in the tiny ashtray. "How's your ma doing?"

I didn't know how they would've known each other, except that everyone knew everyone in Wishbone, and you just asked those kinds of questions. "She's pretty good. She likes her job at the bank." I shrugged my shoulders at Sylvie and Denise, hoping to quickly drop the whole subject of my family.

Denise's mom took a wide left turn onto the highway, and it felt as if the big car was a large boat floating across the sea. "Used to be that the wife didn't have to work, but now you see all kinds of things is different. Now it's the wives are doing everything."

"Yeah," I said, and looked out the window at the black dirt in the fields. I could sense that Denise wished her mom would be quiet, and I felt for her; I understood it only too well. Luckily, Teacherville wasn't even a mile out of town, and soon we pulled into the horseshoe-shaped road that all the new houses were built around.

"There you are, door-to-door service," Denise's mom said. "Have a good one. And don't do anything I wouldn't do." She laughed at herself, and we thanked her and waved and walked up to the black shiny door that actually had a brass knocker. The doorbell was lit up soft orange like sherbet with curlicue gold designs around it, and in the center was a pearly white button.

Carla answered the door, wearing faded jeans and a tight red scoop-neck T-shirt. Her hair was all loaded up on top of her head, twisted tight in a bun. "Hi, you guys," she said, and without showing us around the house, she led us immediately to the basement. "Katie's the only one here so far." I did manage to look out the sliding doors in the dining room and saw a deck connected to a bright blue swimming pool. Behind that, a hill tumbled with grass and led down to a little stream. I fantasized about what it must've been like to live in such a great place, but Carla whisked us right past without even glancing. Besides, it was October and too cold for swimming, so it didn't really matter.

Downstairs, the basement was decorated like a penthouse apartment. It was thickly carpeted in a deep brown shag that was so plush my tennis shoes sunk way down and left footprints. There were also sliding glass doors at this level, but these led right out to the lawn. In the corner, there was a black padded bar shaped like a comma with a full stock of shiny liquor bottles behind it the colors of jewels—emerald, ruby, clear like diamonds, topaz, and even a bright blue one, which I had no idea what it was, but it looked like Kool-Aid.

On the other side of the room was a big brick fireplace loaded with fresh birch logs. On the mantel were jars of Brach's candy and root beer barrels and wooden bowls full of walnuts and pistachios. There were huge wildlife paintings on the walls—scenes of mallards in muted golds and greens flying low across some reedy pond, and another of a pheasant, poised, head alert, ready to run across a gravel road. It was a dark and masculine basement, and it felt as if big bottles of beer should've been served there with Texas toast sandwiches and toothpicks.

"So, what do you guys wanna do?" Carla asked. She stretched up on her tiptoes, then flopped down backwards on the big leather couch, giggling. "Are you hungry or what? Because we can eat. My mom bought, like, a million frozen pizzas from the Schwan's guy."

"I don't care," Sylvie said, sitting down in a big rocking chair and running her hands up and down the slick arms.

"Okay," Denise said, but she was far too busy nosing around the room to care about eating.

"Whatever," I said, and thought of how much my father hated Schwan's people because they were his stiffest competition. Instead of people driving into town and going to our creamery, the Schwan's company had all the same stuff, but they delivered right to your door, just like an old-fashioned milkman. They were expensive, of course, but usually people's laziness won out over their concern about the best bargain. That's what my father had said anyway. He'd also said the butter over there tasted like a brick of lard, and that they didn't keep it churning long enough for the right texture.

"Well, I suppose we should wait for the dork Jennifer to get here. Jennifer said her mom is giving her a perm, but don't you think it's going to look kind of crappy? I mean, you can't just get a home permanent out of a box and expect it to look good. I mean, right?" Carla looked at me as if I knew.

"I have no idea," I said, then took a seat at one of the barstools.

"Hey, so what's going on with your family?" Carla said, pressing me, even though we barely knew each other. "Have your parents split up or what? And what about Adam? Why does he live with your mom and you with your dad? Isn't it usually the other way around?"

Katie, who was shy, had braces, had no father, and struck me as being a good and decent person, gave Carla a look as if to scold her for nosing into my life. I had always liked Katie, and used to hang around with her in third grade when both of our moms were in bowling league together. Her mom, whose husband had been killed in a car accident right after Katie was born, would bring Katie over on bowling nights for my father to babysit both of us. She was a sweet, quiet person who would've never wanted to hurt anyone, and somehow I couldn't figure out how she'd gotten in with Carla's cool group, except that maybe Carla felt she could control Katie because she was so meek and mild.

"I don't know what's going on with my family," I said, and twirled on my stool as Carla stepped behind the bar.

"Coke?" she asked, looking inside the small refrigerator below the bar.

"Sure," I said. "Thanks." She handed me a cold wet can, and I snapped it open, sipping. "I guess Adam just likes to stay with my mom at the apartment and I just like to be back at my real house. It's not like we really chose where to go on purpose." Carla poked a striped straw into my can. "I don't know. They'll probably get back together again soon anyway. I hope."

Carla gave me a smirk and rolled her eyes sideways. She looked over at Sylvie, Katie, and Denise, then shrugged her shoulders.

"What?" I asked.

"Just—" Carla said, then looked again at Sylvie. "I don't know if I should say."

"Say what?" I demanded, getting angry now. "Tell me. Of course, if it's that my mother has a boyfriend, I already know that. That's old news." I sloshed the straw around in my pop can and could already hear the bubbles fizzing out flat.

"Well, yeah, but do you know who it is this time?" Carla said, clicking her shiny polished nails against her teeth.

I stood up, ready to walk out the door and hitchhike home if I had to. "What do you mean, 'this time'?" It's not like she's got a whole bunch of boyfriends or anything. God."

"Oh really?" Carla said. "That's not what I heard."

At that point, the doorbell rang, but before anyone could go answer it, Jennifer came bounding down the padded stairs with her firm round breasts bouncing underneath her turtleneck, her new kinky permed hair still wet in the back. "So how do you like my new 'do?" she asked, and we all said fine, although it looked terrible—fuzzy at the ends and like something had raked her scalp in sharp, bald rows at the top.

"Come on," Carla said, "let's get something to eat before my pigass brothers get home and eat it all." We followed her up the stairs, and there was no more mention about my mother or my father or my "controversial" family life, thank god.

LATER, AFTER WE'D EATEN TWO PIZZAS, the six of us went back down to the basement where Carla closed the door behind us. "Don't anyone come down here, either!" she yelled at her brothers, who had stuck three pizzas in for just the two of them.

"Yeah, like we'd really want to come down and see what you

queers are doing," the oldest, Paul, said. I found him to be the cuter of the two with thick sandy blond hair hanging over his round, soft hazel eyes that always seemed as if they were misted with tears. He had a clean, dry smell like deodorant soap and fresh notebook paper, and when I brushed past him before, I'd noticed he gave me a short grin out of the side of his mouth. Still, he was sixteen and couldn't be too interested in one of his little sister's friends who was barely only twelve. But I smiled back at him, too, and probably looked like an excited idiot kid.

Down in the basement, everyone sat around on the floor with cans of pop held on their thighs. There was an actual working jukebox that Carla's mom had bought at an auction, only they had it set up where you didn't have to put in any quarters, so Carla invited us all to pick songs. I went and punched in B-19, which was Debby Boone's "You Light Up My Life," still my favorite, even though it reminded me of the days when Sylvie and I used to be best friends. Everyone picked a song, then Carla went to the wall and turned out all the lights so you could hardly see anything. When everyone started to complain, she pulled out a flashlight and popped it on right under her chin so her whole face lit up orange and her nostrils were a deep, veiny red, her eyes hooded with shadows.

"Now, I can't decide what we should do first . . . a round of Truth or Dare, or start calling boys." She paused, and waited for us to say something, but no one did. Suddenly I was struck by a realization that maybe I didn't even *want* to be in Carla's cool group because not only was she mean, she was also bossy and obnoxious, especially at her own house. "I say Truth or Dare," she said. She started shoving the heavy couch out of the way with her knees. "That's always more fun. Kind of gets the ball rolling." We all helped her with the couch, until there was a large open space on the dense puffy carpet for us to sit in a circle.

"Oh, I almost forgot!" Carla said, and jumped up from her crouched position. With the flashlight in hand, leaving us all in the dark, she rushed back behind the bar and dragged out a cooler, which sloshed and churned with icy water inside like a cocktail. "Beer! I stole it all from my dad's stash over the last couple of weeks, and he didn't even notice. Is that too much or what?" She passed cold cans of Miller High Life around, and we all cracked them open and sipped. It was my first beer, but I didn't dream of admitting that fact, even if asked for a Truth.

Carla got to start the Truth or Dare by asking anyone, she said, because it was her place and her party. She took a big sip of her beer, wiped her mouth, and let out a slight belch as if she'd been a beer drinker all her life. "Okay, I think I'm going to pick Jennifer, and I think I know exactly what I want you to do."

Jennifer, the most developed and mature of all of us, piped up. "How do you know I'm going to pick Dare?" She picked off her beer can's tab and pressed the can to her full, pink lips. "You can't just decide for me." She crossed her arms, and I envied her full breasts as she did this. "Oh, okay. Go ahead if it's such a big deal, Miss Bossy." Jennifer and Carla were both rich and mean and snotty to both their parents and their friends, but Carla was the worst. She tried to control everyone like a den mother.

"Okay, your dare is to lay down—" Carla started.

Jennifer butted in already. "What do you mean, 'lay down'? What are you gonna do, you weirdo!"

"Just do it," Carla said, making a space by pushing us all back. "I promise we won't do anything to hurt you. Come on, everyone, help me get her to lay back."

Finally, after being convinced that nothing bad was going to happen, Jennifer lay down on her back, her arms crossed protectively over her chest. "By the way, it's 'lie down,' not 'lay down,'" she said. "Don't you listen in school?"

"No, do you?" Carla said, laughing. "Besides, Miss, or excuse me, *Ms.* Rickhardt's a dyke. Couldn't you just tell the minute she walked in the first day? She's a total lesbo. And I think she's got the hots for you, Iris. She's always fawning over all your papers since you write like ten times more than anyone when she has us do those stupid exercises. I told my mom we had to pretend we were monsters in class, and she said she was going to talk to the school board because we're not learning anything."

My heart fell, thinking of Ms. Rickhardt's tall bony frame, her friendly overbite, her funky clothes, and how she was the one thing I truly looked forward to in my life these days. I simply had to defend her. "She's not a lezzie. I saw pictures of some guy on her desk. And at least she's fun, unlike most teachers. Would you rather just sit and diagram sentences? They can't get rid of her." I finished the last of my beer and noted how it tasted like bitter tree bark, not pleasant at all.

"Why? Does that mean your *affair* would be over?" Carla asked, laughing.

Jennifer swatted her on the arm. "Get over it, already, you dork. Now what the hell am I lying here for? See, notice my proper use of the word *lying*? So let's get on with it already. If you're going to cut my head off, just do it." She reached up and adjusted her earrings, and we all gathered around her on our knees, as if we were a circle of primitive doctors about to operate. She smelled like chemical hair dye.

"Everyone hold her arms down, okay?" Carla said, and we did, although I started to wonder what was going on. Carla then took Jennifer's brown corduroy pants by the waist and pulled them down, along with her underwear. She then shined the flashlight on what was a virtual forest of coily dense black pubic hairs that not only covered the top of her crotch, but spread down the insides of her thighs.

Jennifer reacted oddly. She didn't fight to be let go, but breathed slowly out of her mouth, as if trying to calm herself down. Finally, she clenched her fists and said darkly, "You're sick, Carla. You really are."

"Well," Carla said, still holding the flashlight right over the center of her crotch. "You're the most mature of all of us, and I just thought everyone would want to see what it looks like. I thought the hair would be more red, you know, since your other hair is kind of strawberry blond, but it's so black."

Sylvie and I exchanged glances, and it became clear that Sylvie hadn't gone this far or this deep with Carla's group before. She shrugged her shoulders and shook her head as if she didn't approve either. Katie and Denise said nothing, but looked curiously, boldly, at the pubic hair. I just wanted it to be over.

"Just one last thing," Carla said, and handed me the flashlight. Her little pig nose twitched. "We have to get the whole picture so we know what it's gonna be like." While I held the flashlight at a cockeyed angle, Carla whipped up Jennifer's turtleneck and hoisted the bra up over Jennifer's bare, full breasts. "There," Carla said, huffing and puffing, "we also have this to look forward to. Shine the light on them better, Iris. Boobs." We all stared in wonder and shock at the soft mounds of white flesh with their broad pink nipples that stood up straight and hard like little pencil erasers. No one, it seemed, looked at Jennifer's face, but I noticed that her eyes were closed and her neck muscles tensed. Before it could go any further, I dropped the flashlight, ran to the bathroom, and locked the door. As I leaned against the sink, I thought of DeeDee and Adam, and how hard it seemed for any of us to stay safe.

More than anything, I wanted my mother back.

Later, Carla said it was all just a joke, and even Jennifer laughed it off, calling us a bunch of lesbians. As we watched TV later on, I fell asleep against Sylvie's shoulder, the closest I could get to home for the time being.

Chapter Nine

Memory: My father lets me ride with him to Reetz's dairy farm to check out their milk supply. It's the middle of winter. Chunks of snow harden in the fields like glaciers. Inside the barn, the cows stand still while machines drain them of milk. I watch it flow white overhead through clear plastic tubing. A balmy ripe smell settles over everything.

My father discusses prices, volume, deliveries. The farmer eyes him hard. My father stands back. Something is wrong. The farmer has already agreed to go with another outfit. I see my father pat himself for a cigarette, but he holds off. Not in the barn.

On the drive home, I watch his profile, but every time I blink it grows darker and darker. He fades like fog. I think of the cows, so innocent and accepting. I think of white milk rushing down my throat.

"Not a make-or-break deal," he tells me, though I haven't said anything. "Don't sweat it."

I finally got it out of Sylvie who my mother was dating, and it about made me sick. It was Ronny Nelson, a guy who'd just graduated from high school last year and was now going to college up in St. Cloud. Apparently he'd flirted with her at the bank, not knowing how old she really was, and she fell for it and even led him on. He was a big jock with huge hands and a basketball player's stoop. I had no idea why or when they saw each other, but it was sick in my book. I also couldn't tell whether my father knew or not, and I tried to gauge by asking really subtle questions like "Have you seen Mom lately?" But he always gave me a straight yes or no, so it was hard to tell. Still, if I read him right, he must've known, because he'd go very silent sometimes and had a generally sad air about him that never went away.

It also seemed like ever since the slumber party at Carla's, Sylvie and I had been on the mend a little bit. Like the other day she'd called me up and asked what I was doing, and I couldn't believe it since it had been months and all of the school year since that'd happened. She ended up coming over, but she couldn't get over how strange it was without my mom or Adam there. She said it felt like they had died or moved to another state, and I couldn't help but agree. So that was at least better, having Sylvie in my life again, although she was still sort of torn about being with Carla and Jennifer and that whole group. She even admitted to me that she'd still probably hang around them sometimes, but that she and I were always going to be friends, through thick and thin.

Unfortunately, I had another problem riding on my shoulders having to do with Ms. Rickhardt. Apparently the day she'd had us crawling around like animals and then writing about it, I'd let go in my paper about Adam and DeeDee and basically spilled the beans about all my worries without even thinking about it. I should definitely *not* have written about it for a teacher, because she wrote at the end of my paper in purple felt-tip pen that she wanted to see me and talk about it privately. I truly had to be ready and not let myself break down crying because that was my tendency these days. I was becoming a real crier. She wanted me to stay after school the next day, and I guessed I really didn't have a choice.

My other big problem was my father. Things were obviously not going well for him with Verne Ott totally taking over the creamery bit by bit and making it into a completely different store. Last week, my father had come home with a twelve-pack of beer, which was unusual for him, and sat down in front of the TV and drank almost every one. He kept asking me to get him a fresh one, and didn't even cook us any dinner that night. I had to make frozen pot pies and cut up apples for myself, and I even brought some for him, but he just smiled, tousled my hair, and cracked open another beer. Later, I noticed he'd eaten it, though. I asked him the next day what was wrong, and he told me that Verne Ott had decided to install two gas pumps out in front of the store, which would mean major remodeling and possibly the end of the creamery. There was even talk of a chain franchise, not a 7–Eleven, but something like it—a Casey's Carry-Out, or a Stop-N-Go—same difference.

He was so depressed that today, a Friday, which was the creamery's big delivery day, he called in sick, even though I was pretty sure he wasn't. I heard him on the phone as I was pouring cereal on my milk, and it seemed like he was trying to make his voice sound hoarse and sore. "Yeah, Verne, I've got the flu real bad here, and it looks like I won't be able to make it in today. Sorry to give such a late notice." He paused, rubbing the back of his neck. "Uh-huh. Uh-huh. Okay, sounds good. See you tomorrow then. Bye." I hunched over my bowl of cereal and looked up expectantly.

"What did he say?" I asked, my mouth full. "Is he mad?"

"No," my father said. "No, in fact, he said it's just as well because he'd like to get his son—he's got an older son, Scott—familiar with the business, so he's going to call him in." My father poured himself a cup of coffee, and sat across the table from me, staring out the window. He was still in his pajamas with his robe wrapped around him. He started patting his pockets, groping around the table as if he'd lost something. He flicked off his eyeglasses, which were only for certain distances.

"Looking for your cigarettes?" I asked. I was too full to eat the soggy cornflakes that floated like little scraps of paper in my bowl.

He nodded. "Next to the toaster," I told him. "And the matches, too." He lit up in the kitchen and stood in front of the sink, exhaling slowly, watching birds twitter and rock the feeder outside the window. When I left for school, he was still standing there, holding himself at the elbows. When I called out a cheery, "See you later!" all I got in response was a low, murmured "Yeah," which worried me—his sinking again. I'd heard my mother talking more than once to my aunts about how depressed my father had been, and it was apparently a depression that demanded medication, which he'd refused over and over. Now I was starting to think he needed it more than ever. As I rushed out the door to meet Sylvie, I wondered if I should've told my mother, but then she was probably too wrapped up with her new studly boyfriend to care.

AT SCHOOL, I HAD A HARD TIME paying attention, even though Ms. Rickhardt had us do some interesting things with vocabulary words. I almost cracked up when I saw her come in wearing a long, black jumpsuit with flared legs and a gray, bumpy sweater jacket that went almost to her knees. She paced around the room like a caged animal, the wide legs flapping. She had put us in groups of five, and every time she shouted out a vocabulary word and gave us the meaning—"Archaic: outdated; old-fashioned; of another, past era"—one of us in the group had to write the word down in a sentence. Since I was the best at English in our class and everyone knew it, my group made me start. I wrote, "Although it was an <u>archaic</u> way to do it, Robert liked the feel of dirt under his fingernails, and tilled the entire one-acre garden by hand." Then Ms. Rickhardt shouted out another word. "Propensity: inclination; tendency; partiality," she said, rubbing her long spidery fingers up and down. "Now the next person has to use the word in a sentence, but his or her sentence must also fit along with the first person's sentence. So, in other words, you're building a collaborative story.

Got it?" Everyone in my group, including Jennifer Barnes—who I had a hard time looking at ever since the slumber party and seeing her dark pubic hair and silent humiliation—looked at me dumbly for an interpretation of what Ms. Rickhardt was asking us to do. Jennifer sat tearing at her cuticles and nibbling the little pieces of skin that came off.

"So what should I write?" Bill Dutton asked, rubbing his oily black hair with a pencil eraser. "This is dumb. This isn't even like school. Here, Iris, you do it. You're Miss Brownnose anyway."

"I am not," I said, twirling my hair between my fingers. "Just write something like . . . how about write . . . Whenever Julie's father had too much to drink, he had a propensity for violence. Say something like that," I said, but I could tell he was copying down every word exactly as I said it. Then I sat up and put a hand on the paper. "But wait, no. You can't write that because it doesn't match my first sentence."

"Huh?" Bill said dumbly, and looked around the group. "I don't get it."

"Just write something about a gardener or his family or something," I said, growing impatient with his density. Ms. Rickhardt was also giving us sidelong glances and probably knew that I was the one doing it all. I whispered, "Just write something like: Robert's cows were a smart herd and had a propensity to take shelter at the first sign of bad weather."

"That's dumb," Jennifer piped in. Her blond perm had softened up a bit by now, but still had a raked effect at the part, which clearly showed where each row of curling rods had been placed. She also had a pimple on her chin, which she must've just popped because there was a tiny, oozing bead of oily blood poised at the tip. She wiped it casually away with the back of her hand. "It sounds like a big farm story. Make it more exciting or something, or we'll probably get a bad grade. I'm sure." Jennifer sat way back in her seat and crossed her arms over her chest. Then she pressed on the pimple with the back of her hand again.

"Like what?" I asked, feeling a little defensive, despite myself. At least I didn't have pimples.

"I don't know. Just write something cool. Write something like: Cheryl and Rhoda always went shopping at Ridgedale Mall on Saturdays, and had a propensity for buying colored bikini underwear and black lace bras." Jennifer sat back, satisfied that she had made a great joke. Everyone in the group laughed along uncomfortably.

"Whatever," I said, and looked up at the big clock on the wall, waiting for the day to be over. I liked English and I liked the way Ms. Rickhardt taught us things, but everyone else in the class seemed like they didn't get it.

Bill Dutton scrawled something out in pencil, then, while Ms. Rickhardt was helping another group with something, he leaned over and whispered to us. "My parents said Ms. Rickhardt's a lesbo. I guess someone saw her with her arm around a woman all lovey-dovey in some bar in Mankato. Gross, huh?"

"That's probably just a rumor," I said. "Everyone's saying that just because she's different, which is apparently not allowed in this town."

Suddenly everyone began talking loudly, and Ms. Rickhardt decided the exercise wasn't going very well. She made us rearrange the desks, then took me off to the side and whispered, "Remember to see me after school." Bill Dutton must've seen this because he whistled and nudged Jennifer on the arm, and I heard him say something idiotic like, "Guess we know who her girlfriend is now." I ignored him and wished it was time to go home. We finished up the assignments individually, and by the end, I thought I had a pretty good story cooked up about Robert the gardener and his cows and garden and family. Besides, I loved new words like *surreptitious, agility, xenophobia,* and *precipice.*

They sounded beautiful, like their own flavors, and slipped off the tongue like iced fruit.

After the final bell had released everyone from their seats, I sat at my desk in the back, chin in hands. The wind had almost completely stripped all the leaves from the maple trees, and only a few golden tough ones hung on, fluttering like flags. I saw the school buses lined up along the curb below, and wished I got to ride the bus like the kids from the country. I'd always wanted to, and could imagine myself sitting with my knees up, gazing out the window as all the scenery passed by, maybe listening to my tiny portable radio that was shaped like a large grapefruit and was lime green with little daisy stickers all over it. The kids from the country seemed to share a sort of bond, and always looked out for each other when there were blizzards and other bad weather. It seemed more interesting than being a town kid. We were all on our own, even in the rain and cold and snow. Every day I trudged up and down Main Street, and never had a big group of people to hang around with like the bus kids did.

Ms. Rickhardt closed the door and came swooping back to me in her big flared jumpsuit. She smiled, holding on to my paper, but the look on her face was one of determination and concern. "Iris," she said, taking a seat in the desk right next to me. She sat in it sideways, her bony knees poking out into the aisle. "Thanks for staying after. There's just some things we need to talk about." She stopped, considered, and I noticed that up close her skin was scarred with pockmarks of old pimples. She looked like a sweet overgrown teenager, and I noticed two silver fish dangled from her ears. She looked up at me with her small brown eyes, and raised her eyebrows. "You probably know what I want to talk to you about, right?"

I squirmed in my chair, since I couldn't remember exactly what I'd written and hoped it wouldn't get me or my family in trouble. "I might," I said, "but I'm not sure."

Ms. Rickhardt took my paper, which she'd stapled together and written comments on, and started leafing through it. "You wrote a lot about your family here, Iris, and about your brother, Adam. He's a grade higher than you, right?"

I nodded stiffly, and folded my hands on my desk like lawyers did in movies.

"He's adopted, too, right?"

Again I nodded, not looking her in the eye. She put a hand on my thigh, and I almost lurched out of my seat.

"Iris, you're so nervous for such a young person! Relax, I'm not going to bite." She removed her hand from my leg, and I thought of what everyone said about her being a lesbian. "You can trust me, okay? You didn't do anything wrong. I just want to talk more about Adam, because, frankly, what you wrote about him and your cousin . . . what's her name again?" She leafed through the pages, and turned her head sideways to read the back sides.

"DeeDee." I crossed my arms and looked out the window, waiting for this to be over.

"Right, DeeDee." She put the paper on her lap and gave me her full attention. "What you wrote about him, what you might have seen, is something you should probably tell your parents about."

I nodded, trying to hold in tears. I hadn't talked to anyone about it except for DeeDee in a roundabout way, and it felt as if a door was finally creaking open, but it was hard to look.

"Now, I have to ask you this, and don't be afraid to tell me, because for right now, everything here is just between you and me, but did he ever try to do anything like this to you?"

"Nope," I said. "Just her. Just that one time with DeeDee, I think. And I don't really even know what happened."

"You're sure?" she said, and threw her long hair over her shoulder. "He never tried anything with you?"

"He really didn't, " I said. "I would tell you." I finally got the nerve to make eye contact with her again, and saw that, in a new way, her eyes also had a green cast, like a weedy lake. The oily shine had also developed on the center of her forehead from a long day's work.

"Well, now that I know that," she said, crossing her legs and appearing to relax, "I have to tell you something. As a teacher, I'm required by law to report this, what you wrote here—" She held up the paper again and shook it, and I wished I'd never written it. What could I have been thinking? "I'm going to report it first to the principal, and then she'll report it—and I know this might be kind of hard for you—but your mother and father will need to know, too, and Adam will be brought in for a talk." She leaned an elbow on the desk. "I don't know what'll happen then. Maybe he'll get counseling."

"I see," I said, and fast-forwarded with horror to what Adam might do to me when all this was over. I could see him creeping out of the apartment, wandering over to the house, and getting me next while my father was at work.

"Your parents are separated if I'm not mistaken, isn't that right? I don't mean to be so nosy, but you know how it is around here. People talk."

"I know," I said, and began to feel friendlier toward her. "I don't know if they're officially separated, but my mom and dad live apart right now. But they still see each other. Except . . . well, my mom sort of has a boyfriend right now, and my dad's all depressed because the creamery got sold and it might close completely and turn into a big chain convenience store, and so I don't know. I worry about him. He's different now and . . . Everything's really hard now. I don't know what to do. It's just—I'm trying to . . ." And then the tears started to come and wouldn't stop. They had been building up for so long that I felt myself gasping and really bawling. I threw my arms down on my desk and buried my head in them, but then Ms. Rickhardt stood up and pulled me toward her. It seemed odd to be hugging my teacher, but she was so warm and understanding and kind that I simply let go and cried like I hadn't cried in months. Her thin body was not much to hold on to, and felt like a skeleton.

"There, it's all right. Ssh," she said, and we stood that way in the back of the classroom until I badly needed a tissue to wipe my nose. "Come over here," Ms. Rickhardt said, and walked up to her desk. She gave me a tissue and pulled a small red thermos out of a drawer, along with two paper cups from a basket brimming with herbal teas, napkins, plastic silverware, and hard candies. "Let's have some apple juice," she said, and poured me a big golden cupful. It had never tasted so good. My lips were puffy and numb from a hard cry, and the coolness felt refreshing.

Ms. Rickhardt sat on the edge of her desk, and I sat in her chair. "I just want you to know that Adam, if he really did something inappropriate, is going to be upset and maybe try to deny it. But you did the right thing by telling me. You know that, right?" Then she gulped her juice down to the bottom.

I sipped mine, still calming myself down. "But I shouldn't have said anything. I didn't mean to write all of that. I promised DeeDee I wouldn't tell anyone." My hands shook thinking about Adam's wiry little body and intense black eyes. "Plus, I'm afraid that if you say anything, Adam'll take it out on me. He's like that."

"Well, from what I read in your journal," Ms. Rickhardt said, "what you saw seemed entirely inappropriate to me. And I know you don't want me to say anything, but I have to. *Really,* Iris. This is serious." Then she gave me that sweet crooked smile, and popped a light green candy into her mouth, which smelled like spearmint.

But I worried. Adam had such a sneaky way of winning everyone over that they probably wouldn't even believe that he'd done anything wrong. What would Grandma Laura think? Or Aunt Patty? Maybe she'd never let DeeDee come over and hang out with me again. Maybe she'd think I was involved, too.

I pulled on my jacket and walked home slowly through the dry crunchy leaves. With my hands in felt-lined pockets, I stuck my chin in my collar to avoid the cold biting wind. It was getting dark earlier and earlier, and I wished more than anything that my mother would've been back home, a nice baked chicken in the oven, some whipped potatoes in a pot, a glass of red wine in her hand. She would've been nibbling at the hunk of cheese she always used to keep under a small glass dome. "Hi, honey," she would've said to me as I walked in cold and red-cheeked. "Some cheese?" And she would've chopped off a little corner of sharp cheddar and placed it on my tongue. I would've closed my mouth and let it melt there like cream, like a gift of love, and gone to her and said, "Stay here like this with me forever."

By the time I got home, there was a much deeper chill in the air and the outside light was not on, which it almost always was. I detected a faint light on in the kitchen, but the rest of the house seemed closed up and dead. Maybe my father really was ill, I thought, and when I didn't find him in the living room or kitchen, I padded immediately up to his bedroom to see if he needed anything. The bed was messed up a little, but not unmade, so I checked all the other rooms. The bathroom was dark, as were my room and Adam's room. Downstairs, I looked for clues to see if he'd decided to go into work or if he was somewhere else. The TV room was very tidy, with the weekly guide placed directly on top of the set the way my mother liked it, and the footstool perfectly set in front of the blue chair. The dining room was empty and dark, although I did find a small stack of mail on the table, though nothing exciting: a MasterCard bill, water bill, Mutual of Omaha bill. In the kitchen, I opened the refrigerator to see if there was any new food because we were actually running kind of low, but there was the same old collection of condiments, leftovers, a plate of cold chicken, and milk . . . which, for the first time, I realized, was not my father's milk in a glass bottle with a pleated foil top, but a regular paper carton from the supermarket.

The door to the basement was open, and since he sometimes went down there to work on projects like making bird feeders or planing off a piece of a warped bedroom door so it didn't stick, I flicked on the light, stomped down a few stairs, and hollered, "Dad!" since his workroom was off to the right, behind the water heater and furnace, and he didn't always hear me. I checked to see if his work light was on, but it wasn't. I almost turned around to leave, but saw his shoes there. His tennis shoes, white leather, worn and stretched out on the sides because of his wide feet, sat in the middle of the floor, right in front of the old, musty red couch. I went and picked them up, then saw him around the corner. He was lying on the floor on his side with his arms thrown up to his face. There was a lot of blood, and I saw his hunting rifle just a few feet away. For a minute, it didn't seem real, and I supposed I was in shock or something because I walked right up to him and shook his pant leg. "Dad?" I shook his leg harder, and his whole body felt heavy and dense. I looked around dumbly. On an old stained table where we kept the laundry soap was a tiny piece of notebook paper folded in half. I grabbed it and read, barely breathing. "I'm sorry. Please forgive me," it said.

I dropped the note and stood there, wetting myself. The warm pee slid hot down my pant legs, and the corduroy felt like rich velvet as it soaked up the urine. I could feel it sink into my right shoe, and then, without thinking, I grabbed my father's shoes and ran silently to my mother's apartment, five blocks away, where I found her in the living room, folding towels and watching TV. Food burbled on the stove—split pea soup with a ham hock. Adam sat at the table reading a motocross magazine, and waved to me instead of saying hi. I ran across the room to my mother, and she said, "Iris. Did a ghost get you? What's the matter?" I tried to talk and to tell her, but nothing came out, and I was afraid I'd gone mute. I stood there with my mouth open.

"What is it, honey? Did something happen?" She set the green and pink towels aside and pulled me to her, half sitting me on her lap, even though I was almost the same size as her.

Then I spilled my father's shoes out in front of her, and she knew; I could see that instantly she knew.

GRANDMA LAURA ARRIVED LATE that Friday evening and found us all up in the apartment above Dana's, my mother drinking cup after cup of coffee. After the police and medical examiner had declared the death an apparent suicide and had taken his body away (they phoned her constantly to update her on the process), my mother whisked Adam and me back to the house, and there we watched her nosing around, as if for clues, until late into the night. She had her hands on every letter, every bill, every envelope, what channel the TV was on, what dirty clothes he'd left behind, what food was in the refrigerator—as if any of these things might've provided a clue as to why he'd done it, might've taken away from the terrible guilt and pain she must've felt. No one really went to sleep that night, except for Grandma Laura, who had arrived at the house later, and had dozed off in a chair, her coat still on.

Adam and I trailed after our mother like good little children who wanted to help but didn't know how. I stood at their bedroom window and watched the sun come up in a lavender mist. Frost coated the yard. A big maroon car pulled up to the curb, and the paperboy, Ryan Newberg, ran out and threw the *St. Paul Pioneer Press* onto our doorstep, then ran back to the car, where it drove him up to the next house, leaving a trail of exhaust lingering in the cold air. I envied how cared for and loved he was to have a parent drive him on his route on such a cold Saturday morning. Sighing,

I turned back to my parents' bedroom and noticed my father had left his eyeglasses folded up on the end table on his side of the bed. I picked them up, put them on, and watched the whole world outside the window in a kaleidoscope blur.

When the sun had finally risen, I went downstairs and found my mother in the entryway, where all our coats hung on hooks and a big decoupaged milk can held our scarves and mittens and hats. She pulled a crumpled grocery list out of my father's coat pocket, and as I stood there looking at her, she screamed, "You don't have to tell me it's all my fault! I know it! Don't look at me like that—I know it and I take all the blame! Isn't that what you want me to say?" until Grandma Laura and Aunt Patty, who had just arrived with Melanie and DeeDee and Uncle Robert, took her by the arms and made her sit down in front of a cup of herbal tea.

Uncle Robert, who was hardly ever affectionate with me, took me by the hand and made me sit on the couch next to him and DeeDee. He was still dressed up from work and wore a navy-blue suit and a diagonally striped silver tie and crisp white shirt. "You can't take anything she says to heart right now. She didn't mean it. She's in a state of shock, and this is very hard for everyone." He put his arm around me, and DeeDee nodded alongside him. Uncle Robert was the one who eventually started making everyone blueberry pancakes, and although my stomach was still trembling, I accepted two small ones on my plate, smoothed a swipe of butter on top of them, and watched it melt into a soft white smear. This may've been my father's last butter, and I didn't even put syrup on so I could taste the sweet creaminess of it.

Adam sat beside me and was strangely quiet. Our silverware clanking against our plates was the only sound heard. I stared over at him as I ate—tiny bite by tiny bite was all I could manage—and began to think that ever since Adam had come into our family, there'd been an endless run of trouble, and maybe, in a way, he was the one who had killed my father—in a way. Grandma Laura sat looking at us as if we'd break, and I began to fantasize about living with her in Mankato for the rest of my life. Adam could have my mother, who seemed to be taking everything out on me, and I decided I would never come back to Wishbone as long as I lived. This seemed like the best plan of all for the time being.

At around noon, Aunt Deb and the boys arrived, carrying bags of food. She held a frothy green Jell-O salad in a copper-colored mold—ambrosia, my favorite. Noel, my favorite cousin, lugged in a big bundle of sleeping bags, and for a second it seemed like a blast to have everyone here for a slumber party. He came up to me and set a hand on my shoulder. "You doing okay?" he said in his raspy voice like an old man's. I nodded and swallowed, afraid to speak.

Carter and David also came over and gave me little kisses on the cheek, then drifted uncomfortably into the living room with the others, not knowing what else to do. Aunt Deb threw her arms around me from behind, and I could smell her Juicy Fruit gum, warm and familiar on her breath. "How you doing, sweetie?" she said, and the best I could get out was, "Okay."

The telephone rang nonstop all day, and we spent the afternoon eating Special K bars and blarney bars, which my Grandma Laura always made. They had a springy white cake bottom, creamy toffee frosting, and salted peanuts with the papery red husks still attached sprinkled on top. Everyone watched football in the family room, and somehow it was decided and announced by the women at the dining room table that the funeral would be on Monday. This was the proper, acceptable amount of time for the body to be embalmed, dressed, and readied for the viewing, they said. The wake would be the evening before, Sunday night, and I wondered, Why did they call it a wake?

It was true that my mother did seem like the villain. Even though everyone was being very supportive and holding her close and drying her tears, there was no denying a sense of blame toward her. I could especially sense it from my two aunts, even though they hadn't said anything to make me believe so. It was more of a chilled look in the eyes, and a curiosity about what had made her run around with a college freshman when she was a married woman with two children and a decent husband. But I also thought back to the miscarriages and how hard it must've been for my mother to weed through all of that, and maybe, just maybe, there was no one to blame.

My father hadn't been as close to his family as my mother was to hers—or that was what I'd grown up listening to my mother tell everyone. His parents, who'd owned a good-sized dairy farm, had both died in a car accident about seven years ago, and he had two brothers who lived just outside of Madison, Wisconsin—Richard and Kenny. Even though it was only a five-hour drive, we rarely saw them unless it was a special occasion. I still remembered my Grandma Kauffman pretty well, although I'd been just five years old when she'd died. Unlike my Grandma Laura, who still had a good figure and wore fashionable clothes and knew about current movies and music, Grandma Kauffman (her name was Ellen, but we'd never once called her that) had been a chubby, white-haired grandma who got her hair set in tiny puffy curls every Saturday at the local salon. She'd often wander around the farm wearing a big, flowered work smock that tied in the back, and she'd have things like fresh eggs and interesting-shaped rocks and little sprigs of fresh mint in her pocket. She hobbled on one leg from a horseback-riding accident she'd had as a teenager, and her hands shook when she'd try to zip me into my lilac Windbreaker, insisting that I have the hood tied tightly around my little face. "Oh, you, you're so cute," she'd always tell me. "You're my little peanut." Her big, solid body radiated love, and I could still taste the dark, sweet curl of fudge that she'd let me lick out of the saucepan, ever so slightly hardened on the wooden spoon.

Grandpa Kauffman (whose real name was Elmer, though we also never used that name) had been a tall man with pale blue eyes just like my father's, who always, without fail, wore striped overalls with a blue chambray work shirt underneath. The only exception was on Sundays for church, or an occasional holiday, when he'd slip into one of his many pastel short-sleeve button-ups—mint green, pink, peach, powder blue, soft yellow. He'd wear them with the solid outline of a white T-shirt underneath, and I'd always find it odd to see him hatless, since most days, out in the barn, he would wear his Purina feed hat with its red-and-white checkered logo. He was silent and hardworking and let my grandma do all the talking and Christmas gift buying and family business, but I remembered sitting on his lap one Christmas and the delicate way he'd held my hand up to see the pale watery red polish my mother had let me wear. It was all smeared around on my cuticles and knuckles, but he'd said, softly, "Say, now, aren't you quite the lady." I remembered because I looked down, shy, at my little hand in his big, gnarled, red one. His finger pads were so calloused from work they were slick and hard like plastic, with sharp edges, but I was delighted simply because he had noticed.

They were hit head-on by a nineteen-year-old drunk driver barreling down the wrong side of I-90. They'd only been in their early sixties, and had left behind three grown sons and a herd of two hundred dairy cows with bloated teats and no one to tend them.

LATER IN THE AFTERNOON when I came out of the bathroom, my mother was standing right outside the door. She had finally taken a shower and dressed herself in tan bell-bottoms and a dark green turtleneck sweater. She looked very nice with her hair longer now and pulled away from her face, and she had even put on earrings— big gold hoops. Her eyes were still puffy and red, though, and her eyelids were bloated and looked as if they were filled with water. I noticed she didn't have any makeup on, and looked young, freshly scrubbed, washed out. "Iris, come here, honey," she said, and led me into my bedroom. We sat on the bed together, and she kicked the door shut with her foot. She took my two hands in hers.

"I'm sorry. I really didn't know what I was saying before—it was all such a shock. . . ." She faded off, and when she looked out the window, the light reflected off the big circles of her eyeglasses and I couldn't see her eyes. She turned back to me, and I could see how the dark green of her sweater brought out her eyes. Instead of the pinched light green they usually were, they looked deep and mossy, and the pupil was the sharpest, clearest pinhole of black I'd ever seen.

"It's okay," I said. I wanted to make her feel better, even though it seemed there was little chance for repair between us without my father around to bind us together.

"You saw him in the morning, right?" she asked, and kept my hands tightly in hers. My room was messy with comic books and discarded clothes and a bag of potato chips I'd been eating a couple nights before. I was sure my mother hated that I'd been eating in my room; she'd never let me before.

"Yeah, he called in sick to work," I said, and thought back to him loitering in the kitchen in his pajamas, which he would've never done on a workday. Even on Saturdays, he was typically up and dressed and unclogging some gutter or raking leaves or reading the paper, but always dressed in a nice soft flannel shirt, khakis, and white tennis shoes.

"And so how did he seem? Did he say anything unusual?" She let go of my hands, and I leaned back against the headboard of my bed, thinking. My mother pulled her feet up, shoes and all, and sat cross-legged, her back arched straight. "Did he say anything that would give a clue why he might do something like this?" She wanted so badly for me to tell her why this had happened, but I had no idea. I had seen no secret clues.

I studied the ceiling and tried to remember. I thought of the carton of store-bought milk, but didn't mention it. I tapped my fingers against my lips, which were chapped and dry, and tried to give her as much as I could. "He called Verne Ott at the store and said he was coming down with the flu and couldn't come in, and I remember thinking that it sounded like he wasn't really sick but was trying to sound sick. He smoked a lot of cigarettes, and he just seemed kind of down." I tried to keep my voice steady and calm, even though it hurt to go back again to those last moments I would ever have with him. I remembered how frustrated he would get with me when he'd come and find me playing dead under my bed.

My mother's eyes started to glaze over with tears when I told her he had still been in his pajamas, even though, I remembered clearly, he'd been dressed when I found him in the basement, though I couldn't remember what he wore—just the stocking feet stood out in my mind.

My mother sniffled. She smoothed my hair back from my face, then dropped her hand on the bed helplessly. "Did he—" Her voice cracked. "Did he say anything about . . . me?" She held a hand up over her eyes, as if shielding herself.

"No."

"Did he—ever?"

"Not too much," I said, and I knew this would somehow break her heart, just as she had broken his. My answer made her cry harder, and I watched her shoulders literally shake up and down. "Oh, Iris," she said, out of breath, "it's not my fault, is it? It can't be my fault, right?"

"It's not your fault," I said. Then, without discussing it, we both lay down on the bed. She cupped herself around me, and I curled my arms up to my chest. My west window let in the fading afternoon light, and I felt my mother pulling me even closer to her so that I could feel her heart beating against my back. Eventually I felt her muscles start to relax and twitch as sleep finally came. She had been up all night, and so had I, but I was unable to surrender yet, and lay there, guarded, stiff, waiting for something to clear out the shadows of growing darkness.

THE WAKE WAS SUNDAY AFTERNOON, and we all drove up to Rolf's Funeral Home in a huge car caravan—Aunt Patty and Uncle Robert in one car; Aunt Deb and the boys in one car; Grandma Laura, my mother, Adam, and me in one car; and three separate cars of my father's relatives, all of which were big expensive-looking luxury cars coated with dust. When we arrived no one was there yet, and the place had a rich, though dreary, ancient smell. Suddenly two double doors opened, and I watched Mr. Rolf wheel the shiny black coffin in. In front of the wide, richly carpeted receiving room, Mr. Rolf opened the coffin and nodded to my mother for us to approach. She had shunned the usual black, and wore instead a gray wool dress with a wide black belt around the middle. I had on a dark flowered dress that went down over my knees, and Adam wore a tie that was just a clip-on. We looked, but we didn't know how to react, partly, I thought, because it was such a curiosity to see him there, so unreal. His nose looked sharp and refined, and without his glasses on, he seemed softer, younger. He was in a brown suit, the only one he owned, and his smooth hands were pale and folded over one another very politely. He still wore his wedding ring. We peeked in for just a few seconds. I couldn't imagine how they had managed to make him look so good after what I'd seen of him in the basement. I whispered, "Good-bye," and tried not to pay attention to Adam or my mother crying. Then we walked back to the receiving chairs set up for us in the back of the room. I got through it all remarkably well.

But what I was not prepared for were all the people who arrived clutching Kleenexes and purses, placing cards in white envelopes in a basket, kissing my mother and all of us so tentatively and dearly. Then it started to be difficult, and a huge egg of grief lodged in my throat and ached. Sylvie walked in with her mom and sister, made a beeline for me, hugged me breathlessly, then started to cry. "I'll come over," she said. "I kept trying to come over yesterday, but I knew I couldn't stop crying. Even now, look—"

Then all of my classmates filed in, some with parents, some alone, some in groups: Jenine, Carla, and Jennifer, carrying little vases of roses; Denise and Katie with cards; Bill Dutton from my stupid vocabulary group; Verne Ott. Practically everyone in town must've known my father and liked him, because the place was packed. Even Ms. Rickhardt showed up, carrying a huge bouquet of daisies, and I introduced her to my mother, who was now operating on remote control. She looked at the daisies kind of funny, because most people had brought somber, autumn-colored flowers. "You have a wonderful, gifted daughter," Ms. Rickhardt said to my mother, then pressed a small pink card into my hands. I couldn't wait to open it, and excused myself for the bathroom after she had gone off to talk to some of the other students.

It was a small card with a purple watercolor iris on the front. Tears sprouted in my eyes before I even read it.

Dear Iris,

I'm very sorry for your loss. My father died when I was about your age, and since then, I have never been the same. I don't know if you were close or not, but no matter what, it will do something to you and make you much older than you already are. A suicide is the hardest, because it will always leave you wondering what went wrong, what *you* may have done wrong. But, Iris, you did nothing wrong. I want you to know that since this tragedy has happened, I will, of course, put the issue of your brother, Adam, on hold until a later time, or until you want to talk about it. You obviously have enough to deal with right now, and I want you to keep writing down your feelings, because you are a beautiful writer. I'm always here if you need me.

Yours,
Gloria Rickhardt

I hadn't even known her first name—Gloria. I held the beautiful card up to my heart and breathed deeply. There was more sense in that card than in anything else that was happening at the wake. I went into a bathroom stall, and read it again and again, and felt a surge of importance and hope. I sat down on one of the toilets, which had a small blue toilet mint hanging in its rim, and fingered the elegant paper.

Then I heard the door creak open. "Iris? Are you in here? Are you okay, honey?" It was Grandma Laura, light-footed and heavy with Estée Lauder. I put the card back in its envelope and let her lead me back out.

Eventually, the wake was over, and we went back home for coffee and bars; the night wore on. We did it all again the next day at the funeral, only that time my father was lowered into the ground forever, and afterwards, everyone drove home to where they belonged, leaving the big house quiet and empty with just three of us to fill it.

Chapter Ten

Memory: We're standing in her office while the water boils for tea. My mother hands me pages of the book she's been writing.

"Take this," she says. "I'll probably never finish anyway."

I hold the thick stack of papers in my hand. It's bound together with a big rubber band from the creamery.

"There are things in here," she says, "you should probably know. Someday."

I hold them to my chest. I can already feel her words piercing my heart before I even read them.

Somehow we made it through the weeks that followed. My mother had quickly moved herself and Adam back into the big house with me, and I was grateful. She'd even taken all my father's clothes from the closet and stuffed them in garbage bags for Goodwill. It was a time of cleaning out, of stumbling over the past, and going forward. Adam moved back into the bedroom two doors down from mine, and every night, although he'd been silent and sweet since our father had died, I closed my door tightly and thought of what he'd done to DeeDee. I was still planning to tell on him—when all of this blew over, when we ever just settled down to normal lives again, if that was even possible.

Winter had moved in early so that by the end of November we were surrounded by knee-deep, rock-hard snowbanks that had nearly become chunks of ice. But I liked winter. I liked the feeling of working to stay warm and not feeling obligated to go out and enjoy the weather all the time. When I was little, I remembered my mother prodding me to go out on sunny summer days and dig around in the sandbox with my little pail and shovel, even though I preferred the cool, quiet peace of reading or drawing at her big, smooth desk. "Iris, it's too nice outside for you to be cooped up in here all day. Why don't you go out and do something? You should go out and get some sun. You're too pale." Now I liked to sit on the couch and look at the dark, icy street as cars crept down it. I liked that it got dark early so that sometimes the sky was navy blue, then close to black when I dawdled home from school with Sylvie.

Sylvie and I had been back together ever since my father died. Even though it had been hard at first, she came over all the time, despite my mother's crying fits and the general chaos of our days. Right after he'd died, I found myself, in the middle of talking to Sylvie about people in school or boys we thought were cute, crying without any warning. She would hold me and pat me on the back in her awkward way, but then she was always very good at distracting me somehow. "Let's organize your sock drawer, or let's make a list of all the people we can't stand," Sylvie would say, and I'd go along with her, drying my eyes on my shirtsleeves.

One Saturday, Sylvie and I were up in my room trying on some of my clothes, and I realized again that she had a bra on. I'd noticed it before, but this time I actually saw it when she took her shirt off. It was a white stretch lace thing with a tiny rosebud appliqué in the middle of two triangle-shaped panels. Her breasts weren't very big, but the bra seemed to make the pointy shapes rounder. "What?" she said. "My mom said it was about time I got one. She's been through it with my older sisters and just drove me up to the store and picked it right out."

"In town here?" I asked as I tried to hide my own small breasts that were like hard nuggets and pointed downwards. The left one was bigger than the right one, and the nipples seemed too large. I turned my back as I slipped out of a blue-and-white striped rugby shirt so Sylvie wouldn't see them. "Weren't you afraid somebody would come in and see you? How embarrassing."

"No one did," Sylvie said, throwing a pink turtleneck on my rocker. "It's no big deal. You should probably get one, too, you know. You kind of need it." She glanced at me over her shoulder, and I noticed how white and veiny and pale she was. Blue veins squiggled all over her tiny, narrow back. As she got taller, she was also getting thinner and more beautiful, too. Her sharp chin and jawline were her best features, and her high cheekbones made her dark eyes look big and intelligent, just like her mother. For the first time, I felt a flicker of jealousy and imagined myself a washed-out shadow of Sylvie for the upcoming endless duration of high school. "Well?" Sylvie asked me.

"What?" I put a big blue T-shirt on and pulled on a tan cardigan sweater that my Grandma Laura had given me.

"I said you should get a bra. You're kind of bouncing around," Sylvie said. She got back into her own clothes—a red turtleneck underneath a black sweater with snowflakes on it. I knew for a fact the sweater was a hand-me-down from her older sister Jayne, because Jayne used to wear it all the time and even wore it on yearbook pictures day. It was in all the group shots of FHA, choir, yearbook staff, and Spanish club. Now it was all pilled and had a long snagged piece of yarn coming out the elbow. "Doesn't your mom notice or anything? That's what moms are supposed to do."

"Ha," I said, and flopped down on the bed. "Not my mom. She only just had her husband commit suicide, and she only just has a boyfriend fresh out of high school. She doesn't notice anything I do. I could die for all she cared."

Sylvie lay on the bed next to me, her head at the opposite end. She grabbed my foot and shook it. "Oh, stop being so melodramatic.

She cares about you. She's just got a lot on her mind."

"Obviously." I kicked my feet up onto the wall and let the blood rush out of them. "She's always had a lot on her mind. I bet she wishes she would've never even adopted me or Adam so she could just live her life and do whatever she wants to."

Sylvie rolled off the side of the bed and jumped to her feet. "We have to get you out of here. You're getting too whiny for your own good. Come on."

"What do you want to do?" I asked, leery.

"Let's go up to Chester's and get you a bra."

"No way!" I said, but I knew there was no stopping her now. Plus, ever since she'd mentioned my breasts, they seemed to have grown huge in my mind, and I had to keep walking around with my arms crossed over my chest to cover them.

My mother was sitting on a stool hunched over the phone when we walked in to say we were leaving. She didn't say anything or ask where we were off to, but gave us a quick wave, then got back to her call. Adam was nowhere to be seen.

Sylvie's coat used to be a nice red ski jacket with geometric green, yellow, and blue inserts at the sides, but now it had a big white bleach spot on it. I knew Sylvie was embarrassed about it, but her family couldn't afford to buy her a new one until that one wore out. I felt kind of sorry for her because although my family had never had a lot of money, I always—through Grandma Laura or my cousins—managed to have very nice clothes.

"How much money do you have?" Sylvie was always the wise, street-smart one who knew how much bras were, knew how to French-kiss, knew where girls in high school went to get abortions. This was the advantage of being in a large family, unlike me, having grown up practically by myself, knowing nothing. There'd never been any chaos or commotion to teach me, at least not until lately.

"I've got about fifteen bucks. Grandma Laura gave me another ten dollars last time I saw her. I was supposed to give Adam half, but I forgot. He'll never even know."

"That'll be plenty." Sylvie slipped her rainbow-striped scarf over her mouth and nose. It was so bitter cold it hurt to breathe. We took the shortcut downtown, which wasn't really that much of a shortcut, but just meant you didn't have to walk down all of Main Street to get there. We cut through State Street, then crossed over the railroad tracks, then maneuvered through the cement works. I hated walking that part because there were always forklifts driving around beeping with a million stacks of concrete blocks on them, the drivers all bundled up in insulated coveralls trying to keep warm. After that was the public school, and I could see the big glass doors of the swimming pool were all steamed up, probably beginner's lessons or water aerobics.

Our boots crunched through iced-over puddles, and for part of the walk, we slid across solid patches of ice with our hands clasped behind our backs, like Olympic speed skaters, who always looked like Spider-Man to me in their slick little zip-up, hooded suits.

"So, what's up with your mom and her boyfriend? Have you seen him around much?" Sylvie asked as we took a side street up past Warner's Cafe, where all the old men gathered on Saturday mornings for eggs and coffee. The place was always full of cigarette smoke and newspapers rattling, and they lingered around until it was time for lunch, then played round after round of Sheepshead, a card game I'd grown up hearing about but had no idea how to play.

"I don't know what she's doing with him," I said, and tiptoed up to peer in the cafe window just to see who was in there. "I've seen him driving by our house a lot on weekends, but the only time I've ever seen him in our house was two weekends ago, late on a Saturday night when I was getting up to watch TV because I couldn't sleep. He and my mom were sitting on the couch, and when I walked in I just stared, totally confused. She introduced me to him and everything as her *friend*, but I didn't stay. I turned around and went right back to my room."

"You'd think she'd have broken it off with him since your dad died," Sylvie said as we turned the corner onto Main. Lots of cars were pulled into the diagonal parking slots, despite the cold weather and warning of a possible blizzard. I thought they must've been stocking up on canned foods and candles before the storm, but mostly they seemed to be socializing outside of the stores, complaining about how cold it was and how much snow we'd had. We walked past the drugstore, then Ben Franklin, which I remembered my father saying would be the next store to go. He said it would be taken over by a big chain, just like everything else in Wishbone would be eventually. Maybe that was part of the reason he didn't want to live anymore. He'd loved Wishbone the way it was, and hated to see it changing into city ways.

"I think my mother feels guilty, but what can she do? She can't bring back my father. Although you'd think she could find somebody more her age."

"No kidding," Sylvie said. We had arrived at Chester's, the only real clothing store in town. In the windows were very old, outdated mannequins with molded Ken doll hair and deeply tan skin with seams where the plastic parts had been fit together. The clothing advertised was pretty out of it. They only had Wrangler jeans, no Levi's, and mainly solid-color polyester shirts and sweaters. The old-fashioned bell rang above the door as we entered. First were the baby clothes, followed by the men's clothing section, which was always fully stocked because of all the farmers. Stacks of hard, crisp overalls, which seemed like they'd never lose their creases, were stacked high on metal racks. The same for chambray work shirts, painter's pants, suspenders in red, white, or black, T-shirts by the five-pack in V-neck, crew, or tank, and a nice assortment of various work hats and bandanas. In the back, they had fabric and notions, the section where my mother went immediately when she used to love to sew me outfits out of calico and checks, but that hobby of hers had faded sometime between kindergarten and first grade. I could still remember the last thing she'd made me—a tiny brown-and-white checked dress with gathers at the chest, capped sleeves, and perfect, tiny pearly buttons going down the back. That was also the first year I'd gotten my hair cut short and wore it in a blunt, swingy bob with straight, feathery bangs. Two yellow butterfly barrettes were clipped high up on either side of my temples. I remembered my mother wetting my bangs down with a comb then pressing with her fingers so that they stayed straight.

The women's clothing section was off in its own little alcove on the right. It was painted white, had high ceilings, and two dressing rooms on either end. It was crammed tight with racks of pants, skirts, dresses, blouses, and sweaters. On one wall there were boxes of bras hanging on hooks with photos of women with no faces on the front. Not a big selection, and I whispered to Sylvie, "Which one?"

Sylvie ruffled through boxes, acting like she knew what to do, but soon the salesclerk came over, Mrs. Scheffer, who went to St. Luke's Lutheran Church where we used to go to. "You girls need any help?" she asked, and then stood there, with permed red hair and droopy eyelids, leaning on a rack of pants.

"Just looking," I said, browsing through some sweaters.

"Say, how's your mother doing?" Mrs. Scheffer asked, then began studying her long red fingernails.

"She's doing pretty good," I said. "As well as can be expected." It was a phrase I'd heard Grandma Laura use whenever people asked her how she was doing, and I thought it worked well to remind people that we'd just had someone die in our family. I glanced at Sylvie, but she was way in the back of the room, stalling.

Mrs. Scheffer wouldn't let up. "We miss you in church. We've said a lot of prayers for your father and for your family. God knows, you must miss your father. I'm so sorry, honey." Everything she said dripped with phoniness, and I looked up suspiciously into her hooded eyes. In catechism class we'd learned that if you committed suicide you went to hell. Ever since I'd learned that, there were a lot of things I suddenly didn't know if I believed. My mother didn't like the church because only men were allowed to vote on things, and she thought that wasn't fair. Just like Ms. Rickhardt, my mother was fast becoming a "Women's Libber." She'd recently stopped shaving her legs and armpits, and even Sylvie thought that was going too far. My father had been only a little religious, and I was more than happy to sleep in on Sundays and read in my bed until I smelled bacon and eggs downstairs.

"Well, thanks," I said, forcing myself to be polite. I could tell she wanted to keep asking me questions, probably pumping me for good gossip, so I tried to get away. "So, I guess we're just going to look around a little."

"All-righty," she said, putting on her glasses, which hung around her neck on a gold chain. Her red dress with tiny black polka dots all over it looked decades out of style. "If you're looking for brassieres, there's some teen ones over in here." She pointed to a deep, metal drawer, and I wondered why they had to make such a big deal of hiding them when the big women's ones were out for all to see.

I sidled over to Sylvie and said, "Sylvie, come on. Let's get this over with before someone comes in." We rooted around in the metal drawer until Sylvie found me one like hers in size 28AA. I brought the flimsy Bestform box with me to the dressing room while Sylvie stood guard. There was nothing much to it but a band of soft spongy cotton and a pulley of solid elastic at the back where it hooked. I clamped it on around my stomach first, then spun it around and pulled it up over my small, hard breasts. There was a cute little satin triangle in the middle of it, which gave it shape, but it felt tight and suffocating when I inhaled.

Sylvie knocked on the door lightly. "How is it?"

"Tight," I said.

"Well, let me see." I cracked the door open and made her have to struggle to get in. She inspected, front then back. "Nope. It looks right. That's how mine is. It's supposed to be tight, only you can loosen it a little in the back. Here." She moved it over two notches and I could breathe easier. "How much is it?"

I looked at the price sticker on the box. "Seven ninety-nine. Should I get it? What will my mother say?" With my back to Sylvie, I slipped it off and shoved it into a ball and into the box. It was still warm from my body.

We made a speedy purchase, trying to ignore Mrs. Scheffer's stifled amusement. She seemed to take a deliberately long time ringing it up, removing the price tag, and wrapping it up in a big flat brown bag, which she folded in half. "Thank you much, girls," she said, then looked at her watch.

We rushed down the street to Warner's Cafe where some of the men were still playing Sheepshead at a back table. There was a large knotty pine women's bathroom in back, and in one of the stalls I whipped up my shirt, hooked the bra around me, whipped my shirt back on, then disposed of all the packaging, receipt, and the bag in the garbage can. I shoved it way down, and then threw some balled-up paper towels on it just to be sure.

Sylvie and I sat there and had two Orange Crushes with ice and shared a slice of cherry pie between us on an old green-rimmed cafeteria plate. Outside, it began to snow, then sleet, then snow again. "Now what do you want to do?" Sylvie said, slurping every last drop out with her straw. "This town's a bore."

I knew this was a line she'd picked up from Carla and Jennifer, and I rolled my eyes. "Wanna go to your house?" I asked, since there was always action of some kind over there. Usually her mom was cooking some big feast of cookies or stew or making bread dough ornaments in the oven and painting them with melted suckers.

"Okay," she said, and we bundled up again to face the weather outside. As we walked down Main Street, I swore I saw my mother inside a red two-door car, and suddenly she saw me, leaned over to the driver's side, beeped the horn, and must've made the driver pull over. "You guys want a ride?" she said, and I could see her boyfriend, Ronny Nelson, behind her. The car smelled like pine air freshener, and I saw he had about five hanging off the radio knob. "It's freezing."

I shrugged my shoulders, feigning indifference, and Sylvie and I got into the black-fur backseat. The car was warm and stuffy, and Ronny turned down the volume of the tinny rock. "So where were you guys heading?" I asked, trying to be both polite and mean at the same time.

"Just cruising," my mother said, a word completely new to her vocabulary. Only high schoolers said that, much less *did* it, and I couldn't believe she wasn't embarrassed.

After a short uncomfortable silence, Ronny cranked his head back a little and asked, "So, how do you two like school?" He was working very hard at being chummy.

"Oh, we love it," I said, then asked to be dropped off at Sylvie's. I had nothing more to say to either of them and asked Sylvie, whispering, if I could stay overnight. Throughout the entire conversation, I was focused on my bra and its gripping little elastic holding me in. Finally, Ronnie pulled up to Sylvie's big, white house. Snow swirled lightly on the street and began to collect against the curb.

"Well, good-bye, Mother," I said. "Good-bye, *Ron-ny*."

"Ciao," Sylvie said. We stood in the middle of the street, now glazed and slippery with ice, and watched them drive away.

INSIDE SYLVIE'S HOUSE IT WAS WARM and steamy and smelled like broccoli. The windows were fogged up, and we quickly peeled off our layers and threw them on the couch in the living room.

"Mom?" Sylvie shouted, then turned to me. "Just stay here a sec. I'll ask." She went into the kitchen while I waited on the couch, feeling like everybody's charity case. I heard her ask her mom if I could stay overnight, and of course her mom, Elizabeth, said yes. Sylvie came running back into the living room in her stocking feet. "You can," she said, and we settled down on the couch to watch reruns of *Three's Company*. As usual, I craved having hair like Suzanne Somers, who wore a long, blond ponytail out the side of her head. My hair was damp and musty-smelling from being scrunched up under a stocking cap all afternoon.

"I made out with Adam," Sylvie said out of the blue. She wouldn't look at me but stared at the TV screen.

I sat up, alert. "You what?"

"You heard me," she said, and flashed her big brown eyes at me. She picked at a hole in her socks. "It was no big deal. We just kissed and stuff. Kind of a dare thing. At a party Carla had one time. But I always thought somehow I should tell you."

"But—" I started, then realized I didn't know what to say. Suddenly, the television beeped, and an emergency weather alert scrolled across the bottom of the screen, interrupting the program. BLIZZARD CONDITIONS EXPECTED ACROSS THE FIVE COUNTY REGION. BLOWING, DRIFTING SNOW, WINDS EXPECTED AT 30–40 MPH, FREEZING TEMPERATURES. THIS AREA INCLUDES LE SUEUR, NICOLLET, SIBLEY, BROWN, AND BLUE EARTH COUNTIES. NO UNNECESSARY TRAVEL REPEAT NO UNNECESSARY TRAVEL UNDER ANY CIRCUMSTANCES.

"Cool," Sylvie said. "No school on Monday, I bet." She pulled an afghan from off the back of the couch and tossed it over us. It had orange, cream, and brown wavy stripes and smelled like cinnamon and old wool.

"So when were you with Adam?" I asked, not ready to let her off the hook yet.

Sylvie shrugged. "I don't know. It was awhile ago. Maybe over a month. I hope you're not mad."

"I'm not *mad*," I said. "Just surprised." I toyed with telling her about Adam and DeeDee, but simply couldn't. But I did want to make sure she wasn't planning to do it again. "So it was just that once? Just like a dare at some party?"

"Yeah," she said, the TV lights glowing off her eyes. "Just a stupid thing we did once. He still kind of irritates me. You know? He thinks he's so cool or something. So much better than everyone else."

I nodded, agreeing silently.

"But I kind of feel sorry for him, too," Sylvie said. "He seems so lonely."

I nodded again, agreeing with that, too.

"Girls!" Sylvie's mom shouted from the kitchen. "Are you hungry?"

"Yes!" Sylvie answered for both of us, and I followed her to the kitchen. Sylvie's sisters, Jayne and Janelle, were setting the table—big, brown soup crocks with tan stripes around the sides. Instead of napkins they folded paper towels in half and set big spoons on top of them to keep them flat.

"Hi, Iris," Sylvie's mom said, as she transferred the big kettle of soup from the stove top to the table. "You're definitely staying overnight here, because nobody's going anywhere in this storm."

"I know," I said, and slid into the seat against the wall. I always felt extraneous in their big family. Soon, the two little boys, Ryan and Joseph, came pounding down the stairs to eat, too. Sylvie poured everyone glasses of skim milk, which I could barely drink because of its lightness and blueness. I remembered my father saying skim milk was like colored water, like watered-down paint, and that we should refuse to drink it. But I drank mine, and tried to forget all of that for now.

The whole family said grace and I mumbled along, not knowing the words. The older girls, Janelle and Jayne, served the soup. "I hope you like broccoli and spinach," Janelle, the older one, said. "Sylvie here is such a little fussbudget she usually has to have her own little can of SpaghettiOs from the cupboard. Is that enough?" she asked me. "That's good," I said. "Thanks."

Sylvie piped up. "I like the soup! God, you always have to try and make me look bad in front of my friends." Sylvie stirred her soup and didn't look up, and I wondered why she was so upset, but then realized it was probably just a sister thing. I actually envied it.

It was a heavy cream of broccoli-spinach soup, and shreds of green swirled around the pale, white base. A yellowish skim of butter coated the top in little oily bubbles, and I stirred mine to try and mix it in. Sylvie's mom passed a basket of sliced bread around, and we all took a slice and dunked it in our soup. The boys wiped out their bowls with the bread and asked for more. They punched each other, and Ryan played fake drums on the table with his fingers while he was being served more. The soup was delicious, and I told Sylvie's mom that, too. I told her I loved it, that it was the best soup I'd ever had.

"Good, good. I always think that soup is so nourishing and good for people. It makes you feel loved, I think. Or safe. Something." She spooned up her last bite and seemed to relish it. I couldn't help but feel her comment was directed right at me. I needed love. I needed nourishment. I needed to feel safe while my mother was driving around on a date with her young boyfriend. I could tell they were trying to be extra nice to me and make me forget that my father was dead and my mother had all but abandoned me. I took another bite and tried to change the subject again to the weather, which everyone loved talking about on days like that.

For dessert we had instant pudding in small gray Tupperware cups. Sylvie's mom put on a pot of coffee, and she and the older girls drank cups of it with cream and sugar. If only I'd had a family like this, I thought, and looked at the bright reflections of everyone in the dark windows. If only it was still me, my mother, my father, all together in the big house like it used to be. Maybe Sylvie's family would adopt me, I thought, feeling a strong surge of hope rising in my chest. Maybe I could just come and live here and forget about my mother and Adam. But it would never happen. As we ate, the windows rattled and shook off and on as tiny, icy snow sprayed against them like sugar. Sometimes I thought of my father in the basement and could barely figure out how I'd get through the next minute.

After helping with the dishes, Sylvie and I watched some more TV with everyone, then I decided to call my mother so she wouldn't worry. I let it ring sixteen times, thinking at least Adam would answer, but no one picked up. I even tried the old number at the apartment above the salon, but got a recorded message that it had been disconnected. She was probably with her new boyfriend, Ronny, although I couldn't imagine he had his own place. He probably still stayed with his parents on their farm, but my mother certainly wouldn't go out there—at least I hoped not. But I wanted to call *somebody*, so I dialed up the creamery number just to see. Of course there was no answer, and I could imagine the big, black wall phone ringing endlessly right next to where the dairy cooler used to be. Right next to all our orders for real butter, real cream, huge tubs of ice cream with my father's Kauffman's Dairy label on the lids in red and black letters.

"Nobody home?" Sylvie said to me. She stood on the phone book, which was tossed on the floor, then acted like she was surfing on it.

I shrugged my shoulders.

"That's weird," she said. "Where would they be? Even Adam's not there?"

"Yeah," I said. "But I'm not worried. My mom's probably out whooping it up. It's no big deal." We headed upstairs, stepping over stacks of clean clothes and schoolbooks, and inside I felt fear, as if my mother had left me for good. With my father gone, she probably thought she could finally be who she wanted to be. It was just like I'd always thought from the moment they'd told me I was adopted: she didn't really want me. She wanted her own baby that would come from inside her. Maybe Ronny could help her make one that wouldn't die this time. Just thinking of it made me dizzy.

"Let's go listen to music," Sylvie said, and I followed her into her messy room. Dirty clothes lay all over her bed, on the floor, thrown over the furniture. She flipped on an Olivia Newton-John greatest hits record, and I started to get swoony and sad when she sang "Please, Mr., Please." Sylvie patted me on the back and told me to slip into one of her flannel nighties. I obeyed her like she was my parent and lifted off my clothes, one by one, not caring if she saw me. I unhooked the bra, which still smelled new and felt rubbery, and threw it on the floor with all the rest.

"Just lie down and relax," Sylvie said, walking around the room, rearranging clumps of mess. "It'll be okay. You'll feel better in time, after days pass and it's not so new. You can miss your dad. Just miss him. Ssh, it'll be okay." She turned out all the lights except for the little ballerina night-light on her dresser, which cast a warm orange glow over the room and made my eyes, so red and sore from crying, finally close.

IN THE MORNING WHEN I WOKE UP, Sylvie's side of the bed was empty and rumpled. I instantly ran to the window and saw how bad the storm was. It was still snowing, and a lot had accumulated overnight, but the wind had let up. The sun was out off and on like a roving spotlight. My mother must not have cared where I was; she hadn't even called. I breathed on the cold window, smelled coffee and hot cereal downstairs, and still in Sylvie's too-small nightie, pulled on yesterday's socks and tiptoed down the stairs.

It was quiet, too quiet, and somehow I knew something was wrong. No one was in the living room, although the TV was on, so I pressed on to the kitchen and did a double take when I saw Grandma Laura and DeeDee sitting at the large table with Sylvie and her mom and sisters. How had they driven from Mankato in the blizzard? Didn't they know nobody was supposed to travel? But then again Grandma Laura had never been one to worry about the weather. She used to drive in hailstorms to get to our birthday parties if she had to—to my mother's worry and dismay. I edged over to her suspiciously.

"Honey," she said, and rubbed my hair. "How are you?" DeeDee touched my back and ran her fingers up and down the soft flannel of Sylvie's nightie. I didn't ask what was going on, and for a long time, nobody told me. Sylvie's mom stood nervously over the stove, brewing coffee in the percolator, refilling Grandma Laura's cup, even though she'd barely had a few sips. She poured me and DeeDee glasses of water, even though we didn't ask for them or drink them. Sylvie stood against the refrigerator, hands behind her back.

Finally, Grandma Laura spoke again. "It's your mamma," she said, and for some reason, since I'd never called my mother "Mamma" in my life, it hardly registered who she was talking about. "She's had some problems, see, so many problems, and she . . . well, she had to leave. Just for awhile. Really, not to worry, Iris. It's a hard time for her right now." I felt Grandma Laura's grip tighten around me, and DeeDee rested her head on my back.

I didn't do anything but look around as if for some explanation. Then I asked about Adam.

"Well, Aunt Deb'll take him for awhile," Grandma Laura said in a voice that was gravelly and worn out. "You know, she's got the boys. They get along so well."

I thought for a minute. "Did she go with Ronny Nelson?" I asked.

"Well . . . ," Grandma Laura said.

"Where to?" I asked.

"We're not exactly sure," she said. She rubbed her elbows with her hands.

"So what will I do?" I asked. "Where will I live?"

Grandma Laura took me by the shoulders and looked me in the eye. "You'll stay with me. Just like old times. And you can see DeeDee and Melanie all the time. It'll be fun."

"Okay," I said. "I just need to think for a minute." I knew they were all watching me, but I walked out of the kitchen, through the living room, and opened the front door. I sat outside on the stoop, which was coated with snow. I liked the cold. I liked the sting that traveled through my thin socks and into my tender feet. I liked that I could feel it, and it mattered. I could freeze to death if they let me. If they locked me out. If I ran away and hid behind some bushes and fell asleep in the cold.

Instead, I sat and thought and shivered. My mother was gone. My father was gone. Adam would be gone; I wondered about Ronny. I remembered my father telling me it wasn't nice to play dead, but I always did it anyway because it felt so good, so free. Now, I did it instinctively. I lay down in the deep snow and felt it press below me, wet and dry at the same time. I flapped my arms like angel wings, then wrapped them across my chest. I looked up at the sky, such a large gray stew, such a deep and faraway world. I closed my eyes and listened to the wind. I didn't know if they were watching me from the windows, worried, giving me just a few minutes to myself before they came and saved me and warmed me up. I didn't know how long it would last, but it felt good, this freezing from the underneath, this silent melting and falling, this little death.

• • •

ACKNOWLEDGMENTS

I would like to express deep gratitude to my mother, Barbara Panning, who raised me to believe in good dairy products, love, and patience. Also, my grandfather, Henry Griep, was an award-winning butter maker in Minnesota, and it's to him that I owe the greatest debt of inspiration for this novel. Although the story line is fictional, the creamery and its machinations, the dairy products and their smells, tastes and textures, all came from him and a collection of 8mm home movies unearthed one day that started it all.

My friend Wendy Miles gave her feedback on this novel early on with generosity and kindness. She read the whole thing, over and over and over, and provided me with voluminous typewritten notes. I will be forever grateful.

My family in Minnesota is always with me in heart and mind whenever I put pen to paper. My deep thanks and love to my sister, Amy, who answers all my constant questions about our past, who texts me on a daily basis, and whose big green eyes feel like home to me, and to my brothers, Jim and Mike, who inspire me with their knowledge about things like wild boar hunting, how to skin a deer, which berries are poisonous, and where to catch the best sunfish.

Also, my thanks to Steve Fellner, Phil Young, Sarah Cedeño, Gail Hosking, Sarah Frelich, June Spence, Nancy Zafris, Sam Bell, Silas Hansen, and Noelle deJesus-Chua. You make the writing journey less lonely. Also, many thanks to the late John Mitchell, who taught me how to break the rules.

Thank you to Susan Vasquez, the English department secretary at SUNY-Brockport, who is always there to help me when I'm rushing around in a panic trying to get everything done (including make copies of my manuscripts).

Thank you also to editor in chief of Switchgrass Books, Mark Heineke, who has been a true pleasure to work with on making this book possible.

I owe my deepest gratitude, however, to my husband, Mark Rice. We've been through so much together and he continues to support me through it all. Thank you for taking the kids hiking while I wrote. Thank you for being fun, generous, loving, and supportive no matter what. Thank you for always making me laugh.

A special note here to my two children, Hudson and Lily. It's hard to explain, but everything I do, I do for you (even when it means I have to hide away in my study for hours at a time and you don't see me). I love the kind, interesting, engaged people you are both becoming.

Lastly, in memory of my parents, Barb and Lowell Panning, who gave me an interesting life and a good heart. No one would be more tickled about this book than my mother—the daughter of a butter maker.